# THE TEST!

Windham had heard that dumb animals were unable to meet the eye of man. He sat down one day and stared fixedly at the wolf-dog for fifteen minutes. Never altering his glance, except for the mere flicker of the eyelid, when the ball of the eye became dry . . . he stared.

Chinook answered with a glance as steady. For fifteen minutes Chinook's direction never wavered. His eyes turned neither to the one side nor to the other. Only toward the end of the time, his lips curled back a little from the white of his teeth. And in his eyes came a blaze of yellow fire.

A chill crept through Windham. He jumped up from his chair and rushed into the open for air. His brain reeling, Windham realized that his face was bathed in a cold sweat, and that he was trembling.

He had been fairly met . . . and, to his horror, beaten!

# MAX BRAND

## MIGHTY LOBO

**WARNER BOOKS**

A Warner Communications Company

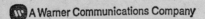

# CHAPTER ONE

When the irresistible force meets with the immovable object, the result is immeasurable heat. That is a law of physics and it is also a human law.

In this case, the immovable object fell into the hands of the irresistible force. But the object really assumed charge of the force and took it to Alaska.

There the heat was developed, enough heat to melt the Muir Glacier and raise a fog. People will tell you yet—oldtimers from the interior—all about what happened. Alaska burned with it for a long time.

The irresistible force was Ned Windham.

There was no doubt about his force. You could feel it from a distance, radiating. When he came near, his physical dimensions dominated everything, included the most imaginative minds.

He stood four inches over six feet. He weighed nearly two hundred and fifty pounds. He was made of thoroughbred bone, tough as sword steel, tendons that were like woven steel cables, and muscles of the finest India rubber.

Considering the quality of his make, he was fairly to be called a matchless machine, irresistible as far as most men go.

It is a temptation to dwell upon Ned Windham. Men still talk about him, a whole evening at a time, slowly, tasting the feats of the man, pulling at their pipes, wrinkling their eyes like misers computing a stock of golden savings.

They would treasure up foolish trifles that had belonged to him—the coat that once had fitted his massive shoulders, a huge boot that had grown battered upon his foot, or his cap, likely to fall down over the ears when placed upon a normal head. We like the gigantesque. And Windham was such a giant that other men did not feel envy. They measured themselves by the monster, and even strong men merely laughed and shrugged their shoulders.

He was the ugliest man, as well as the strongest. A crag of a jaw, beetling brows, great, solid cheekbones, and a wide, grim, determined mouth—that was Windham. He was so ugly that his ugliness removed the envy of other men.

He was fairly well educated; he had read a good bit; he spoke correct English; sometimes he could even be eloquent. But his mind moved slowly. Impressions seized upon him and worked for months inside his brain, fermenting, growing, possessing him. After the months of incubation, the idea burst forth with a rush, in words or in action.

He was doing very well when he met the immovable object. He started out without any money at all, and one day when he was hunting through the foothills in northern California, under the white heights of the Sierras, striding mightily along, he came to a little valley all sowed with evergreens and rocks, with mere patches of grass growing among the surface crop of stones.

But the grass grew sweet and thick, where it had a chance. There was something, too, about the loneliness of the place, the beauty of the mountains, and the pine-scented purity of the air that ravished the soul of Windham.

He was only nineteen then. He spent a year working and brooding. He found out who owned that little valley, and finally he bought it for a dollar an acre—two thousand dollars for two thousand acres. The only thing that gave it any value at all was the timber growing on it. The timber was not big, and there was no road, no waterway that approached the land for transporting the timber. One might, therefore, say that Windham was a fool. But he was not.

You or I, looking upon that land, would have thought of a gang of trained ground-breakers, of powder, drills, fuses, and all of that. But Windham made himself into powder and drill and traveling crane, combined. He exploded those big surface rocks with the might of his back and shoulders, and he began to fence off the valley with the uprooted stones. This was not an easy or a quick work.

He used to run sheep and a few cattle in the valley, increasing the numbers as fast as he could. They throve upon the fine grasses. The cattle, particularly, got fat as pigs, and he used to drive them off in small batches and sell them directly to the butchers in the small, nearby towns. That beef got a fine name. Everybody was glad to buy Wind Valley beef. He had called the valley after the first half of his own name. In every way possible he wanted to leave his impression upon the place. It was himself, do you see? He owned the valley, and the valley owned him.

He cleared two hundred acres a year, a steady average. At the end of six years he had cleaned out the whole bottom of the valley, where the most level and the richest land lay.

He had done other things. He had two hundred acres under actual cultivation, and he used to count on twelve sacks to an acre when he planted wheat. He got it, too.

He had increased his cattle and his herds of sheep. He got in a low-browed, dark-faced Basque to handle the sheep for him. There's nothing like a Basque for that business. They're as hard as the rocks they wander among, and they're the only people in the world who don't go mad from loneliness. Besides, they know sheep. They must have an instinct for them.

Windham had built himself a good two-room house of logs. He had a fine chimney of stone and cement—the cement carted in more than a hundred miles!

Then he began to look into the future. He constructed a dam at the head of the valley and backed up the water in a narrow, deep canyon. It was a whacking big dam. He blew in part of a rocky hillside on either side with dynamite, and the wreckage filled up the mouth of the gully. That was how he did it.

That dam gave him a water reserve with which he could

9

defy the water famines in summer. Furthermore, one day, he would use that piled-up water power to turn a saw mill, or grind flour, or perhaps for some other purpose.

He had now a good blacksmith shop. He used to spend his spare time, times of blizzards and such, fiddling about in the blacksmith shop, and there he hammered out everything from wagon fitting to plowshares. He was one of those tough, independent fellows who like to make everything with their own hands. He wanted to weave his own cloth. He was that sort of man!

Jumping on to the end of the sixth year, however, is no good. For that was when he left Wind Valley and went to Alaska. The point to make the break came along at the end of the fifth year. He had then cleared well over a thousand acres.

Not counting the other improvements he had made, consider what that meant. To be sure, it was a long haul to the nearest market but, even so, the land now must have been worth at least eighty or even a hundred dollars an acre. And nothing in the world could keep Windham from clearing the rest of the two thousand acres by the time he was thirty. Also, the railroad was planning a branch that would bring him within twenty miles of a shipping station. And that would double the value of everything he produced.

That was the position of Windham when he was torn away from his home. It is a thing hard to believe. When a man becomes infatuated, however, his common sense as a matter of course deserts him. Wind Valley disappeared from his dreams, and another object gradually took the place of his love of the valley.

It had been noted that he was a fellow in whom passion was only slowly aroused but, when it came to the full bloom, it occupied every bit of his mind. That was true concerning the new infatuation which took the place of his home-building instinct that had driven him forward, as if with whips to the making of his farm.

Poor Windham! Those who saw that valley and the work he had done in it never could believe the story they heard. For, when he left it, he never returned to it. He was gone from it once and forever.

10

But, then, isn't it true that most of us cannot compass, with our weaker imaginations, the ways of larger natures, huger passions? Of one thing be sure—that there never was a real regret in Windham over what he had given up.

Like the perfect gambler, he put that earlier part of his life behind him and turned his iron face steadily toward a new future.

# CHAPTER TWO

And now for that immovable object which ended by uprooting the giant—it was not a sudden passion that obsessed the man. It was rather a thing that grew gradually upon him, striding further and further into his mind from day to day.

Ir began upon a moonlight night in the early spring, when the snows had melted off the upper acres of his farm, though the cold mountain wind still scooped along the course of the valley and whistled through the chinks of the cabin.

On that night, an hour or more before the dawn began, he heard the howl of a wolf near the cabin, and the sound pulled him out from his blankets.

Well, he had heard many a wolf before that time, to be sure. During the earlier years, there had been a veritable pest of the great, sly timber wolves which came down to murder his sheep, or cut the throats of his calves and his colts. He had driven the beasts away, in part with his accurate rifle, in part by patient and cunning trapping. Now his farm was a bit of taboo range. The wolves knew perfectly well that it was a danger line and they feared to cross it, except once in a while during the dead of winter, when famine scourged them down toward the richer lowlands.

So he knew all about wolves and their ways, all about their songs, whether in the mating season or on the blood trail, or when they were simply singing down the wind because of the happy devil inside of their coats.

But this wolf's voice was different from any he had heard. It was vastly more powerful, for one thing. The sound seemed to leap up through the floor of the cabin. It seemed to bring the bristling monster right into the house.

Wolf? By heaven, the howl died off and changed into the loud, hoarse barking of a dog! By that time, he was stepping into his boots and reaching for his rifle.

He went out into the broad glare of the moon, and there in the nearest corral that he had built, he saw a black wolf, if wolf it was, standing with its forepaws upon the shoulders of his prize bull; that is to say, the bull lay upon the ground of the corral. And the lobo stood over it, like a fighter over a dead foeman.

When it saw the big man coming, it laughed at him, as only a lobo can, and disappeared on the farther side of the huge carcass of the bull.

"You're dead, nevertheless," said the big man to himself. And he started to walk in a short circle to get a view of the killer again.

He was impressed as he never had been before in his life. It was a combination of circumstances. In the first place, there had been the volume of the howl and the savage quality in it; then the barking, like the barking of a whole chorus of big dogs. Finally, there was his prize bull dead on the ground, and over it a wolf that looked as big as a bear!

But who has ever heard of a wolf that could kill a powerful and savage bull? A pack of wolves might, now and then, but not a lone hunter! Yet, here was the miracle right before his eyes.

Then, there was the cold brightness of the night, the cut of the wind that seemed to drive through the great body of Ned Windham; so that he had an eerie feeling of being in contact with the supernatural; not a very strange feeling, either, considering all the elements present at the moment.

12

He got to a sufficient angle presently, to see the big lobo sneaking away toward the farther fence of the corral. It did not look back, but the instant that Windham was in line with it, it seemed to know. For it jumped up and streaked for liberty.

Windham got the rifle to his shoulder. Moonlight shooting is not the easiest thing in the world, but it was not the first time that he had done it, and at moving game, too. He was as sure of stretching that wolf hide in the morning as he was that he was standing there at that moment with the rifle in his hands!

So he drew the bead and pressed the trigger just as the big scoundrel jumped the high fence.

He fired just as the wolf landed, but he missed! For the lobo, though it had not looked back, had had sense enough to dodge. A devilish intuition appeared to guide it! It also dodged the second shot, in exactly the same manner.

It was still within range for a third bullet, but the rifle simply slipped out of the numbed hands of big Windham.

The mere telling of the tale does not make it seem so strange, but the actual fact was enough to fairly paralyze that big hunter.

Well, Windham stood there for a moment, staring, and then he began to rub his eyes. He walked over to the fence, and vaulted it.

He went to where his bull lay, and there he saw that both hamstrings had been slashed by the lobo. He stood in front of the carcass, then, and saw that the throat had been ripped wide open, apparently by one tremendous slash of the fangs.

No wonder the bull had not bellowed in terror for help! The stroke that slew it had stifled it as well.

Then, on the ground, he saw something that made his eyes start from his head.

The dust of his corral was very white. The moonlight silvered it still more. And in this shining dust, just under his nose, was etched the print of a wolf's forepaw, delicately and accurately outlined by the shadow which the

13

slanting moonlight cast on the rim of the dust. It was as clear as though it had been drawn upon white paper with the blackest of ink.

He was not staring, you may be sure, because he recognized it as the print of a wolf's paw. As a matter of fact, the thing that staggered him was the suddenly born conviction that this was no wolf at all!

He had reason for his conclusion. He knew that a wolf whose forepaw has a four-inch spread is a good-sized and mature animal, able to kill calves and colts with the best. He had seen some four-and-a-half-inch spreads, too, but these were giants of their kind. He had not seen, but he had heard of one almost fabulous monster whose print was five inches from edge to edge. And he furthermore had heard it alleged that the weight of that king of wolves was actually a hundred and fifty pounds.

About these dimensions, about this weight, he always had had doubts. But here, before him, was a print exactly six inches across. No wonder that he could not believe it! He tried to build again in his mind the picture of the monster as he had seen him here in the corral, but his wits failed to serve him well. He could not recreate the beast! He determined to follow the trail when the morning broke. He wanted to know something more about the habits and the work of the destroyer.

As he cooked his breakfast, scowling at the stove, he pondered the problem. It was not pure wolf. Wolves never bark. The muscles of their throats seem to forbid the making of the sound. Therefore, this lobo must have been crossbred with some large domestic animal.

In this manner he could explain the freak, but after all of his logical processes, there remained something inexplicable in the impression which had been made upon his mind.

He could hardly wait for the day to begin. And the dawn was still pale rose when he mounted his toughest mustang and jogged away on the trail of the big brute.

He intended to be back by noon but he was gone for three days. On the way, he counted four killings by the ravager. All were on his own land! For the lobo, leading him back into the hills as though traveling straight for his

14

home cave, would suddenly double back and come on the preserves of Windham again.

Besides the bull, he killed a good heifer, an old cow, and a husky maverick which Windham had caught up the year before, there being no brand upon it whatever. Also, he slaughtered a silky young two-year-old which, on a day, promised to be big and strong enough to carry the weight of Windham under the saddle!

Even this was not the hardest blow. The wolf got into a herd of the Basque's sheep and cut a dozen throats out of sheer blood lust before it was through.

So Windham finally gave up the trail at the end of three days.

No, he did not really give it up. But he thrust the thing back in his mind. He would take up that same trail later on. He did not dream, then, that it would be his obsession for an entire year.

But that was the case. And for the entire year following, the wolf lived upon the thinning ranks of the Windham cattle. Not a week went by without at least one major slaughter. And nothing could be done! Traps, poisoned meat, waylayings, were all in vain.

He saw the monster several times. Once he was in company with Tod Brewster, an old-timer who had hunted and trapped the Sierras from one end to the other. He had stopped in at Wind Valley for dinner, and the next morning he rode out a way with Windham.

Far off, between a pair of rocks on a hillside, they saw the mighty shoulders and the wise head of the lobo. They could see the red flash of his tongue as he laughed at their poor human wits.

"Now, look at that," said Windham. "Can you believe it?"

Brewster sighted from beneath the shadow of his hand, measuring the distance and the proportions of the wolf.

"Yeah. I can believe it," he said. "That's Chinook."

"Who's Chinook?"

"He's the devil, done up in a wolf's fur. You go down the line a ways and get to the ranches. They'll tell you plenty of stories about him. He comes out of the mountains like the wind, raises the devil, and goes back again.

That's why they call him Chinook. You never know when he'll come. And you feel pretty sick till he's gone again. Go down there and ask 'em. They'll tell you about Chinook!"

"I don't want to hear about him," said Windham. "I want him."

"The devil you do!" said the trapper. "What would you do with him?"

Windham stared at the apparition on the far-away hilltop. He unsheathed his rifle from the long holster and leveled it; the brute vanished.

"I don't know what I'd do with him," said Windham. "I'd like to talk to him, I guess."

Brewster grinned.

"That'd be some talk," he agreed. "You ever trap that lobo, take my advice, put a bullet into his brain before you get close, or he'll cut your throat to the neck bone. He can bite five pounds out of the side of a running beef. What would he do to a man?"

Windham did not answer. In fact, he had been amazed at his own words. He had been thinking that he simply wanted to kill the marauder. Now he knew that he actually wanted to break the heart of the wolf.

And it was that realization that led to all the disasters that followed.

# CHAPTER THREE

For a whole year Windham matched himself against the wolf. For a whole year he lost steadily—time, sheep, cattle, horses. As a matter of fact, he hardly cared about the losses. The importance of Wind Valley was shrinking day by day in his eyes. The importance of this duel between himself and the brute was magnified at the same time.

Then, when he was exactly twenty-six years old—the fact that it was his birthday gave the event a peculiar significance—he came upon Chinook when he least expected to find him.

There was a hard wind cuffing across the valley, and he had ridden against it, making his way to its head where the dam was filling. He got very close to the place when he heard a wild snarling that came out of a dry draw near by.

He recognized that voice. It was a mountain lion tuning up. He was surprised to hear that song in the middle of the day, but he snatched out his rifle and went to investigate.

He pushed straight through the screen of dust, still on horseback, until the noise seemed to be rising up out of the ground at his feet. When he came to the verge of the brush and the edge of the draw, he looked down. There, crouched among the pebbles and the boulders of the draw, was one of the biggest mountain lions he had ever seen; young, in the height of its power, its sides sleeked with fine living. Chinook was not the only murderer on that range, you may be sure.

This tawny devil was lashing its sides with its tail, its mouth yawning open and showing teeth as sharp as needles and long enough to find the jugular of the biggest steer. Its round eyes burned with a yellow fire, and it kept turning about, slowly, to keep its face to its enemy.

That enemy was Chinook! The scoundrel had stepped out of his class, it appeared, to make trouble, single-handed, with the big cat. The rancher knew what the teeth and the quadruple set of claws on a mountain lion could accomplish. He had seen half a hunting pack mangled by one of them in a single charge. But Chinook did not appear to be afraid.

This was the first time that Windham had a close and special look at the wolf in open daylight, and he marked down every feature.

It was the biggest thing in the way of wolf or dog that

17

his experienced eye had ever seen; but, despite the bulk and the six-inch spread of paw, the whole mass of the animal was so neatly and smoothly proportioned that he seemed as active as a cat. He had the wolf's head, with the round, wise eyes, and the lobo's true, leonine wrinkles between the eyes to increase the philosophical air. His coat was almost black, but at the breast it was mottled with brown and white, and there was a snowy stocking upon the left foreleg. He was in perfect condition, due undoubtedly to his beef and mutton diet. When he moved, a ripple of power ran through him, from hindquarters to shoulders.

Now, after a year, there he stood in the hollow of the hand of Windham. Such a shot the big man could not miss at such a range, and yet Windham had not the slightest temptation to shoot. He actually thrust his rifle back into the holster and took his rope from the horn of the saddle, beginning to calculate his chances of breaking out from the brush, driving the mustang down the slope, and shooting that noose over the powerful neck of the wolf dog. For dog there certainly was in him. No wolf since the beginning of time ever had such markings upon the breast and upon the foreleg.

In the meantime, Windham grew so interested in the struggle between wolf dog and cat, that he almost forgot his own relation to Chinook.

It was not exactly a fight of tooth and claw; it was, at this point, merely a clashing of opposed wills. This was the manner of it. The great cat, crouched, every muscle straining, slowly turned to face the circlings of the other, ready at any instant to spring out and rend the wolf to pieces. And Chinook continued to circle, warily, vigilantly, hanging out his red tongue, laughing at the prey, sometimes licking the slaver from his lips, as though he had tasted cat meat before and intended to enjoy it again.

Windham shook his head in bewilderment. Then he noted that the puma was no longer lashing its sides so furiously. It crouched lower. A tremor appeared in its sleek body and in its stalwart legs. Windham vaguely understood. The whole cat family is made for sudden efforts, not for long strains. The cat kills with a spring and a dash. It fights with a moment's insane frenzy. Then it is exhausted. It gives an antelope a twenty-five-yard head start and catches it in a hundred; but at the end of a hundred yards of sprinting, even a man on foot could run away from it!

So the long strain of facing Chinook was proving too much for the nerve strength of this yellow devil. Now it shook with the continued tension. Every moment Chinook appeared about to rush in. Every moment he postponed the attack.

Finally, the puma turned its head and looked up the bank through the brush toward the place where the man on horseback lurked. It was an odd thing, almost as though the hunted beast asked the man for help in the crucial moment.

That instant, Chinook darted in. The great cat, with a howl of fear and excitement, bounded stiff-legged into the air to meet the rush, and Chinook instantly halted and backed away.

The cat, back humped, head held low for the spring, began to turn slowly around and around to meet the ceaseless circling of the wolf dog.

Sometimes Chinook reversed his direction, swinging a little nearer, and this change always brought a great convulsion of spitting and hissing and howling from the puma. It was a picture of two murdering devils facing one another. Through minutes the thing went on.

Then Windham saw that the cat strove to follow the movements of the wolf by mere turnings of its head, without twisting his shaking body around. But always, when Chinook was just to its rear, that cunning devil knew exactly the feint, exactly the growl to make the mountain lion whirl screeching about!

For half an hour that seemed half a day that odd duel went on, and never a dull instant in the eyes of Windham! Then he saw that the eyes of the puma were beginning to narrow to slits of weariness; a foam appeared on its mouth. Once, when the wolf rushed in a feint, the yellow cat merely shrank and shuddered. That instant Chinook made his dash.

There had been so many feints, so many delays, that

even the watchful eye and brain of the man were not prepared for the climax when it came.

Chinook bounded, like the driving of a great, dark spear which carried in the haft the solid weight of a man's body and which for a lance head possessed two white, naked, knifelike fangs.

Just across the scruff of the puma's neck, where the neck bends and the neck muscles are most taut, just there Chinook, like a clever surgeon, struck with all his might.

The puma howled and twisted.

Then Windham charged! He stuck his spurs into the sides of the mustang and went down that bank, scattering the pebbles right and left.

Chinook was in the throes of mad joy over his victory against this monster. The forequarters of the mountain lion already hung paralyzed. The rear legs were merely scratching feebly. Yes, victory was all upon the side of the wolf!

But, even in this moment of hysterical joy, the keen wits of the wolf were on guard; for he left the dying cat with a bound and whirled to face the new enemy.

He saw it was Man, and whirled again to flee. Then the thin finger of the noose whipped around his throat and the tug of the rope tumbled Chinook among the pebbles.

The rider, wheeling his horse about, sent it galloping wildly down the draw.

Looking back, Windham saw the dark monster striving to get to its feet, but the jerking rope tumbled it again head over heels. And on they went, the mustang gathering speed as it went along, and the bulk of the wolf battering against boulders, thudding here and there, still struggling to regain its feet.

With a cruel caution, Windham looked back until he marked the instant when Chinook was trailing at the end of the rope, a limp and helpless weight.

Then he dismounted.

He ran back and tied the big creature with short lengths of cord, binding the forelegs together, the hindlegs to the fore. After this, he twisted the large rope again and again around the head of Chinook, making the most effective of muzzles.

He could leave the animal now.

For Chinook was not dead. He was badly battered. There was a rip across his skull where he had collided with the edge of a rock. But he was far from dead, and his heart pounded steadily under his ribs. All silk he seemed to Windham. His fur was like the silken gloss of a black fox. The pads of his feet were hard as tanned leather. The nails were worn short and blunt by ceaseless travel through the hills and over the mountain rocks.

He was hard all over! Even in this moment of relaxation, the muscle of hindquarters and shoulders stood out hard and strong like bundled masses of sinew.

Windham thumbed them and examined them with an expert's knowledge. Then he stood up and surveyed his prize with a deliberate joy such as he never had known in his life, not even on that day when he took the paper that made Wind Valley his own!

He stood up and stretched his arms above his head, like some old Indian brave, appealing in silent prayer to the thunder gods of the mountains above him.

But there was no prayer in the iron throat of Windham, you may be sure. There was only a rush of resolve that he would make the monster his own, body, mind, and soul—his slave, to come to his heel like any house dog, reared under the fear of a whip!

Oh, Windham, that was where pride and folly put their thumbs to your throat!

# CHAPTER FOUR

He rushed his mustang back to the house, harnessed a pair of horses to his toughest buckboard and drove them back at a gallop. His heart was in his throat for fear lest something should have happened in the meantime, for fear, perhaps, that the puma had recovered enough to come down the valley and kill its bound and helpless enemy. Or, perhaps, those steel springs, the jaws of the wolf, had worked the muzzling rope loose and those knife-like teeth had clipped the bonds, strand by strand.

He was sweating with anxiety when he drove the buckboard recklessly down the bank and into the draw, but, when he got there, he found the wolf as he had left it.

Not exactly in the same spot, for the dragged pebbles told how Chinook had been twisting this way and that to escape; but every bond was in place.

There was this other change. The eyes of the wolf were wide open, and they looked at Windham with the red-rimmed, awful hatred which all the animals of the wilderness feel for man. Windham laughed. The lobo shuddered!

Windham laughed the more heartily, the more fiercely. He got down on one knee and laid a hand on the shoulder of his prisoner.

At that, such a snarl tore out of the throat of Chinook as rasped even the resolved and prepared nerves of the man. But Windham laughed again.

"That's it," he said. "Talk to me, fellow. You cattle lifter, you throat-cutter, you nighthawk. I'm ready to listen."

He laughed again, and actually slapped the shoulder of Chinook.

But not a sound came from Chinook!

His eyes opened with rage, with a cold, steady hate, yet he made not a sound! And that was the beginning of the long silence that fell between them, one of the strangest things, surely that ever befell in the relations of man and beast. Windham was startled. For he recognized something in the silent pride of the wolf that resembled his own nature—the six almost silent years which he had spent up in the valley, tearing the rocks from its breast, preparing it for fertility.

Then he gathered the weight of the big animal into his arms. Not until the full heft of it was pulling at his shoulders and the steel cables that bulged in the small of his back, did he realize the actual mass of Chinook, and it fairly took his breath. No wonder that the wolf had cut almost to the life of the puma at the first strike of his fangs, with such a driving force behind the teeth!

He got the wolf into the buckboard. He put up the tailboard. Then he drove to the house.

He worked a day to fit shackles and chain hobbles to Chinook. He worked another day to prepare a powerful iron muzzle and a strong club. Of the club he was proud. It was a real device. For it consisted of two thicknesses of rubber taken from a hose he had used for siphoning, laid over the knobby head of a hardwood bludgeon. With a stroke of that club he could fairly trust to stun Chinook in a fight, without shattering the skull.

He devised a second muzzle, a broad, strong strap, which would enable the wolf to eat, but without permitting it the full opening of its jaws.

It took him two days to make these things, working hard, for long hours each day. During that time, he offered his wild beast not a morsel to eat, not a drop to drink.

When the period had ended, he placed water before the wolf dog, and slippped over its head the strap muzzle. And Chinook drank, long and deeply. The pan was refilled, and he drank again. After that he lay down, licking his lips dry. Then he raised his head once more to watch the man.

There was no alteration in his expression. The same deathless hatred was there for human beings and, above all, for Windham. It was not a blind, sneaking, around-the-corner hatred. It was open-eyed, considering, thoughtful, as though the dumb creature were devising ways and means for the future, studying the mind of man for reference. If ever that strength were turned loose to do battle, what would happen to the man who ventured to face it?

Windham set his teeth, his wide, thin lips stretching in a grin. He, Windham, would be the one to stand before the monster, when the time came. But there must be a period of probation first.

Then began the first circle of hell, into which Windham was to go deeper and deeper, beyond all of his imaginings.

23

Poor Windham! You see, he had made up his mind that no living thing could stand against the united power of his will and of his great hands. He looked down at those brown, calloused, powerful fingers, and asked himself what task was beyond them?

Chinook was to furnish the answer to that!

Windham had a natural instinct for the training of dogs. He was, moreover, methodical and patient by nature.

He laid out a scheme, and then he followed out the scheme to the letter.

One thing he left out of his scheme. It never occurred to him to try to win the love of Chinook. He wanted the submission of the brute, and that was all. This was what he worked toward from the first, and this alone. He envisaged the day when Chinook would guard the flocks which he had once despoiled, when Chinook would run down his brother wolves when they dared to descend into Wind Valley, and when Chinook would lie before the bright hearth in the hut, of an evening, stretched at the feet of his master.

That was the ultimate picture which brightened the eyes of Windham; that was the picture which he tried to paint in reality.

He gave Chinook his first lesson on a stomach which had been empty for two days. But Chinook failed to respond. He simply lay prone and refused to notice the man, except with that steady, thoughtful stare of hatred.

Windham starved him for a week. Every day he spent hours with the great brute, but, though Chinook grew weak and his ribs thrust out, still he did not surrender. He did not even dream of surrendering, as it appeared!

Fear came into Windham then. It was the first real fear that ever had come into his life, this new dread that he might fail.

So he made his first surrender, grimly, bitterly, with a dark heart.

However, a dead wolf was of no use to him! And he gave lobo a great deal of raw meat.

Chinook devoured it, cracked the bones, licked the

24

marrow out of them and curled up for a twenty-four-hour sleep.

At the end of that time, it was as though the week of famine never had passed over his head.

But what Windham chiefly noticed was that before, during and after the famine, the expression of Chinook's eyes never altered. It was the same alert, wide-lidded regard, the same prying as it were, into the mind of the man before him.

Everything about the beast was strange. He had no fear, no weakness of will. He was adamant, as Windham himself was adamant.

Once, therefore, Windham decided upon a vital test.

He knew well enough that dumb beasts were rumored unable to meet the eye of man and, therefore, he sat down one day and stared fixedly at the wolf for the whole of fifteen minutes, never altering his glance, except for the mere flicker of the eyelid when the ball of the eye became dry.

So he stared at the wolf, and Chinook answered with a glance as steady. Through all of those fifteen minutes, his direction never wavered. His eyes turned neither to the one side nor to the other. His head was high.

Only, toward the end of the time, his lip curled back a little from the white of his teeth, and into his eyes came a blaze of yellow fire.

Suddenly, a chill crept through the great body of Windham. He jumped up hastily from his chair; he rushed into the open and stood there with a reeling brain, so that the hills and the white-headed mountains beyond them seemed to be whirling before his face.

He had been fairly met and fairly beaten. He had striven to terrify the dog with that dread of the unknown, of which man is supposed to have some knowledge, that power of thought which is termed a human thing. Instead, he himself had been crushed. A strange and unreasoning terror had possessed him and he had been forced to leave the house.

Mysteries upset any man. But physical mysteries upset most the physical man. That was the nature of Windham.

25

The problems which he had set for himself were problems which could be solved by the might of his hands and the brawn of his broad shoulders. But this matter was entirely different.

As he stood there, the horrid thought which possessed him was: "Is there such a thing as a werewolf? Is the mind of man ever reincarnated in the body of a beast? Is such a mind now working behind the fur and the teeth of Chinook?"

He answered himself with a negative, but only part of his conviction was in the negation, for he remembered the fight between this Chinook and the mountain lion, and he told himself that not even a famine-driven wolf ever before, single-handed, had attacked such a creature, to say nothing of destroying it.

The picture came back to him with vividness. But, this time, he seemed to see himself in the teeth of Chinook, his own neck crushed in those terrible jaws, his head and arms hanging limply, paralyzed, and his legs making an impotent, feeble struggle.

He realized, as he grew calmer, that his face was bathed in a cold sweat; that he was trembling. And he remembered how the mountain lion had trembled under the steady gaze of the wolf.

Was he not in the same state?

He went rapidly back to the door of the cabin, determined to sit down and outstare the brute this time but, when he came to the entrance, the cold swept in a wave over his heart once more. He shrank from the test and hurried off into the kind heat and brightness of the sun.

# CHAPTER FIVE

A brave man is not content with one defeat. He rises from the floor of the ring after the first knockdown and struggles again. Fierce pride rises in his heart. Pride strengthens his limbs. Pride wipes the mist from before his eyes. Pride renerves his muscles for another struggle. So many a defeat is turned into a victory.

Now, in Windham, there were both pride and courage of the most indomitable sort. The foundation of these traits was not in the mind; it was in the body. Nevertheless, both his physical pride and his physical courage were enormous.

So Windham brooded for a day upon the matter and decided that he must fight the battle out.

He could not manage it with the sheer force of his eye. There had to be some other way, and the way that he chose was to lock and bolt the door of his cabin, clear the furniture from one room, lock the door to the next chamber, and bring in the wolf.

When he had done that, he removed the hobble shackles and the hobble chains. He removed the muzzle, also. Leaping back, he stood prepared with his rubber-shod club, ready for the attack.

He felt that he was acting desperately enough. He had bulk enough. He had strength enough in his arms and his shoulders to brain the beast. But the padded club would steal nine tenths of the shock from his battering blows.

Against him, there was the devilish cunning, the weight, the four-footed activity of the wolf. In addition, there were the teeth, ready to tap the lifeblood of the man at a single stroke.

It is not easy to imagine the condition of Windham's

mind when it is realized that he could actually accept such a duel, make of it a thing worthy of life and death! But, then, Windham was of a different cut. In speaking of him, one speaks as of some ancient barbarian, some follower of Attila or Alaric, whose deeds may be chronicled, but whose motives remain hidden.

Having been downed in that battle of the eyes, so it seems, he had to redeem himself by a more physical test, and this terrible one was what he chose.

He stood back, as has been said, and waited, and then he saw that the wolf was in no haste.

First, Chinook stretched and braced his legs, then strained his belly toward the floor, to loosen his jumping muscles. Finally, when he seemed to feel that he was fit in all his parts, he opened his mouth, his long, red tongue lolling, and laughed at the man!

It was a grisly thing for Windham to see. Then a more grisly followed. The wolf slid to the door, sniffed under it, ran and leaped up to the height of the window, and, as though making sure that there was nothing else for it, turned and began to stalk the man; that is to say, he moved in a broad semicircle that gradually narrowed, coming closer and closer to his quarry. And there stood big Windham, with his club poised, his mind alert, and every faculty of nerve and body prepared for the attack—when the wolf feigned an attack.

Blood rushed blindly hot into the brain of Windham, the club trembled in his mighty grasp—and then the assault did not materialize! Instead, the wolf slunk back, sat down on his haunches, opened his white-fringed mouth, and laughed again at his quarry.

Yes, Windham was the quarry, and the wolf was the master! At least, so it seemed. And the man remembered how the mountain lion had tensed itself, not once, but many times, prepared for the attack itself, not once, but delayed. Was his experience to be similar?

Suddenly he went berserk. He rushed wildly forward and struck with the full swing of the club, and missed.

In return, that black giant shot up and in at him, and laid open his left shoulder to the bone!

The gushing of his own blood sobered Windham. He stood back once more and saw Chinook standing in a corner licking his lips clean of human blood, the first taste of it!

What was to be done now? The blood would madden Chinook and make him fight for a kill. The loss of blood would also weaken even so huge a man as Windham.

He could back to the door, open it, and show the wolf the irresistible temptation of the open way. But Windham would not do that! His frame of mind was what in another man would have seemed sheer hysteria. But it was not hysteria in Windham. It was mere logic, so far as he was concerned.

He hefted the club once more in his hand. He feinted a step forward and, as the wolf dodged with incredible speed, Windham struck at the blind blur of the beast in motion.

Luck helped him more than skill. The rubber-padded club descended fairly upon the head of the wolf, and Chinook sank to the floor. He was up again in a moment, shaking his half-stunned head. When he tried to dodge the next blow, he failed again.

The impact rolled him into a corner, and he tried a trick worthy of some rough-and-tumble fighter. With his four legs, he kicked himself violently backward and came at the man rolling over and over with incredible speed, his teeth naked, prepared like swords.

Windham bounded far off, and managed to miss that whirling peril, and, as he recovered his balance again, Chinook was on his feet.

He did not charge. Instead, he started the slow circling, as he had done before in his fight with the mountain lion. And it made Windham grit his teeth with rage and with despair.

In that moment, when the nerve of most other men would have been broken, he made a silent and solemn vow that he would not give up this contest until he had beaten the wolf senseless, or until his own throat was mangled by Chinook. He was a man, was Windham, a strangely twisted, half brutal caricature of a man, but still

29

a man. He himself charged for the second time, but checked himself on braced feet and smote at the shadow that rose at him from the floor.

It was not mere luck, this time. He was seeing his target. He was adapting himself to the problem of this sort of fighting. And the club head went solidly home upon the skull of the wolf dog.

Down went great Chinook. No doubt a frailer skull would have collapsed under such strokes, and even Chinook was more than half-stunned this time. He rolled upon his back, and kicked himself with difficulty to his feet.

Windham ran in to take advantage of this opening and got for his pains, from the snakily darting head of Chinook, a gash that ran almost from his thigh down to his knee.

He felt the slicing of the teeth, like the cut of a knife. Shortening the club, he smashed it down on the head of Chinook again.

It knocked the big wolf away. It unbalanced him for a moment, and in that moment, Windham tossed the club away.

He was not thinking now. He was fighting as blindly, as furiously as any beast. He simply threw the club away and, hurling his body forward, he gripped the throat of the wolf with his right hand. The left had missed its hold.

He got, for his reward, a slash that made the blood spout from his forearm. Then he fixed his left hand deep in the throat, high up under the jaws of Chinook.

That finished the biting powers of Chinook.

Now, I have seen Chinook, and I know what he could do in a fight. Everybody else in Alaska knew, also, in after days. But also I have seen the grip of Windham. There will be more to tell about it later on. And I can understand how even Chinook's terrible jaws were helpless with the hands of Windham collaring him.

He had four feet armed with four claws, however.

In half a minute the clothes of Windham were rent from his body. Then his skin began to fly. He was furrowed from head to foot with small, broad, tearing gashes. He seemed to be on fire. But he kept to that terrible grip until he saw the fire die out of the bulging eyes of the wolf.

Then Chinook turned limp as a rag.

When that happened, Windham calmly flung the wolf into a corner. He retreated to another himself. Then he took a bottle of iodine from a shelf. He parted the lips of his wounds, one by one, and poured them full of that liquid fire. Then he bathed the multitudinous scratches which he had received.

It must have been an exquisite agony. I know how iodine feels even in the throat of a shallow cut. And Windham was literally torn to rags.

But he said, afterward, that he felt nothing. He was contented. He had asserted himself and he had won.

When he finished putting the iodine upon his hurts, he found that the wolf was standing upon his feet again, watching him. He caught up the club again, with a shout of rage. But Chinook did not show his teeth.

Neither did he begin to stalk the man again, but remained exactly where he had been standing, with his head tilted a little to one side, but held high, and in his big yellow eyes, there was that same thoughtful, curious look.

It was an odd thing to see. It baffled Windham, but it rejoiced him, too, for suddenly he guessed that Chinook had accepted one lesson. He was matched against a force which he could not master, not in open battle, at least. There was no surrender in those eyes of his, but there was infinite patience, infinite ability to wait—until there was an opening through which he could let drive at the tender throat!

Windham saw all of this in the grim moments following his conquest.

He went into the next room, dressed himself again, took up the collar and chain and, returning, limping because his wounded leg was already stiff, he went straight up to Chinook, poised club held firmly in hand.

Chinook gave one glance to the right and one glance to the left. The room was not small. Apparently he must have been tempted to flee from danger and trouble and that clanking chain whose links he had chewed to brightness for so many hours before.

31

But he did not flee.

He simply stood there and let the great hands of his master fasten the collar about his throat. There was just one tremor, one turn of his head when the man leaned over him, and so brought the throat closer. But apparently the wolf did not think that the chance was good enough. He waited patiently while the collar was fastened on him again.

So ended the second great battle between them. It was not the last. But at least it was the beginning of the remarkable education of Chinook.

# CHAPTER SIX

About the education of the dog a great deal could be said and should be said. But it would take too long. However, it's worth while to remember that many officers in an army wish to inspire in their subordinates neither love nor fear, but simply a strict and impersonal attention to duty. That impulse, they continually feel, is bound to work for the best in drawing from their men their greatest efforts. Love breeds a familiar contempt, too often, and fear is worthless except when the whip is actually suspended in the air.

Now Chinook, from the first to the last, had certainly no fear of his master, but he had recognized, after that battle of blood and blows, that in the man there was a power which he could not overcome except when a favorable opportunity offered. He sat down, as it were, to wait until that opportunity might come. In the meantime, he submitted to commands. The months which he spent with young Windham at this time were crowded with training, and Chinook learned his lessons with a brain already sharpened by the solution of ten thousand problems of the trail, of battle, and of all the stratagems of the wilderness.

He had always been a lonely liver, a single-handed hunter, and such creatures are sure to develop the keenest wits. He had not been, like Windham, superior to all the brutes of the wilderness, as the man was to all the other men. Indeed, a tap from the flexible steel of a grizzly's forepaw could have torn out the ribs of the wolf, and Chinook knew it. There were other creatures, too, smaller than itself, which the lobo had learned to avoid. It knew the ways of the wolverene, for instance, and strictly avoided that hump-backed, thirty-pound lump of devilishness. So Chinook had grown subtle of mind, and this subtlety easily accommodated itself to the demands which Windham made upon it.

But it is easier and quicker to tell what Windham taught it by referring to the account of Steve Murray, when Steve paid his first and last visit to the Windham shack. This story was told by Murray himself to a crony of his, Jay Drew, and Jay repeated the tale broadcast, including its disgraceful feature toward the end.

"I'd gone back from the inside," said Steve to Drew, "half froze and starvation thin, but still rememberin' some of the dust that I'd washed out of the tundra. I went clean back to San Francisco. I wanted to get the coin for a real outfit. I wanted enough money to clean up, and to pick me up some good dogs, above the rest.

"Well, what I thought of was the timber camps in Oregon, finally. You know those big bohunks, they rake in their monthly pay checks, and then they go and blow 'em in a day. That was what I was ready to do. I was ready to help them get their pockets lighter. If the cash didn't go to me, it'd go to somebody else. And so, why not to me? That's what I decided.

"So I went up to Oregon, and I done pretty well. I collected a big enough stake to get me back to Alaska and outfit me; I would have collected a still bigger one, but one night I got careless and dealt myself four aces, and that hand looked pretty big to the boys at the camp, specially because I'd dealt four queens to one of the lumberjacks.

33

"They give one another a look, and then they go fo me. I had to do a dive through a window to get clear, an left a coupla hundred dollars in stakes there on the table It makes my mouth water still to think of what I misse by being a hog and trying to rake in everything at once.

"Well, they got on my trail, and I had to hit for th mountains to get clear of them. Finally, I wandered of south and picked me up a mule, and come down throug California, humping that mule along the way and gettin half froze going over the passes. I drop down into a nice sunny valley, with the flowers all over the ground, som sections of black plowland here and there, crops beginnir and a little shack down in the middle of things.

"I got up to the house about the fag end of the day an bang on the door.

" 'Who's there?' says a voice from the inside, the kin of a voice that I'd never heard before, a big, thick voice that seemed to be wellin' out of a cave. I said who I was and that I was hungry, and pretty soon I hear a rattling c chains. Then the sound of the door being unbarred.

"There in front of me stands the biggest thing that ever looked at. Now, then, this here big fellow tells me t come in, which I done. I step into a room full of th steam and the smell of cookery. It tasted good to me. mean, just the smell of it. My mouth begins to water.

"He tells me his name is Ned Windham—you fellow have heard about him before—and he shows me a home made chair to set in, while he chucks some more ti plates and cups onto the table.

"About this time, I look into the corner by the stove and there I see a dog that mates up with Windham i looks. When I say that, I mean that it's the biggest dog ever laid my eyes on, and I've seen some heavy walloper among the Mackenzie River Huskies.

"I go over close to him, and Windham says: 'You min yourself, friend, or the dog'll take off an arm for yo He'll take it off at the shoulder, if he can reach that far!'

"I backed away. I asked some questions, and Windha tells me a cock-and-bull story about he trailed that do for a year, and finally caught it while it was killin' off mountain lion.

34

"I swallered that, though. For the looks of that dog was enough to warm up a man's imagination. Nobody would like to tell no common or garden lie about such a whale!

"I set down, and we et pretty good, and I ask Windham why he has the dog on a chain, and he says that it's because he can't take chances, with a stranger in the house.

"After dinner, I say that I'd like to see that dog off the chain. Windham don't take so much persuading, after all. He goes over to the dog and he reaches over and catches him by the collar, and I see him stiffen his arm, in case the dog should make a sudden slash at him.

" 'Ain't he likely to take your arm off?' says I.

" 'No,' says Windham. 'He's got his lesson about that. He's only likely to try to cut my throat, if he thinks that he sees a good chance.'

" 'Has he tried for your throat, too?' says I.

" 'Only three times,' says Windham, and he touches a long red mark on his cheek. 'He only came close this once,' says he, 'and that time he was just a little high.'

"I took another good look at the dog and the man. Yes, they were both cut out of one piece of goods. Big as all outdoors, and yet silky smooth and fast. You know there are plenty of big fellows. But most of 'em are weight lifters.

"Now then, I asked Windham if the brute could be trained, and he said that he'd already taught him a little. So he shows me, when he's unhooked the chain at the collar and stepped back. The first thing that the dog done, when he was free, was to stand still and give me a look out of his yellow eyes, a long, long look straight into my face, until I began to get a freeze up my backbone. After that first look, he paid no more attention to me. He centered the rest of his attention on his boss.

"Windham told him to go bring his boots, and that big dog slides away, without even making a rattling of his claws on the floor, and he comes back, pretty pronto, with a pair of boots.

"I'll tell you how big he was and how much he knew. Those boots were whales, but Chinook, as they called the dog, had hold of a bootstrap in each side of his mouth, and by raising his head a little, he kept those boots from dragging. He puts down the boots at the feet of his boss. Then he edges in a little closer, his big yellow eyes right on the face of Windham. And Windham hooks an arm across his chest, as though to guard his throat, and orders the dog back; and Chinook backs up right away.

"Then he fetches other things for Windham. And he winds up by standing on his hind legs and picking some chicken eggs out of a dish and bringing them over and laying them on the table without breaking a one of them; and then he goes and puts them back where he found them.

"I was pretty surprised by all of this. But that wasn't all. Windham lines that dog out and sends him around the room by orders. Like a single line leader, but better than any jerk-line mule that ever I seen.

"He'd send him right with a 'gee,' and left with a 'haw.' The louder he yelled, the sharper the dog turned and the farther. He stopped with a 'whoa,' backed up at 'back,' and spun about and came right in at 'come.'

"He had no parlor tricks. He didn't speak, he didn't sit up, and he didn't beg. He lay down when he was told, and he knew kneel.

"But the thing that laid a chill up and down my spine was when Windham takes my bandanna, gives the dog a smell of it, and tells him to 'grab!'

"What you think he done? Why, the beggar just turns and makes a bound for me. I got out of my chair with a screech, you can bet, clawing for my gun. But Windham had yelled again, and the wolf seemed to stop right in the middle of the air and sailed right by me!

"I never seen anything like it in the world.

" 'That dog is worth money to me!' says I, thinking of him leading a line of my dogs through the Alaska snows. 'What'll you take for him?'

" 'I don't know,' says Windham. 'I've never been able even to think of the right price to put on him. I guess there's not enough money to buy him, stranger.'

" 'Well,' says I, 'can you let the devil run loose? D'you have to keep him chained all the time?'

36

" 'He won't run away,' says Windham. 'There's nothing that he's half so interested in being close to as to me.'

" 'Is he fond of you, then?' says I. 'Didn't you tell me that he tried for your throat, now and then?'

" 'It's not fondness that keeps him close to me,' says Windham.

"And he said no more. He didn't have to. He just stood there staring at the brute, and the brute stared back at him without blinking. And I understood."

# CHAPTER SEVEN

That account which Steve Murray gave to Drew ended with the tale of how he, Murray, arose in the middle of that night from a dream in which he saw his sled being pulled up the White Horse Pass by a wolf dog as tall as a horse, how he dressed, slipped into the living and dining room of the shack, and there fitted the muzzle over the head of the brute; how he softly undid the bolt of the door, and led the lobo outside; how he "borrowed" the best horse he could find in the Windham corral and, with Chinook on a long lead, galloped away to the south.

It was the middle of the night when he started. He had several hours before daylight began. By that time, people were striking abroad in the lower valley. So he kept to the smallest trails, avoided the roads, and only after twenty-four hours of steady trotting, galloping and walking, did he reach the railroad far to the south, abandon the horse, and put the dog into the train. He himself sat crouched beside it until the train reached the Oakland Mole. There he led the wolf onto the ferryboat, and finally walked off at San Francisco through the Ferry Building with a feeling that he was already two thirds of the distance back to Alaska.

But he was by no means perfectly at ease.

It was true that there was the ranch to tie big Windham to the ground. It was true that the rancher was likely to place the affair in the hands of the police. On the other hand, he could never forget the strange manner in which Windham had looked at the dog, and the dog back at the man, as though there were between them some unsettled battle of a desperate importance. Constantly, in the back of the miner's mind, there was the gigantic picture of Windham following him with seven-league boots, stepping across rivers, blotting out the mountains behind him. Such an impression had been made up by the power of that man!

For his own part, Murray could not have given up the dog. He had made the pleasant discovery that the commands which Windham had taught the dog would be obeyed even when another voice uttered them. The whole attitude of Chinook, moreover, seemed greatly altered. Much of the ferocity had left him. He seemed suddenly very logy and sleepy, and would lie, breathing deeply, for hours at a time, eyes closed, every now and again rousing with a convulsive twitch, staring about him as though to seek for danger; then, slowly lowering his massive head upon his paws and sleeping again. It was as though all strain and care were taken from his life, now that he was away from Windham. The only time that there was a keen expression in his eyes, was when he lifted his head and looked far off into some distance which, Murray very well guessed, might conjure up thoughts of Windham.

In the meantime, Murray booked passage on the first outward steamer, and blessed his stars that one sailed the very next morning. He spent the interim lying low.

Only when they passed through the Golden Gate and saw the nose of Alcatraz Island disappearing in the sea fog, did Murray at last relax. He could rub warmth into his hands, then, and take one deep breath. Then he resumed his attentions to the dog.

He had guessed that nothing but sheer power had been used with Chinook. He determined to try the effect of affection and caresses. But he discovered that he might as well have wasted tenderness upon an iron statue. For

Chinook, he simply did not exist. He was neither pro nor con on any matter whatever. The food he gave was accepted. Nothing else that he could do was of importance.

His heart was warmed, however, by the admiration which was showered upon the dog on the way north. For the boat was filled with men hurrying to join the gold rush. And many of them had picked up dogs. There were dogs of all kinds in the motley array.

There was not much sympathy in the hard heart of Murray, but when he saw a leash of greyhounds on board, he could not help telling the owner of them, a proud young fool, that those dogs would be killed by the first cold snap as surely as though bullets were fired through their hearts. There were other short-haired dogs, street mongrels, little black-and-tans. Among the long-furred ones, were useless little spitzes. Twenty of them would have been needed to make even a light team!

But it was a mad world that was sending forth the gold hunters. Murray was accustomed to that madness. And he was glad to walk up and down the deck with Chinook, thoroughly muzzled, walking on a stout chain lead behind him. More than once, he saw an old-timer lean down and measure accurately the spread of the dog's print upon the wet deck.

"Them feet," said one sourdough, "if you can make a leader of him, will break trail and do the leadin', both."

It was the very thought of Murray. He would not have to take a companion with him, even on the most arduous trails. He could afford to trust to Chinook, out there in the lead—if only he could persuade the monster to leave the throats of the other dogs uncut!

He had a flash of Chinook's fighting quality before the boat reached Seattle. There was on board an old-timer who had made one stake in Alaska already. Coming south from the land of blizzards and gold, he had brought out with him his huge leader, a Mackenzie River Husky of the first water, a hundred and sixty pounds of brawn. Now, his money all spent, the miner was returning to the white North, and with him went his faithful leader, as a matter of course.

"He's my luck!" the man was fond of repeating many

times a day. "He's the most luck that ever I found in the world! And my bodyguard. There ain't any three men in the world that he can't lick, single-toothed, if I give him the word!"

This formidable Husky, one day, gave Chinook a side glance in passing and followed the side glance with a charge.

The lobo had no teeth with which to meet the attack. Nevertheless, he leaped to meet the onslaught and, throwing his head low and far to the side, he hurled all his weight behind the massive bones of his shoulder, straight into the Husky's charge.

The latter shot backward, spinning head over heels. It landed against one of the stanchions supporting the lifeboats and lay there for a time, gasping to get back its wind. It was as though it had been smitten by a pile driver. And Chinook walked calmly on behind his smiling master!

From that moment, muzzled or unmuzzled, the other men with dogs gave the monster plenty of room.

The old-timer complained a little. He said that it was wrong to take wolves to Alaska. The beasts chewed up too many good dogs, and they never had any working sense themselves!

So Murray, overcome with pride, forthwith gave a working demonstration of what Chinook could do.

He felt a little ashamed, at first, when he thought of how the giant in the cabin had made the dog perform, he who had the right of ownership. It was as though he had stepped, now, into boots too big for him. But Chinook gave a flawless performance. And the admiration of the onlookers warmed the very cockles of Murray's heart.

Suddenly he almost loved Chinook. And he felt that that dog would literally drag him into fame!

What of great Windham? Even if the man did by chance pursue and overtake him, a very faint possibility now; bigger men than Windham had died when a .45-caliber slug struck their foreheads!

So, every day, Murray nursed the thought of his revolver, against the future, and used to spend much time when he was alone in his cabin in practicing fast draws.

He was a notable man in the Southwest, in years before this. Murray was not his name in Arizona, but under various aliases he had gathered a sufficient reputation among the wearers of six-guns.

He had a face like an Indian, this Murray, with a swarthy skin, high cheekbones, and slanting eyes. I have always thought that there was a good deal of the half-breed in his make-up. For one thing, his ability to endure cold weather pointed to something more than the pure Caucasian name. For another thing, the only thing that made him fight quickly was to be called "Canuck"!

He had done about all the unsavory things that a man can be accused of, and ten years in a penitentiary had helped to sharpen his wits and supple his mind. In a word, he was as dangerous a man as one could wish to find.

Before the boat left Seattle, he was so proud and excited about his ownership of Chinook, that he had almost forgotten that the dog was stolen property. He felt a strange right to the big beast. By this time, he was firmly determined to kill the rancher sooner than give up the lobo!

There seemed little chance that Windham would overtake him, of course. From Seattle, the ship, loaded now entirely with miners, gamblers, and dance-hall girls, also provisions of all sorts for the Far North, headed straight up for Dyea. On a day when the mist rode high, and the sun was a small red disk behind it, they reached that dingy harbor and began to unload on the lighter.

Murray went ashore on the first load, his pack and his wolf dog with him.

He did not remain there long. He picked up six dogs as good as he could find, and he did not spare money on the purchase of them. Men are free-handed enough when the cash they spend is made at a gambling table! Furthermore, there are reasons enough for having nothing but the best in the way of dog flesh when one treks from the coast into the white heart of Alaska. So he got the best, harnessed them up, took Chinook on a lead, and drove straightaway for the interior.

Once on the way, he took his time. Every day, he shifted the greater part of the light load on the second sled and, harnessing Chinook to it, he put the big creature through his paces. Before the very first day of that practice was ended, he knew what a treasure he had.

Four days later Chinook stepped into the traces for the first time as a leader. A peerless one he was to be!

There was only one accident, and that occurred the second day after he assumed the number one post. Then the largest and fiercest of the other Huskies dared to snarl in the presence of the lobo, and Chinook stretched him dead with one stroke. The throat of the poor husky was literally torn out!

After that, there was no rebelling on the parts of the other dogs. They had seen the lightning strike once. They had no wish to see its white flash again!

# CHAPTER EIGHT

This was in the days of Alaskan "luxury"; that is to say, the important trails had been marked out, staked, and to some extent worn in. After many packings, even when a considerable snow fell, a good leader could poke his head deep down in the snow and find the scent of the teams which had traveled that way before. There were not many leaders who possessed that faculty, of course. One who did was worth his weight in silver, at least.

In the lobo, Chinook, Murray found that he had come into the possession of a wolf dog that could do the thing. He was amazed by it. Ordinarily, it was a trait possessed only by dogs bred and raised in the cold North, that come to learn its ways, beginning with their puppy days. But Chinook had passed a considerable part of his apprenticeship among the snows of the Sierras, where the wind is

42

as strong and the thermometer often falls almost as low as it does in the arctic.

Nature had gifted him with an ideal coat to withstand the Northern climate, except that the under fur was in a nascent state, but as soon as he stepped out on the freezing trail, he began to grow that important undergarment which lies like wool or softest feathers next to the skin.

He had his strength, of course, and his tricky wisdom. Above all, from the viewpoint of Murray, he had instinct —and a nose! He first showed that instinct one time, when they were going down the bed of a stream and Murray was urging the dogs confidently along. It was almost dark. The ice seemed perfectly strong; there was a thin incrustation of snow upon it that made the runners slide easily and smoothly, without gripping too much.

Suddenly, as they whooped along, without any direction from his master, Chinook began to swerve out from his course. Murray shouted, but he shouted in vain. Chinook continued to turn until he actually came straight back to the sled, and there he paused. When Murray ran shouting, club in hand, to administer reason and justice to the brute, he saw before the team, not far away, a dull dark shadow upon the ice. He stopped with a gasp. He knew very well that it was water and that Chinook had smelled it from afar!

It is an instinct that one leader in a thousand possesses, and it is as valuable, fully, as the instinct which enables a dog to smell the trail that lies deep beneath the snow. For when a team dashes into water, at a low temperature, there is nothing for the driver to do but to camp at once, build as large a fire as possible, and then work frantically to remove from between the toes of the dogs the pellets of ice which have formed there. Foot by foot, over every dog of the pack he must go. Otherwise, there will be a frozen foot, and the next morning the crack of the rifle will announce the death of another Husky.

From that moment, Murray began to develop an almost blind trust in his new leader. So had the rest of the team. They had no use for the grim, silent monster, when he was out of harness. They kept carefully away from him

43

and, if one of them blundered near, one flash of his white smile was enough to send the biggest of the Huskies scampering. When he was in harness and at their head, however, they seemed to know that he understood his work, and they followed him faithfully, with tails up and pricking ears, just as men will gladly follow a leader whom they dislike but whose brains they respect.

The trails in Alaska, since the early days, had been made comfortable, not only by staking them out, but also by the construction of way stations where a man could put up and, for a rather stiff price, get food for his dogs and himself and a blissfully warm shelter for the night. Such halts did the driver and the team much good; they put heart into man and beast.

At one of these stations Murray put up on his march toward the Yukon. He arrived rather early, ate supper with the rest, listened to the admiration bestowed upon Chinook, and then retired to his room. In this place the rooms were a special luxury. Usually such a station consisted of a single big apartment, with bunks built in around it. But here, besides the central room, there were other little cubbyholes, constructed of light logs. Into one of these, Murray went, for he wanted to write some letters to send back by the stage.

With him he took Chinook. Usually he kept the monster well muzzled, but on this night he dispensed with this precaution. After chaining him securely to a leg of the built-in bunk, he sat down to his writing, spelling out the words painfully, the pen uncertain in his swollen hands. He had kept at it for some time, when Chinook became restless.

He rose to his feet and slid out to the length of his chain. When Murray looked down, he saw the big fellow bristling, the hair along his back erect. In a moment the head of Chinook swung about and he gave Murray such a look as he never before had received from man or beast. The eyes of the lobo were aglow with a yellow flame, and they seemed to be saying: "Why are we anchored here? Don't you see that I have to go on?"

"You have to go where?" muttered Murray, actually out loud, as though he had heard the question.

For an answer, Chinook fell back a stride and then took up the slack of the chain with such a lurch that the leg of the bunk snapped off. Murray himself rolled upon the floor and, getting up with a curse, wiping the dripping ink from his hands, he saw that Chinook had attacked the door of the room with his teeth! He was afraid that the big fellow had gone mad, a common thing for Alaskan dogs to do.

"Chinook, you fool!" he said. "Are you going to eat wood? Didn't you get fish enough to fill your belly?"

Chinook, in the meantime, had sunk his fangs well into a projecting rim of wood and, jerking back upon it, he ripped out a whole panel from the door. The noise caused an outbreak of astonished voices in the big room, where still some of the mushers were sitting about the stove, completing the thaw before they turned in.

In a far corner of the room, one big fellow, with shoulders a yard broad, looked up from the plate of beans that he was eating. He had come late. There was nothing left except the stewed beans, the dregs of the coffeepot and the heel of a loaf of bread. But he did not complain. His capacity was ten times as much provender as this, but he merely nodded and took his pittance.

The others had looked at him, when he first came in, because of his bulk, but they had quickly stopped their examination. For there was a grim and settled fierceness in the face of the stranger that did not invite questions. About his forehead, creased with three knife-cut wrinkles in the center, there was a look of brutal and animal wisdom, like the forehead of a lion. Words seemed to come uneasily to his lips, and presently no one looked toward him except with furtive glances.

Now, as he heard this rending of the wood, he raised his head, slowly, and stared at the shattered door across the room.

"What the devil is that?" asked the owner of the place. "Hey, you in there, are you drunk? You'll be paying me for a new door, you young idiot. Leave off that smashin', will you?"

"It ain't me. It's the dog. He's runnin' amuck!" Murray shouted back.

45

The big man in the corner softly laid his coffee cup and polished plate upon the floor. He placed the last of the heel of the bread in his mouth. He dusted his knees and rose to his feet. From the deep pocket of his coat he took a short truncheon, with a rubber padded knob at one end of it.

Now his eyes burned! The shadows about them only made their fire more apparent, as when candles burn in the pitch dark of the night.

"Down, Chinook!" shouted Murray, inside the room. "Steady, there! Here, damn you! Chinook! Leave go of that door, you fool!" He broke into gasping, furious imprecations.

Suddenly the door was ripped again, this side and that, and through the gap which was made leaped Chinook. The hole was not large enough to let him through, but the weight of his burly shoulders smashed in a way. He came with a lurch into the room, Murray, yelling, and on his knees, crawled through the aperture behind the wolf.

He was yelling: "Don't shoot him, boys. He's just got a streak on him. He's a five-thousand-dollar dog. Don't shoot, or you'll have me to shoot afterward!"

There was a rush for the wall and the far corners of the room in the meantime. Those who were already in their bunks had been awakened by the clamor, and they sat up, wadding their blankets together, as a shield in case the dog should rush for one of them. Every man present reached for a weapon!

Only the big man, the newcomer, stood passively waiting, with his eyes fixed upon the dog.

Chinook, in the meantime, had frozen in his tracks. After jumping through the shattered door, he stood there just for an instant, glaring across the room at the stranger. In that moment, Murray looked up and saw across from him the last thing in he world which he had expected to see—the giant figure of Windham!

He could not believe it. His brain spun. He looked back, in a flash of the mind, over the thousands of miles which he had covered and told himself that his trail could not possibly have been found so soon, or that any human could have tracked him so quickly as to overtake him upon his way to the Yukon. But there was the fact before his eyes—six feet and four inches of fact, and two hundred and fifty pounds of proof!

All thinking ended for Murray. In the place of his mind, he began to use his hands, and from under his coat he snatched out a long-barreled six-gun, his old and familiar friend, every corrugation of whose handles was a kindly blessing to his fingers.

Yet Windham was not looking toward the thief. He had eyes for the dog alone!

Afterward, so the men swore, as Windham stared at Chinook a smile came upon the face of the man, a sort of desperate smile, as when a brave man faces great odds. For a moment, the jaws of Chinook himself parted, his tongue lolled out, and he gave to Windham the red and silent laugh of a wolf.

Then he lunged across the floor straight at his first master.

# CHAPTER NINE

Not a breath or a word came from the others who watched that scene. There was only the scratching of the nails of the brute upon the floor, with neither growl nor snarl. He was that same, silent fiend which Windham had known before. He seemed to have forgotten all about the formidable qualities of this man. All that he remembered, in a flood of ecstatic hatred, was the scent and the form of that detested creature—man as man first had come into his life, with rope, starvation and club!

Chinook sprang. Windham did not side step, but the short, rubber-padded club smote like a thunderbolt between the eyes of the wolf and Chinook dropped to the floor, a sodden heap of unstrung nerves and loosened muscles.

Then Windham took from his pocket a long, rather light, but very strong chain, made of the finest steel forged by himself, in his own shop far off there in California. He snapped the chain into the steel rung of Chinook's collar, and then he stood by to wait for the dog's return to consciousness.

A loud, half-crying, nasal voice across the room broke in on him.

"You sneakin' thief, leave go of my dog, or I'll drill you!" Windham looked over at Murray, saw the gun leveled upon him, but merely smiled at the smaller man.

He had scarcely taken a step from the chair in which he had been sitting. Now he sat down in it again, picked up his coffee cup from the floor, and drained the last of it.

"Get hold of yourself, Murray," he said. "You're not going to do murder with so many witnesses looking on."

And he settled back comfortably into his chair. Perhaps he was foolish in doing so. Murder had been committed before crowds larger than this in Alaska, and little done about it. For there were few settled communities, and rarely have any but settled communities the sense of law. These men would all be scattered on the next day. Every one of them was accustomed to looking upon acts of the rawest violence in that wild Northern land. Only from the keeper of the place, a report might be sent back by the stage, and a marshal might journey out after days or weeks, to look into the matter and make a probably futile search for the slayer.

Murray knew these things, if the big man did not. But now Murray held his hand, for the moment, at least. For he heard the keeper of the place saying, grimly, to Windham: "You aim to hang onto Murray's dog, stranger, without payin' him his price?"

"I've paid the only price that ever was paid for that dog or wolf, or devil. My name is Windham. I come from Wind Valley, up in northern California. I caught that lobo off the back of my own horse, on my own land, with my

48

own rope. I tried to starve him tame in my own house. I fought it out with him and beat him with this club."

He took it from his pocket again, and showed it to them, a strange instrument.

He went on, slowly: "I made this chain, here, with my own iron, on my own forge. I made the collar he has on. I've got the mark of his teeth all over me. That fellow, Murray, I took in for the night. He stole Chinook before morning. I've traced the two of them this far. And now I've got the dog!"

This speech, being delivered without the slightest emphasis, carried a good deal of conviction. And when Windham touched, upon his cheek, a long red scar that showed through even his dark beard, men nodded with agreement.

Murray saw that he was crowded against the wall.

"He lies," said he. "He had that dog. He was broke. He can't do nothing with the brute. I stop by and see it. I offer him a hundred bucks for Chinook, and he jumps at the price. He's never heard of a dog costing that much before! He takes the money and counts it three times. Why, partners, what would I be doing stealing a dog in northern California to take all the way up here to Alaska? I ask you that?"

There seemed to be equal logic upon the side of Murray.

The keeper of the place, a pale-eyed and pale-haired Nordic, looked from one man to the other. He liked Murray the better of the two. For no man could take easily to Windham's bulk of body and brow of iron.

"You mean to say, Windham," asked the keeper, "that you came all this way just for the sake of getting your dog back?"

"That's what I mean to say," answered Windham.

The keeper smiled and shrugged his shoulders, then he turned a little, and by his gesture he invited all of the others to contemplate the absurdity of this statement. They, in turn, nodded sharply. The case was growing dark for Windham.

Murray was quick to take advantage of this attitude.

"You see how it is, fellows," he interposed. "This fellow gets the gold fever in his blood. He comes up here. He happens along to this place. The dog gets the smell of him and tears his way out to get at him. Would any man want a dog that tries to do murder every time it sees its boss? No, and that's why Windham sold me the wolf. But when he gets up here and he sees the dog, he decides that he'll take him back again. He knows that there ain't much law around here and he's a good deal bigger man than I am!"

He put out both his hands. He seemed to be appealing for justice. At the same time, his sense of an advantage gained made his voice smooth and easy. Windham watched him closely and carefully. His blood was rising fast, and what he saw began to be tinged with red. He was holding himself hard, as he answered:

"You lie pretty well, Murray. But you don't lie well enough to get back this dog. Fellows," he added to the crowd, "if I didn't come up here for the dog, why did I bring along this club, that I made specially for keeping him down, without cracking his skull?"

And he showed the strange weapon. Then, he pointed to the chain.

"I made that chain myself. Look at it, and you'll see that it's homemade. If you've got a forge handy, I'll show you how I work and you'll recognize it. Why did I make that chain so strong, except for such a wolf dog as Chinook?"

Several heads were shaken at this.

"It looks like a toss-up," said one man to the keeper of the place. "You better keep out of it, Mike. Let it slide."

"I ain't going to let it slide," said Mike. "I've made up my mind. No big ham is goin' to bully a smaller man inside of my place!"

"That's right," joined in several of the others. "We ought to have justice around here! There's been enough bullies around this trail already!"

Chinook, at this point, got slowly, sullenly to his feet. He looked at his old master and his upper lip curled and showed the white fangs. The old, undying hatred burned yellow in his eyes.

"Look!" cried Murray. "Does that look like the picture of a dog or of a four-footed murderer?"

He pointed, and those who watched, grunted in assent. They never had seen a grimmer picture than Chinook made just then.

Said Windham: "I'll tell you what, Murray, if this is your dog, call him over to you!"

Murray nodded assent. "Here, Chinook, here, old fellow!" he called. And he added a sharp whistle to reenforce the command.

Chinook, slowly, swung his massive head about and favored his second master with a long stare. Then, without moving a foot, he looked back at his owner. It was a telling stroke for Windham.

"What's the matter, Murray?" asked Mike, the proprietor. "Can't you make your own dog come when you holler to him?"

"He's got Chinook hypnotized," said Murray, sweating with eagerness and with fear. "Look at Windham, I ask you to! Is there a man of you that would want to be alone on the trail with him? Ask him why he lived ten years alone in the mountains? Because he's got the evil eye. Because folks won't have nothing to do with him. That's the main reason. Now you ask me to call my dog in, when the dog's stood there under the eye of Windham! Of course, I can't. It ain't in human nacher to beat a hypnotist except at his own game—and game as dirty as that ain't a game for me!"

It was, on the whole, a silly speech, but those who listened to it were not men of analytical minds. They merely realized, when they looked at the deep brows and the shadowed eyes of Windham, that they never before had seen a face so ugly or so powerful. A feeling of revulsion swept over them.

"I dunno," said Mike. "It sort of beats me, but I got a feeling that Murray is right."

He advanced a step toward Windham.

"Hey, you, what we know is that Murray drove that dog onto his sled up to my way station," he said. "As far as the law goes, that's enough for me. This here is my

51

house. I ain't gonna stand by and see you put it over on a smaller man than yourself. Unhook that dog, take your eye off of it, and hand it over to Murray, here, or you'll have to fight the pair of us!"

Mike came of a fighting race, and he was fighting mad. It was not for nothing that he maintained law and order among the rough gangs that gathered every night at his house. He knew his fists and he knew his guns. Upon guns he would depend, in this crisis, since mere hands seemed impotent against such a monster as this stranger from the Southland.

Moreover, the decided stand of Mike seemed to have convinced the wavering minds of the rest of the crowd. The ugly face of Windham was distinctly against him— that crag of a jaw, that beetling brow, with the triple deep-set crease between the eyes, brutal and savage and seemingly filled with animal cunning.

So Windham ran his eyes over all of the faces, and among them all he saw not one probable supporter. He was alone against a crowd, in a strange place, in a strange land with which all of the others were more or less familiar.

Murray was saying. "You've put up a good bluff, Windham. But it ain't gone through. Just unhook your homemade chain, as you call it, and turn that dog back to me. You know I paid you good money for it."

Now Windham, looking thoughtfully down before him, seemed to be studying the shadow of the stove in the center of the room. Then his glance shifted from the shadow to the lamp which hung suspended from the ceiling, swaying a little from side to side in some unperceived draft, the one point of illumination in the place.

Suddenly, without warning, he picked up the chair from under him and, half rising, hurled it right at the lamp. There was a tingling crash, and the room was swallowed up in darkness.

# CHAPTER TEN

Now the instant the chair was flung, and the uproar started, the night blackness was split through by the bark and flash of Murray's gun, but he fired too late, half blindly. At the same moment, Windham snatched the rubber-shod club from his pocket and struck into the darkness before his face.

For he knew what would happen. He had been with Chinook too many months not to know the devilish habits of the beast. The darkness through which no man could see would only be as a twilight to that cunning hunter, and this was his chance to get at the throat of his master unseen.

True enough, Chinook had sprung up from the floor, and the blow which Windham struck landed. It was, however, only a glancing blow; it did not stun Chinook. It merely told him, it appeared, that he had been wrong, and that this mysterious devil of a man was able to see, against all precedent, in the dark of the night!

The lobo did not spring again and Windham, in a stride, was at the door.

Other men were there before him. He heard them shouting. Their wild voices guided him like a light.

"We've got the door safe!" he heard voices yelling. "Strike a light, somebody. A light! A light!"

He strode on. He reached the men before the door. Easily he brushed them away to the right and to the left.

They tumbled headlong, cursing, while he felt for the knob and found it, but the door was locked and the key gone. Somebody had had wits quick enough for that! No matter! He put his shoulder against the door and it burst wide before him. Out he sprang, into the icy night air.

He had no time to think of hitching up his own dog team to his packed sled. What difference did sled and pack and team make to him then? He had Chinook, his enemy, yet his own property, running lightly before him, giving the chain a good pull. Holding to the chain, commanding the dog with quick, sharp words, he followed swiftly on.

He heard the uproar spill outward from the way station into the open. Plainly, he could hear Murray's whining, snarling voice, like a furious beast, yelling out an offer of a thousand dollars' reward for the death of the big man or a chance to get at the dog.

Then the guns cracked. Bullets sang like wasps in the air about him. He stooped a trifle lower and sprinted with all his might, and ever the pull of the wolf dog on the chain lengthened his strides. He gloried in the full expenditure of his powers of body. Now that he was once started away from them, let them take Chinook away from him again, if they dared!

He could have laughed, but the labor of the running turned his laughter into a groan, as of pain.

At that sound, Chinook turned suddenly under the brightness of the stars and looked back at his master, the chain slackening. And again Windham understood.

If that groan had been of pain, indeed, or weakness, that monster would have been at him in a flash, to finish the work another had begun.

But he was neither wounded nor weakened. Loudly, he cursed Chinook and the lobo leaped ahead again to tighten the chain.

It was the most ironical thing in the world—the patient slave-labor of the dog at the behest of the man whom he hated, whose heart's blood he wanted, the only thing that could possibly quench his deep-seated thirst!

They headed straight on. There was much running strength in Windham. As has been said, he was one of those few bulky men who are, nevertheless, in such perfect proportion that their own weight does not kill them. He could run, and he could run to a distance, like any Indian. His toiling through the mountains, over trails where even a mule could not have gone, in pursuit of game, had given him both wind and leg muscles. And never did he use them as on this night.

For, though he was green to Alaska, he knew well enough that the pause in the pursuit did not mean that it had been given up. Rather, they were rapidly harnessing their dog teams to a sled. Attached to that sled would be three or four men, and every one of them excellent rifle shots.

They would bring out a dozen of the finest dogs that happened to be at the way station on the single sled, and then they would fly down the trail. When the shooting commenced, it would be their rifles against his revolver!

That was his conclusion. He knew that his chances were slim, indeed. Therefore, he legged it up the trail as fast as he could go.

He might have turned into the snow on either side of the trail. But that would have made little difference. Rather, it would have been worse for him. They could follow his trail only too easily in the snow. They could not mistake it, either, for such a pair of mukluks as he wore would not readily be duplicated in the arctic, and such tracks as Chinook left behind him could be made by no other animal in the world.

He could only trust to his speed, and he knew that that speed could not be matched against the whirlwind rush of the long dog team that would follow. Moreover, he could well recall the tough look of the crowd in the station. A dozen of those men would be fit to take the trail, and surely only the best of all would be chosen to accompany Murray in pursuit of the so-called thief.

That was the most maddening part of all—that he, Windham, who never had cheated a man of a five-cent piece, who never had injured a fellow being by word or by blow, should now be placed in the wrong by the adroit lying of such a fellow as Murray, the criminal!

But there was behind Windham a life of labor, and there is this to be said of physical labor. It is the curse of Adam, but it is also the blessing. It wears upon the very soul, but it also teaches an almost divine patience. This year's bad winter may make next year's good harvest, and the day's work is not ended until the sun goes down!

So Windham said to himself, calmly, with a brave man's quietness, that the battle was not over until it was actually ended by bullets. Nothing but bullets should take Chinook from him, this time! He was sure of that.

As he watched the magnificent animal straining ahead of him, giving of his power as gallantly as though his heart swelled with love and devotion to his master, it seemed to Windham that he was looking at the most beautiful creation of the Maker. He had seen fine horses; he had seen beautiful women; he had seen magnificent men; but it seemed to Windham that Chinook was the consummation of all that was physically perfect in the universe.

Now he pulled in a straight line, tail stretched straight out, hindquarters and withers on a level, head well forward, and shoulders and quarters driving splendidly. A worker himself, Windham recognized the patient strength of another laborer.

It hardly mattered that, instead of love, there was hatred in the soul of the wolf dog. What was important was that the animal was peerless and that he, Windham, was with it, to enjoy its might and profit by its wisdom.

It was very cold. His breath began to freeze on his beard, but he did not make the mistake of trying to break it off. It was a bitter process, while the ice was forming, but once it was made, it would form a sort of chilly protection for his skin. Old-timers had told him that. He had asked advice, on the way up from the coast, from those who seemed best qualified to give it.

He watched the thin, white mist of his own breath puffing out, to blow back and settle as frost upon his shoulders and he saw the white cloud of the constant panting of the wolf dog before him.

Small, dark evergreens stood on either side, shaped, many of them, like the flame of a candle or of a tall fountain, unblown by the wind. And these slid constantly by him, as he worked over hill and dale. He had no streamside, easily graded trail to follow, here, but a white undulation.

That was bad for him. Over such going as this, the numbers of the pursuers' dogs would give them a vast advantage. If only it had been a dark night, all would have been well, he told himself. But it was not dark. The stars seemed, above his head, a dazzling white sheet of fiery freckles. He would have sworn that they even cast shadows!

Now, rounding a sudden turn, at the foot of two hills, he came straight upon two sleds. There were eight dogs in all. Standing alongside the first sled, there was a driver; in the second, another well-wrapped figure.

Over to the left, he could see the dull smoldering of a fire, recently put out. Apparently the team had just been harnessed, camp had been broken, and the two travelers were about to take the trail. The word to mush was on the verge of being given to the dogs, it seemed, but at the sound of the snow crunching under the feet of Windham, the stranger whirled about. The long, gleaming barrel of a rifle steadied, at his shoulder, to a single point of starlight.

"Back up, partner," said a quiet voice. "You can't have her!"

# CHAPTER ELEVEN

Windham stopped. The man before him, he noted, seemed well dressed, after the arctic fashion; that is, he was well furred. The team of eight dogs, a big number for only two sleds, looked fit for fast and hard travel and the pack on the front sled was lashed on in the most masterly and well-balanced fashion.

These things Windham noted, as a man will at a crisis, with a single glance.

As for the man in the furs, he was of about middle height, rather broad in the shoulders, and looked well knit and competent, a quality which the sound of his voice seemed to emphasize.

His face, partly shadowed by his hood, was totally indistinguishable in the starlight, but Windham had an impression of early middle age.

"Whatever she is," said Windham, "I don't want her, or any other she. Put down your gun and let me by."

"Go by if you will," said the stranger, "but I'll just keep this gun on you while you pass. Better wait here. I'll soon be out of your sight. Great Scott," he added, "what a dog!"

He said the last under his breath.

"Can that dog run?" he asked, suddenly.

"Like a horse," said Windham, "but he's not for sale, if that's what you mean."

"I've got a little pack of fifty ounces of dust here," said the driver. "Does that talk to you?"

"Not if it were five hundred," said Windham.

"I see," said the stranger. "A fanatic, eh? Well, wait here. I'll soon be out of your sight around the curve. You're sure about your dog?"

"I'm sure," said Windham. "Watch yourself! Jump sidewise!"

For he had noticed the evergreen just above the place where the driver stood bending under its load of snow, and now, as though the fibers of the branch were weary, like muscles tired of a long strain, the branch sagged and commenced to give way. It was heavily loaded and, even as Windham spoke, the whole burden of the snow descended with a rush. There was, also, a heavy incrustation of ice which held in the looser particles like a sack. So it was a solid shock that the driver received and he fell flat, totally lost in the snow, floundering about blindly. Windham started forward to help him to his feet, but here the seated figure on the sled stood up.

"Let him lie!" she cried. "He's done harm enough in this world. Don't give him a chance to do more. Let him lie! Start the dogs! Help me, for the sake of Heaven! I'll make you rich if you will! I swear that I'll show you a place where the gold is fairly pushing out of the ground and asking men to take it. Start the dogs—give 'em the word."

With this she came running back toward Windham, holding out her hand. He could not see her face, but he knew that she was young, and he felt that she was good to look on. But he shrugged. Women were nothing in his life. They never had been.

"Keep away," he ordered her, curtly. "Keep away, or this dog of mine will slash your throat."

Then, reaching through the smother of the snow, he found the arm of the man and closed his hand over it. Through the thick padding of the furs, he could feel the swell and the sliding of powerful muscles. With one lift of his hand he raised him to his feet.

There stood the stranger, gasping a little, with one hand raised to his head, where the snow had struck him. He shook himself, and the powdered snow flew off in a cloud. Then he faced the girl.

"I heard you," he said, with a ring like the clanking of iron in his voice. "Get back on the sled—you—"

He mastered himself before the word was spoken.

"Get back, and don't stand there gibbering at me!" he repeated. "I heard what you said to him. But he wasn't a fool. Mostly, you've had to do with weak wits. But this time you happened to blunder onto a man!"

The girl hesitated for a second, looking earnestly upon the face of Windham. But enough of his features could be seen even by the starlight to reveal the harsh and almost brutal cast of his countenance. With a sudden shudder, she shrank from them both and returned with bowed head to her place, slowly settled there, and pulled the robes about her.

A faint sound reached the ear of Windham. She was sobbing.

In the meantime, the driver turned back to Windham.

"If I'd taken your first word, I'd have got from under," said he. "But I thought you were trying a dodge on me. I'm glad you pulled me out. I'm gladder still that you had the good sense not to listen to that—"

He indicated the woman with a gesture.

"If it seems a strange thing to you," he said, "that I'm carting her along through the night by forced marches, I'll tell you this—that whatever happens to her, nothing can be bad enough. Of all the devils out of hell, no one is worse than she is. And that's gospel!"

His voice went hard as he spoke.

He held out his hand, but Windham did not heed it. His head was tilted. Far away, he heard the sound of voices shouting to a team of dogs.

"There they come!" said the stranger, gritting his teeth audibly. "I knew that they'd be on the trail soon, but I didn't expect 'em as soon as this."

"It's not you. It's myself they're after," said Windham, gloomily. "And now they have me, and be damned to them! You haven't an extra rifle on that sled that I could buy from you, partner?"

"What do they want of you?" asked the other, snapping out the words.

"That dog," said Windham. "I've followed him four thousand miles and got him back tonight from the thief who stole him. Now they're after me, with rifles. And I've a Colt, only, for talking back to 'em!"

He laughed a little, but cut his laughter short, for the quick intake of his breath threatened to freeze his lungs.

"A Colt—and the crooks want the dog, eh? Say, is it your dog, man?"

"Yes," said Windham. "A wolf dog, wild caught by me and, therefore, it's mine."

"I've a set of extra harness," said the other. "A set made for the biggest Mackenzie Husky that ever walked, and it ought to fit that brute almost. Shove him into the team."

"He'll eat the dog ahead of him," said Windham, calmly, knowing that the truth would out.

"Can he lead?"

"I don't know. I've never worked him up here. But he'll answer any right command."

"We can use those legs of his," said the stranger. "And if we can, he'll help to lift you out of range of those fellows behind. Get him up there ahead of my leader. We'll see what he can do. It's an easy trail. He doesn't have to be a number one leader for this sort of a road. He only needs a set of feet, and pulling power."

But Windham was already on his way to the head of the team. By the time he got there, the driver had joined him with the harness.

It was a big harness, strongly made, but it was not large enough for Chinook. The driver grunted with amazement when he saw the tightness of the fit.

"But it won't choke him," he said. "We'll try him. Quick, now! They're coming fast! They must be running with an empty sled!"

"They probably are or almost," said Windham. "Chinook, go on!"

And Chinook, stepping forward, made taut the whole line that hitched him to the sled and, leaning hard against the collar, scratched his way down to a solid footing.

The line creaked.

"By thunder!" said the driver. "He's trying to pull it all!"

It was a heavy pack upon the first sled. Upon the second sled there was a smaller pack, together with the girl. But suddenly there was a groaning from the runners of the sleds. They stirred, they gradually, inch by inch, began to move.

And still Chinook had not left his tracks!

He was simply leaning and lengthening! That is the trick of pulling, for a horse or for a dog, to get the traction low, steady, driving as close to the ground as possible, so that there will be less lifting angle.

"It's not possible!" cried the driver, appearing to forget all else. "Is there a down grade?"

Perhaps there was a slight down grade. Otherwise, truly enough, the thing appeared totally impossible—one dog, looking small indeed, in spite of his bulk, contrasted with the great load on the sleds—one dog, and the rest of the team idle, not having received the word of command.

"He's done it!" shouted the driver. "Look there! It walks!"

And so it did! For both of the sleds were now slowly but surely under way, and the panting breath of the wolf dog shot down, and spread along the ground in rapid gusts, like the breath that shoots from the smokestack of a locomotive.

"No other dog in Alaska could have done it!" exclaimed the stranger. "I'm not believing my eyes. With that one dog, I could go to the pole and back and laugh all the way—yes, and ride on the return trip. Mush, the rest of you lazy, worthless, shriveled up, good-for-nothing curs. Mush!"

As he pronounced the last word, every one of the eight leaped forward and gave their weight to the initial pull.

But the sleds already had been broken out by Chinook alone, for the snow had not frozen hard around the runners, it appeared, and as the eight lunged, the sleds fairly leaped away, at a running pace that threatened, for a moment, to drag it straight over the wheel dog.

That slow but worthy puller, instantly began to scamper for dear life, and the whole of the eight strung out in a dead race to catch up with the flying, monstrous form of the new leader, the ninth dog from the sled.

Run they might, but catch him they never would. If it came to trotting, the long stride of the lobo brought him effortlessly over the packed snow. And when there was a question of galloping, he fairly flew, with bounds that covered distance in an amazing manner.

Both the driver and Windham had to race after the rear sled to catch up with the rapid flight of the team.

"He'll wreck the whole outfit. He's running away! Stop him!" shouted the driver.

"If I stop him, the rest of the team'll pile up on him," said Windham, truthfully.

"He'll never take the curves. This part winds like a snake. The devil!" cried the driver.

But here the girl, sitting straight up, cried in a wild, strange voice: "He will take the curves! Look, Andy! He's taking them now! Watch him go! He's a real leader! Oh, what a beauty! Go it, old fellow!"

In fact, the few lessons which Murray had given to the great wolf dog were now bearing their fruit. Murray knew his business in the Far North and Chinook could absorb teaching like a human being, well-nigh. For now he was taking the curves perfectly, swinging well out to keep the sleds from cutting against the banks on either side, some of them looming well above the packed trail; at other times, speeding straight and true down the center of the way.

"Hurrah, Julie!" cried the driver. "You're right, he's an old-timer. I never saw a better. Now we'll fly. Let them all be damned. They'll never catch you now, unless they put on wings!"

# CHAPTER TWELVE

Along that curving trail, dogs hardly could have set a finer pace. The two men could not have been called drivers in that violent race. Rather, they hung onto the rear sled and were jerked around corners like little boys at the end of the line in the game of snap-the-whip.

Only when a steep ascent was reached did the runaway change to a steady trot, and Andy, the driver, could call out to his companion: "He'll make his name in Alaska, that Chinook! Look at him now!"

For Chinook was leaning hard forward, pulling with all of his great strength.

At the top of that rise they looked back, and behind them they saw, curving out from the last twist of the trail below, a team of twelve dogs and an outfit of four men, dimly outlined under the starlight. Neither was that crew so far away that the fugitives failed to hear the wild and tingling cry which they put up when they saw the leaders!

But Andy laughed, panting and choking with his running.

"They'll have the heart taken out of 'em now. Watch these devils fly down the grade!"

And fly they did. Even Windham, big, strong and sure-footed as he was, could hardly keep on his feet. With gigantic strides they rushed on, holding to the sled, helped by the speed of the dogs in front. Finally, reaching a long level, they shot through it with scarcely abated speed and then slid rapidly up a long slope beyond.

Before they gained that second crest, the dogs were not spent but the men were nearly finished. As they looked back, they had their reward for that hour of frantic mushing. Far, far behind them, almost indistinguishable, they saw that the twelve-dog team of the pursuers had halted and that three of the four men had flung themselves down for a rest.

"Winded!" said Andy, himself hardly able to speak. "Winded, the pikers! But we're not. We'll peg along. We'll peg along. It's the steady pegging that brings home the bacon!"

It seemed to Windham, his lungs burning like fire, that it was high time to make a halt, just as the distanced pursuers were doing, but he was too proud to speak of his fatigue. He pegged on, as Andy desired, swaying himself a little forward, so that the leaning of his body would compel his legs to drive ahead.

He had thoughts to fill his mind, somewhat, and lessen his care for his body. Besides, being in the most perfect training, he gradually recovered his wind, breathing was more easy; and the dogs had at last reduced their terrific pace. In a few words, he communicated to Andy the right words for guiding the big new leader of the dog string. After that, it was a simple matter to keep Chinook under control.

What Windham meditated on was the enthusiasm of the girl as she had watched the lobo running so well in the lead. It was as if she and Andy were of one mind and soul upon this trail. He could not have guessed, from her joyous outcry, that she was being compelled to accompany the man on the journey.

The more he thought upon the problem, the more it caused him to ponder and to shake his massive head. But he knew nothing of women; he wanted to know nothing. It was only that the ringing joy in the girl's voice, her joy over the performance of Chinook, had set up a musical echo in his heart and lifted it in the strangest manner.

He remembered an old proverb: "The wiser the man, the fewer are his hours with women!"

This one was evil. There had been a blasting rage and scorn in the voice of Andy, when he spoke of her. No one could doubt the sincerity of Andy, to be sure!

Besides, he never could doubt or question Andy so long as he lived. For he owed his life to the sudden generosity of the smaller man!

Also, with the passing of every moment he found more and more to admire in the ways of Andy. He had run evenly with Windham himself—to be sure he had been fresh at the start—and now he sent the team along in the manner of one who knows what his business is from the ground up.

Then he discovered that there was much to learn from the manner in which the other marched. Silently, Windham regarded the short, quick steps with which Andy went up slopes, the long but cautiously slouching strides with which he navigated the downward pitches, and the beautifully rhythmic swing of his trot across the level. It was his habitual gait, and it seemed to Windham that it was modeled upon the trotting of the wolf dogs of the arctic.

Without a word, he set himself to the imitation of his companion. Being in perfect physical trim, with a surplus of the needed strength, he soon was picking up the way of Andy. It was a trick which could not be thoroughly mastered in a moment, but with every hour he was more at ease. A few days of this, and he felt that the trick would be his.

Every moment or so, his glance ranged ahead and found the lofty form of the dark-coated wolf dog, and the heart of Windham leaped in him. Chinook was his!

An odd feeling came to him that this was the place for Chinook, up here in the wilderness, where his strength could be put to a useful service in behalf of man. Was not Chinook like this country, dark with the evergreens, huge, bold, over-awing to the eye of man?

And he himself, Windham—why was it that such a happiness flowed through him as he measured his strength against the length of the trail and did not find himself wanting? He felt as though it were his country, his native land; yet how new he was to it!

Also, there was the golden secret here, that thing which so many men had hunted for, and so many already had become rich from it. The girl had said that she could lead him to a place where the gold thrust out from the dark ground. It well might be. For a man could tell, with a single glance, that every mystery was possible here, good and evil!

It was a grinding march and a long one. After a time, as the pace steadied down, the girl dismounted from the sled, and she, too, began to trot along, lightening the load for the dogs.

Dressed like a man, a boyish figure she made. Though she had not a man's stride, still she seemed to make up in lightness what she lacked in size and strength. Even Andy was not the master of the graceful, easy run of the dog musher as she was. There was no wearing out to her! She seemed made all of elasticity and fire.

At the rate they had traveled, Andy declared that it was very unlikely that the pursuers would now overtake them, and that they could at last rest both themselves and the dogs. But, first, he pulled off the trail into a thick copse of trees, small and close-growing. He need not worry about the trail they left, for from a gray, low-hanging sky a steady snow was falling, and this would soon blot out every sign of the runners as well as the tracks of man and dog.

They pulled on until they found a small opening in the trees and there the team was halted.

Instantly all three fell to work, Andy assigning the tasks. First, Windham unharnessed Chinook. The big fellow gave one sidelong, venomous glance at his master, then rolled in the snow, leaped up, and was instantly off among the dark of the trees.

"Is he gone?" shouted Andy, looking on at this with alarm.

"He'll come back," said Windham. "He won't leave me until he's had a few more chances at my throat, damn him!" He laughed a little, a faint, green gleam coming into his eyes.

In a way, he hardly wished to gain the affection of

66

Chinook. As long as the monster was held, was it not as well to hold him by hate as by fear or by love?

Only, as time went on, he would discover the way to creep inside the mind and the spirit of the dog, and so to subdue him. Time, patience, and a firm will, these were needed, he kept telling himself.

So he had let Chinook go, then had started cutting wood. But cutting was too slow a process. He grasped shrubs, and ripped them out of the earth, the roots crackling like the explosions of rapid musketry. Then he hurriedly tore the shrubs to pieces, and flung the pieces in a heap.

Andy Johnson—he had learned the rest of the name during the trip—was putting up, with the girl's expert help, two small shelter tents and kindling the fire in the little portable stove, which held some dry kindling to start making the fires, a seasonable precaution followed by all wise Alaskan travelers.

When Windham came up, he heard the girl saying: "Does that dog really hate you, Ned?"

It was the first time, since their meeting, that she had directly addressed him. But she had heard Windham and Johnson exchanging names and in that Northland formalities do not endure long!

"Yes, he hates me, Julie," said Windham.

"Why should he hate you?" asked Julie.

There was sympathy in her voice, a sudden kindly warmth that startled Windham and impressed him. He looked hard at her.

The light was not good. A purple-gray mist filled up the forest like water. They were in a sense like creatures submerged. But as one looks through water and sees the wavering image, so he looked at the girl, hard and straight, for the first time and saw her.

She was as dark as the half-breed, Murray. She had the same hue of skin and eye, saving that in her a glow of color shone through. Though the eyes were somewhat almond-shaped, they were very large, and appeared even larger because of the length and the thickness of the lashes. She had a bright, keen look, as though she were very cheerful, and only waited for an occasion to smile.

At once, he felt a sense of friendly intimacy, but before he could answer her last question, Andy Johnson was snarling: "Listen to me, Julie, you hell-cat. Keep your claws off Windham. Leave him alone. He's not for you, d'you hear?"

She turned her head a little toward Johnson and smiled at him. Windham could hardly see the smile, but rather the flash of it, and suddenly he thought of the baring of a knife.

"Dear old Andy," said the gently caressing voice of the girl. "How careful you are of your friends—and your guns!"

# CHAPTER THIRTEEN

They had the usual trail meal; that is to say, Andy first cooked over the little stove the bacon, while the teapot was heating at the back of the fire, and while the girl stewed the frozen fish for the dogs at another fire between the two tents.

When the bacon was fried, a sack of flour was opened, a hole made in the top of it, and the grease poured in. As it cooled, Andy worked up a great ball of soggy dough, which was seasoned with salt and baking powder. This he kneaded well, and then he made it into three huge pancakes, which were put into the frying pan to simmer until they were half done. The raging appetites of the mushers would never allow them to cook long enough.

The tea was now made. It was not the pale, insipid tea of the Southland. But a good quantity of leaves were put into the water and allowed to boil thoroughly. When the tea was poured into the drinking cups, it was almost the color of strong coffee, with more of a tawny hue to it, of course. That tea washed down the bacon and pancakes.

Then there was dessert, which showed that they were not far from civilization. A heel of rye bread was brought out, a heavy, hard and badly baked loaf, and with it, a can of blackberry jam; and the three of them devoured the jam and the bread, silently.

The dogs had already been fed. The cooking utensils were cleaned. And now the three sat together without a word. Above their heads, and near to the stove, hung their footgear drying. It would not be completely dry by morning, but at least it would be better than sopping wet. They had on their feet, now, pairs of soft, deliciously comforting slippers made of the hide of young caribou, the fur turned inward. Johnson had given an extra pair to Windham. They were oversize, but he was barely able to squeeze his great feet into them.

The men filled their pipes and lighted them. The steam of their drying garments, smoke escaping from the stove —acrid woodsmoke—and the stench and clouds of the strong tobacco filled the little tent. They began to see one another through a fog, but pleasant warmth stole through their bodies. Windham could feel his tensed muscles relaxing. He was far more tired than he cared to admit. It seemed to him that Johnson was just as erect, as jaunty as ever. And so was the girl.

Well, he had made a double march, and they had made only one. Yet he was vaguely troubled. He was accustomed to wearing other men down more than twice over! And still he usually remained fresh at the end.

But this was a new life to him. He knew, now, that he would have to study most carefully the ways of it.

"That dog, Ned," said the girl.

"What about him?" asked Windham.

"He came in for his share of the food."

"I'm glad of that. When I saw him fading off into the woods," replied Johnson, "I was afraid that it might be the last of him, in spite of what Windham said."

"No," replied Windham. "He'll never leave me."

He smiled, half bitterly, as he spoke. "Not unless he's stolen."

Johnson looked wistfully toward Windham.

"He'd be worth a lot of money to me," said Johnson.

"Look here, man. I'd pay you a fancy price for him. You didn't mean what you said about never selling him. Four or five more years, and he'll be an old dog, anyway. What'll be the good of him, then? What would you do with him, away south, where there's no sledding work?"

Windham saw that the girl had leaned forward a little to wait for his answer, as well as to listen to it. And her dark eyes widened a little, holding steadily to his face.

He glanced down. There was something about her that made his heart leap. Then he put out his big hands and studied them, himself wondering a little.

"I don't know just how it is," said he. "That lobo cut a lot of throats down on my place in California. He hamstrung my prize bull. He slaughtered sheep. And I started out to get him."

His voice trailed away.

"Well, you got him," said Johnson. "What next did you want?"

"Look," said Windham, puckering his leonine brow. "If he'd been all wolf, I'd have shot him, I think. But when I saw the brown and the white in his coat—well, I changed my mind."

"Changed your mind to what?" asked Johnson, rather sharply, as though he did not relish this misty way of speaking.

"I decided that I wanted to do something with him," said Windham, stirring restlessly.

He never before had asked himself these questions. He could not exactly find the answer.

"What did you want to make of him?" snapped Johnson.

Windham made a helpless gesture.

"Look here," he said. "D'you ever see a mountain that you wanted to climb?"

"Sure," answered Johnson. "What of that?"

"Well, was there any good of climbing the mountain?"

"Yeah, you could see the other side of it, anyway," said the musher.

"You know," replied Windham, "that was the way I felt about Chinook. I wanted to see the other side of him. The dog side."

"Have you?" asked Johnson.

"No," said Windham. "But I'm still trying. I'll keep on trying. I usually keep on at a job, once I've tackled it!"

He said it without emphasis, but suddenly the girl leaned back with a sigh. It seemed to Windham like a sound of content, and when he stared across at her he saw that she was smiling down at her slender hands, which were crossed in her lap.

Johnson noticed the direction of Windham's look. "You're softening a little, aren't you, Ned?" said he.

"How?" asked Windham.

"The girl, eh?" said Johnson.

Windham scowled.

"Look here, Johnson," he protested. "You talk as if she were a wolf!"

"A wolf's mild," said Johnson. "A wolf's nothing, compared with her."

"If you're going to tell him about me," said the girl, indifferently, "I'll go to my tent, Andy; that is, if it'll make you any easier."

"I've said it before your face before," said Johnson. "I'll say it again!"

"I don't mind at all," replied the girl. "I was only thinking about you. It's warm, in here, so I'll stay on, if you don't mind."

"I don't mind," said Johnson. "I'll tell you about her, Windham. You've seen her. She's pretty, ain't she? You think that, now. But you see her dolled up, slim as a colt, and as graceful—a dress with some color in it, maybe— and then she's not pretty. No, she's a beauty. She turns the head of a man. She sends 'em away dreaming day and night. That's the kind she is."

She put her chin in her hand and nodded her head a little toward Johnson.

"You've never been so poetic about me before, Andy," said she.

"Shut up!" ordered the dog-puncher, brutally. "Shut your face, till I'm through!"

"Don't talk to her like that!" rumbled Windham.

"You shut up, too, you big freighter!" barked the excitable Johnson. "I'm trying to open your eyes. You just listen, and open up your ears. I say that this Julie Fernal is clean bad, all the way through. Comes of a bad family, too!"

The girl raised her head.

"You might leave that out, Andy," she said.

Ah, how silken smooth was her voice, and yet Windham could sense the rippling bright danger beneath the surface. He looked at her with new eyes. His heart leaped no longer. It began to ache.

"Bad family, I say," said the other. "There's her brother, Bert Fernal. Goes up North. Gets in with the Indians. Throws up his life as a white man. They say he had killed his list of decent men. So he goes out and packs in with the dirty Indians. That's what he does! Well, it's a good riddance for the rest of us, but it's hard on one person. The girl! This one. You know. You know, even the worst of 'em will stick by their own blood. I'll say that for her. She wanted to get her crooked brother back, no matter how many murders were on his hands.

"So she picks out one of the best dog-punchers that ever hung onto a gee hole in this part of the world. That's what Winslow was! And she says to him: 'Go up there and bring my brother back, and I'll show you where the gold is breaking its way out of the ground.' 'Damn the gold,' says Winslow. 'I want you.' 'Well, you can have me, then,' says the girl. 'I'll marry the man who can get Bert back to us!'

"You see what it meant, Windham? Twenty men had gone in among that tribe of Indians, and never a one had ever come back alive. And you knew that, Julie, didn't you?"

"I knew it was dangerous," she admitted, calmly. And she yawned!

Ice ran through the blood of Windham as he noticed the graceful care with which she covered the yawn.

No, Johnson must be right. There was a devil in her!

"She knew what it meant, but she sent poor Winslow up there and Winslow died. He's never been heard of since then. And he was worth the whole Fernal tribe, multiplied by ten!

"But that's not enough for her. What's one man's death

72

to her? Nothing! She gets hold of the whitest man in the North; she gets my old partner, Dean Carey, as straight as a string, as brave as a lion. A man to mush with, a man to fight with, a man to die with, I tell you. But she gives him her damned smile and her promising eyes, and sends him mad, too. And he goes out among those Indians, the devils! Finally he comes back to Fort Yukon, and there he lies, dying by inches, the sickest man that I ever saw. And he says to me: 'Andy, if only I could look on her once again, it'd feed something that's starving in me. I'd die happy, I think, if I could see her again!'

"So I slide out from Fort Yukon, I race all the way to the coast. I find this she-devil. I pretend that I want to take her out for a spin and show her my new team. When I get her loaded on, I start inland with her. And here she is. And I only hope that poor Carey's dead before she gets to him. Because if I see him smile at her pretty, damned, deceitful face before he dies, I'll kill her. I'll strangle her!"

# CHAPTER FOURTEEN

He stared at the girl as he spoke, his teeth set hard, and his jaw muscles bulging. And Windham was troubled as he watched the two, the man almost trembling with wrath, the girl calm-eyed, serene, watchful as though this scene had nothing whatever to do with her and with her affairs.

Windham pointed a finger toward Julie Fernal.

"You tell me your side of it," he said.

She looked calmly back at him. "There's no good in that," she replied, after considering him for a moment. "You don't know enough about women to tell lies apart from the truth. There's no good in listening to me, Ned.

Andy Johnson would talk you around to his side of it anyway."

"Tell me," Johnson shouted at her, "if I've said one thing that's a lie."

"You wouldn't be such a fool, Andy," she answered him. "You know too much to tell lies. You show only one face of the truth, though!"

He gritted his teeth, but did not answer and she, in turn, stood up and stretched and yawned hugely again.

"I'll be going to bed," said she.

"Hold on," said Windham. "Why should she have to sleep in the cold tent? We ought to take that tent, where the stove hasn't been burning."

"You talk like a fool," said Andy crisply. "And you don't know her. She's a seal. She could go to sleep comfortably in ice water. Here's your bracelets to wear; anklets, I mean to say, Julie."

He took out a pair of slender steel manacles and snapped them over the ankles of the girl. There was a small, strong chain connecting them that allowed her to take a step six or seven inches long.

"Sleep tight," said Johnson, cheerfully.

"Yeah. I always sleep tight," answered the girl.

She paused at the entrance to the tent.

"About the big dog, Ned," said she.

"Yes?" said Windham. "He won't bother you at night. I'm the only one that he'll bother around here."

"No, he won't bother me," said Julie Fernal. "I want to make a bet with you. About him."

"What?"

"That I'll have him eating out of my hand inside of three days."

Windham laughed, and his laughter was like a deep thunder which was answered suddenly from the door of the tent. There stood Chinook, bristling, showing his teeth with the tight-lipped grin of a wolf ready to fight.

"Look out!" said Windham.

The girl turned her head, casually, and smiled at him.

"He'll never bother me, Ned," she insisted.

As she stood beside the big fellow at the entrance flap, she laid a hand carelessly upon his shoulder.

Chinook turned his head with teeth ready to clip that arm off at the elbow, but he seemed to change his mind at the last minute. Regardless of the hand that rested upon him, he turned his head again and confined his attention to his master, whose laughter he had just heard.

Julie chuckled softly. "You see how it'll be, Ned," she remarked, and she walked slowly past the big lobo, nudging against him to get room to go by.

Only after she was gone, Chinook turned and disappeared into the darkness. The flap of the tent fell down again.

"You're all covered with sweat, old son," said Johnson to his companion. "I don't blame you. She's a hard case. And she's a queer one."

Windham said nothing. He was still staring at the flap of the tent.

"I'll tell you what's in your mind right now," suggested the other.

"Tell me, then," said Windham. "Only, you'll never be able to come within miles of the truth!"

"You're thinking," said Johnson, "that there must be some wolf in her blood. Am I wrong?"

Windham started violently.

"What made you guess at that?" he demanded harshly.

"Because I've had the same idea myself," answered Johnson. "I've had it almost from the first minute that I laid eyes on her. You can't help getting such notions. It's the slant eye and the way she smiles. I never knew another man or another woman to smile the way she does. Did you?"

Windham closed his eyes, to remember the picture better.

"No," he admitted. "I never did."

"And you'll never see another," said Johnson, "unless there's another devil walking around on two feet instead of four. I put everything about her short, old son. But she's a bad one. Mighty bad. She's the worst sort of poison that I ever saw in my life! She's a thousand dollars an ounce, that's what she is, and every bit of her is dangerous. You take my word for it."

Windham shrugged his massive shoulders.

"You put those cuffs on her ankles," he said. "Why did you do that? Do you think she might harness up the dogs and run away in the night and leave us?"

"That would make too much noise. She wouldn't try to do that," said Johnson. "But she's as likely as not to strike off by herself and go straight through the snow and on her way."

"Alone?" cried Windham. "Without a single dog? Without even a pack?"

"She'd take a rifle and shoot her game," said the other.

"And freeze to death before she'd gone three days!" said Windham.

"Not that girl. She's not the freezing kind. She's got a fire inside of her, more than any Eskimo I've ever seen."

"But where would she find game? I haven't seen a head of any kind," asked Windham.

"No more would I find it," said Andy. "But she's different. She'll see a trail and follow it, when you and I would see nothing at all. And she'll melt into the woods as silently as a moose or a lynx. And before she comes out, she'll have meat of some kind or other to roast at her fire."

"That sounds like a fairy tale," replied Windham.

"I know it. But you'll have a chance to read her better, before we're at Fort Yukon!" answered Johnson.

Windham talked about her no more, except that, as he turned into his bed, he raised up on one elbow and said: "Look here, Johnson, if she starts to get familiar with that Chinook—"

"Don't you worry," answered Johnson, yawning, as though the subject already bored him almost to sleep. "The wolf will never touch her. You were right a while ago. They're altogether too much of the same kind."

With that cheerful suggestion in mind, Windham fell asleep, to dream all the night long of a lovely lady, that turned into a grinning wolf before his eyes and then of a grinning wolf that turned into a smiling girl.

When he awoke in the morning, Andy Johnson was already sitting up, tugging on his mukluks, grunting a little, and groaning a little over the sore places on his feet.

Windham dressed in silence. The flap of the tent was thrown open, the fire was kindled in the stove, and Windham, stepping outside the tent, found that Julie Fernal was already up and stirring, in fact just striking her tent.

She gave him the brightest of smiles, but Windham turned away with a shudder, for the dream of the night before was still too vividly in his mind.

Straightway they started the preparations for the morning. The breafast was cooked, a repetition of the supper of the night before; the other tent was struck, the pack remade upon the forward sled with great rapidity, and they led out upon the trail again.

All day and every day, the same program was repeated —the endless mushing, the pause at the close, when exhaustion was tugging at the tendons of their legs, the tiresome cookery, the feeding of the dogs, the struggling fire in the little stove, and finally, sleep, the great blessing.

But Windham walked on with a growing problem in his mind and that problem was the girl. He had been told sufficiently damning facts about her, and she had not denied a single one of them. She had listened to the accusations of Andy Johnson as though the whole world already were familiar with her character and her career, as though she herself were hardened to all manner of condemnation.

But day by day she maintained the most cheerful manner. She was never sullen or sulky. Even the endless grind of the trail found her with head high, tireless as the most athletic man, ready with a constant smile. There was about her, too, a free and easy camaraderie that appealed deeply to Windham.

"How can she manage to keep up with us on the trail?" he once asked Johnson.

"She was born up here," answered the other. "That's about all I know of her. This whole country was made for her, and she was made for it. But don't you ask me to try to explain Julie Fernal. I couldn't."

Even more than he watched the girl for herself, Windham had an eye out for her maneuvers to win over Chinook. He knew that it could not be done; and he waited to see how she would attempt it.

He saw no efforts on her part. She seemed to pay no

more heed to Chinook than to any of the other dogs in the team. Then, on the third evening, Windham learned something. Inside the tent it was hot and close and he thrust his head out through the closed flap in order to take a farewell breath of the pure outer air. The night was clear; the mists were gone.

There, at the entrance to the tent of the girl, he saw Chinook lying, with head high and the air of a watcher over a treasure.

Windham gazed in dumb amazement. It was more, in fact, than if he had seen her caress the brute and watched Chinook whining and wagging his tail with pleasure.

For the man knew, all in that instant, that Julie Fernal had made the lobo her own!

# CHAPTER FIFTEEN

From that moment, so far as Windham was concerned, the march north resolved itself into two things. The first was the study of Julie. The second was the study of her increasing power over Chinook.

A week after the start the team was given into her hands to drive, and Johnson nodded at his companion, saying: "Watch her now, Windham. You think that you know dogs and I think that I can drive 'em. But she could take a lot of runty malemutes and beat the finest racing dogs in Alaska, if she really wanted to. Watch her travel, old son!"

It was true. When she spoke, a thrill seemed to run in a wave through the entire team.

"What does she do to 'em?" said Windham to Johnson.

"How can I tell?" replied Johnson. "There's hypnotism in her. That's all. Better watch yourself, and keep on watching, because she's not done with you, son!"

Windham said nothing. He began to study the girl and the dogs, and it seemed to him that he could see a special difference between the girl and Johnson and himself. He had told himself that he loved the Far North. But that was probably something which she had never even thought of. She was the Far North, as surely a part of it as the dark forests and the blizzards that whipped them. It did not occur to her to fear the wilderness, because it was in her blood, not an experience grafted onto another existence.

The moment that the team passed from her hands to his own—for Johnson was trying to teach him all the tricks of the trade—it was plain that the dogs lost heart. They seemed to grow physically smaller. Their steps were shorter. Their tails drooped. Chinook, instead of the great, gallant and gay figure which he had presented the moment before, was now a slinking devil, casting slavering looks over his shoulder, from time to time, toward the man whom he so hated. It was always the same.

When he harnessed Chinook in the morning, it was at the peril of his life. But when she called and held up the harness, Chinook came like a dark streak and stood in place eagerly. She would kneel in the snow beside him, murmuring quietly to him as she fitted the straps upon his great body, and once he saw the lobo turn his huge, dangerous head and actually lick the frost from the shoulder of her coat!

"There's something good about her, I tell you," he said repeatedly to his friend, Johnson. "If there wasn't she'd never be able to handle that wolf!"

Johnson looked him full in the face.

"Why not?" he asked. "Is that because the wolf has such a good nature?"

"Why, no," said Windham. "Of course, Chinook is simply a murderer!"

Then he saw where his own remark pointed and was still. It was impossible to persuade Johnson that there was any good about Julie Fernal. Deeply ingrained in his mind was the conviction that she was evil. He regarded her only with contempt.

As for Windham, he became more and more silent.

One thing the long trail was accomplishing for him. It was burning away every scruple of extra flesh. It was consuming every bit of fat. He was turning to iron. He had learned the long and easy gait of the arctic runner, sure-footed, steady, and patient. He had learned to have eyes in his feet, to judge the snow or the ice by the look of it, like a native. It was Johnson who did the oral teaching. It was the girl from whom he learned even more, by watching her steadily.

But he felt that he was embarked upon an endless journey. To Johnson, Fort Yukon was the goal. But to Windham the goal was an understanding of Julie Fernal and mastery of Chinook. If the girl could manage that thing, then he could learn the trick, too.

One day, as they were drawing near to the end of the trip, he fell a little behnd the sled, and went along at her side, up a slope which checked the speed of the dogs.

"Julie," he said to her, "why can't you tell me?"

"What?" she asked him, turning her face suddenly toward him, with a flash of smiling lips and eyes—a habit she had and a startling one.

"You know what I want to learn," said he.

"I don't," she answered.

"About you," said he.

"No, no," said the girl. "Because Andy Johnson has told you everything, already."

"No, he hasn't told me everything," said the big man. He shook his head, looking away from her, down the trail at the white undulation of the landscape.

"What do you want me to say?" she asked.

"Tell me what sort of a girl you are, will you?"

She stared at him.

"I'm what Andy said, partly," said she.

"You're something more," said Windham. "I want to know what that is."

"It's no good asking me," she said. "Why should I make some pretty lies to tell you? Ned, I like you too much to lie about myself."

"They wouldn't have to be lies, would they?" he asked. "Besides, you can be frank with me, Julie. I know what you think about me. You don't have to flatter me at all."

"Tell me, first, what I think about you," said the girl.

"You think that I'm pretty slow in the wits—and it's true," said he. "And you think that I'm not very much of a man, or else I wouldn't let Johnson treat you the way he does. And you think that I'm pretty simple, take me all in all."

"Is that what I think about you?" said the girl.

"Yes," said Windham. "That's about what you think, and one thing more."

"What's the other thing, then?" she asked him.

"You think that perhaps I'd do for the northern trek."

"What northern trek?"

"Out to the Indians, to get your brother."

She stopped short in the trail. She put her mittened hands upon her slim hips and looked fixedly at him.

"Say that again, Ned," said she.

"Well, it's true, isn't it?" he demanded.

He loomed big above her, leaning forward a little, stooping his head, so that he would be a little closer.

Looking back at him, tilting her head somewhat so as to meet his glance squarely, she seemed to shift her look from one of his eyes to the other, as though she saw there a different meaning in each eye.

"Well," she said, "it's true, after all. The first moment that I laid eyes on you, I knew that you might be the man for me. The man to get my brother. That's what you mean?"

"Yes, that's what I mean."

She went on: "But I knew that Johnson would keep you from it. I knew that there was no use trying to talk you into that job."

He shook his big head at her.

"What's the good of saying that, Julie?" he asked her. "Because I know that you understand everything."

"Go on, Ned," said she. "You tell me what I understand."

He flushed, his face burning with a sudden rush of blood.

"You know," he said huskily, "that you could make me eat out of your hand, just as you've made Chinook do. I saw him—yesterday."

Her glance was still moving curiously about his face, as though she were reading every feature.

"Could I do that with you, Ned?" she asked him.

"Well, you know you could," said he.

"What makes you think that I know it?"

"Because I've seen the way you look at me," said Windham. "I've seen you look at me as though I were something that you'd just dropped, and which you hardly knew whether you wanted to stoop and pick up or not. You've looked at me like that. I understood."

"Do you mean," asked the girl, "that you'd undertake that trek to the Indians? Do you know what those Indians are? Do you know what they've done to the last twenty men who got into their territory, prospecting or just traveling?"

"They murdered them," said Windham.

"Well, they were old-timers. And they knew the Indian lingo," replied the girl. "What chance would you have against those murderers up North?"

"I don't know," said Windham. "I only know one thing."

"What's that?"

"That you're going to ask me to go there."

"And you?" said the girl.

"If you asked me, I'd go."

It was the simplest possible avowal of love. He hardly meant it to be that, in fact. But as his glance dwelt on her, he knew that she had given the first profound significance to his life; she and Chinook who had become her dog!

She looked away down the trail.

"I meant to ask you. You're right," said she. "That was because I thought you were only a big—"

She checked herself.

"But now I've changed my mind," she said. "I see that you're a lot more. And I don't think that I'll ever ask you to lift a hand for poor Bert Fernal!"

# CHAPTER SIXTEEN

Johnson was very bitter about it. As the two came up to the sled, he gave Windham one look and then called out in irritated tones: "You've been yapping to her, have you?"

"I've talked to her a little," replied Windham.

"Then, damn you," said Johnson. "I hope that the redskins cut your throat, as they've done with the rest of 'em. You're the biggest and the blindest fool that ever lived!"

For forty-eight hours he refused to speak to Windham. They worked and traveled together in utter silence. The amazing thing was that Julie did not try to break that silence for a moment. She acted, in fact, as though she were afraid of Johnson and did not wish to risk offending him, even by an attempt to make peace between him and his traveling companion.

Then, one night, through the darkness they saw the lights of Fort Yukon, first grouped together in one little haze of radiance, then expanding, until they stretched out wide, warm arms to the trio.

"Now, it's nearly done," said Johnson. That was all he spoke until they had driven into the little town.

The dogs went in on the run, whipping the light sleds behind them. The girl rode. Active as she was, she could not quite keep up with such a long-legged gait as this! So they came, smoking, into Fort Yukon. The dogs, as though the various smells of town, cookery, here and there, had maddened them, let loose wild outcries, which were answered by five hundred wide-mouthed sled dogs of the town.

They slowed, a little, as they passed a pedestrian, a

83

man who looked like a child's image in snow, so clumsy was the fur-wrapped figure.

"Where's Dean Carey?" shouted Johnson. "Living or dead?"

"He's down yonder, in Bud Wagram's house," replied the other.

Andy Johnson yelled to Chinook and he hit the collar hard, the team surging forward behind him. At full speed they shot away and came at last to a halt, as Andy put on the brakes and yelled. They were in front of a house with a wide, low front and a big chimney standing up bluntly above the rest of the building. There was no knocking at front doors.

"Open her up and go in!" called Andy Johnson to his companion and, as Windham made the entrance, Johnson brought Julie in behind.

This part of the building, as Windham saw it, was obviously a store, with heaps of furs, perhaps waiting for the next steamer up the Yukon for shipment. Upon shelves or laid out for show on counters, there were dog harnesses, guns, ammunition, knives, clothes of all sorts to fit the Northern weather and turn the edge of its winds.

This display was dimly lighted by a single smoky lantern in a far corner; a brighter glow and hum of voices came from an inner compartment. As he got to the doorway that opened upon this room, Windham found himself entering a much smaller chamber, with a large stove that glowed red with warmth in the center, and three or four men seated about it. He gave them only a glance.

In a farther corner, he saw a bedridden invalid lying with a wan, thin face, and eyes closed in weariness that seemed more than cousin to death itself. As happens from prolonged weakness, prolonged despair, the very skin of the man's face seemed to be pulling, so that the corners of his lips were drawn in a smile resembling very much that of an Egyptian mummy.

"That's Dean Carey, I guess?" asked Windham, giving no other greeting to the rest of the company.

The sick man opened his eyes wide. He looked at the ceiling instead of at Windham.

"I'm Dean Carey," answered a voice almost foolishly big and strong.

Then he raised his weak head and stared at the doorway. Windham, feeling his companions coming up, stepped aside. The removal of his bulk was like the shifting of a curtain on a stage, for in the gap which he had filled appeared instantly Andy Johnson and the girl.

The sight brought the other three loiterers in the room to their feet.

"It's her!" gasped one of them. "He's gone and got her, all right. Who'd ever've thought it!"

"I'd've thought it," said the sick man. "Andy, he never was the man to go back on his word! Andy, you're gonna let me die easy, at the end!"

"Die?" said Andy, striding rapidly up to the side of the bed. "You'll never die from this, Dean. Why, you look ready to jump out of bed and run a hundred miles."

"All right," said the sick man. "I'm glad that I look that way to you."

But he smiled a little.

"I won't be askin' you how you got her. But I'm mighty glad to see her."

He made a gesture with his thin hand. It dismissed Andy, who stepped to one side, and so the girl stood alone at the bed of Dean Carey.

The latter looked at her, but with what expression the others could only guess, so much did his long drooping lashes veil his eyes. Only the smile was plucking still, in a ghostly way, at the edges of his mouth.

Windham made several steps toward the center of the room.

He wanted to see the girl's face as she talked to Carey, and he was amazed to see that she appeared entirely calm, almost smiling. She actually sat down on the edge of the bed and took one of the bony hands of the invalid in both of hers.

"I'm sorry to see you like this, Dean," said she.

"Are you?" he questioned.

It was an absurdly big voice which came up out of that wasted throat, the big Adam's apple wavering up and down in it, visibly.

"Yes, Dean," she replied. "What happened?"

"Aw, nothing much," said Dean Carey. "Only, they busted my heart for me. That was all. But I saw your brat of a brother."

He opened his eyes more widely. There was visible a glare in them—a steady and baleful glare—which he fixed upon the girl.

"Why didn't you tell me about him?" he asked of Julie Fernal.

"I told you all that I could about him," said the girl.

"You lie!" said Dean Carey. "You didn't tell me what a swine he was. You said that he was a man!"

Windham began to sweat. Yet the heat of the stove had not yet pierced through the arctic chill in which he was armored.

"He is a man," said the girl, calmly and steadily. "He's the bravest sort of a man that I ever knew."

"You lie again, and you know that you lie," said Dean Carey. "He's a throat-cutter, like the beastly crowd of red men that he's living with. He lives with 'em because he likes the life. If he hadn't've liked it, he would've come away with me, when I went there. We had a chance, then. But he wouldn't come. The cur! He sold me to 'em!"

His thin lips grinned suddenly back from his teeth. It looked as though he would snap at her, like a wild beast. Windham grew sick at heart. Yet the girl did not shrink from Dean Carey.

"It's pretty hard for me to believe that, Dean," she said.

"What made you send me in?" he demanded of her, his voice turning hoarse, so that it was almost inaudible.

"To save poor Bert," she answered.

"You lie again!" said Carey. "You wanted to show that you had power over men. You wanted to put your curse on me, the same way that you've put it on other men. You wanted me to be soaked up by the snow. You wanted them to get their knives into my throat. Why, you said what you'd do for me if I brought him out!"

"I said that I'd marry you," said the girl.

"Then marry me now," said Dean Carey. "Because I'd have brought him with me, if he would have come!"

"I made a bargain with you," she answered. "You didn't do your part of it."

"Because of him, because of him!" shouted Carey, furiously. "But didn't I do my part? I'll show you what I paid!"

Suddenly he ripped open his shirt and showed his breast, hideously marked and puckered with scars.

"They did that with coals of fire!" he shouted. "They did that for two days. One coal at a time! They stood around and watched me, and they laughed. And me, I yelled for help the second day. I was a woman. I screamed. I begged! Me, I done that! Me, Dean Carey. I crawled at their feet, I hugged the knees of their chief and begged him to kill me or let me go, but to end it. That's what I done!"

He began to sob. The tears ran freely down his face. "Here, Dean," broke in Andy Johnson, while the other men in the room crowded into a far corner of it. "Here, Dean, old partner, it's not worth while. Nothing you ever did will make the rest of us feel any different about you. You're going to be yourself again, one of these days. As for her, let her be damned!"

Carey waved him and his argument aside. He spoke again, in a broken voice.

"I got away on the third night," he said to the girl, who sat motionless, steadily gazing at the tormented face. "I got away. They took their time hunting for me, I guess. They knew that I couldn't get away far, the shape that I was in. And they were right. Somewhere out there on the tundra I died. The real part of me died. Only this damned thing mushed through to Fort Yukon. That's all! And I've laid here living from that time to this, only waiting for Andy to bring you up, so's I could put my curse on you, before I cash in my checks!"

There was a faint gasp. Windham sucked in his breath with a deep, whistling sound. The eyes of the sick man were bulging from his head, hideously.

"Here's my curse on you," shouted Carey in a terrible voice. "May you love a man as I've loved you, till the heart in you burns night and day. May you crawl on your knees to him, as I've crawled to the feet of the chief, out

87

yonder in that white hell. And then may he kick you away from him, as a man would kick a mangy cur! And may the devil get you at last!"

He fell back, exhausted, and lay still as a stone.

# CHAPTER SEVENTEEN

Windham was never to forget that scene or even that moment. When Dean Carey fell back unconscious on his bed, with his breast still exposed and the scars showing, not a man in the room moved for an instant.

Then Andy Johnson stepped forward. It seemed to Windham that the man had extraordinary nerve, because he dared to stir when the atmosphere of that place was surcharged, as it appeared, by the curse of Dean Carey.

Straight to her side went Johnson. He took her by the arm and shook it. She looked up at him and Windham could have cried out with amazement, for her gaze was perfectly level and calm.

"What is it?" she asked him. "What's the matter, Andy?"

"That's all he wanted out of you," said Johnson, snarling like an angry dog. "He simply wanted to put his curse on you before he died. And I put mine on you, too. So does every other man here, Julie, because of what you are. But there's no weight in ours compared with the curse of a dead man."

She seemed totally unconcerned. The blood in Windham ran ice as he watched her.

He was badly frightened, too, to think that such a woman should have had such a hold over him. That hold was broken now, surely and forever, he told himself.

"You think that he's cursed me and died," said the girl.

"But he hasn't at all. He's cursed me, and now he's going to live."

"He's a dead or a dying man right now!" insisted Johnson.

He pointed to the face of Dean Carey. It was a grim grayish green.

But the girl shook her head.

"You're sentimental, you fellows," she answered, looking at Johnson and then at the others.

Very deliberately she leaned and placed her ear to the heart of Carey, counting out the action of the man's heart, as she did so. Then she straightened.

"He's going to be all right," she said. "His ticker is running along slowly, and not very strongly, but it's steady enough. For a broken heart, it seems to be doing a pretty good job."

She stood up and yawned. Windham thought that Andy Johnson would strike her down, for the man's fist was balled in a knot, and his face was black and working.

"Look here, Bud Wagram," she said. "What have you been feeding him?"

A gray-haired, solidly built man answered: "The best things that we could give him. Clear soup and crackers, and light things like that."

She snapped her fingers. "I thought so," she said. "Here's a dog-puncher who's been living on fried bacon, grease, and flour, most of his working days. And you give him fresh air and clear soup. There's no building power in clear soup, you idiot. You've got some good, fat, frozen quarters of caribou, haven't you?"

"Of course, I have," said Wagram. "But that sort of a diet would just about kill him."

"Don't you believe it! You cut him off a good steak, and don't cook it too much," she replied tartly. "Leave some juice in it. I'll cook that steak for him, because I know how. You take my word for it, he could stow away a pound of steak, right now."

She added: "And coffee. And a good, soggy pancake, such as he'd have out on the march. Make it small. Put in plenty of grease. He needs something to put under his ribs, and you've given him nothing but a lot of kindness. Affection isn't what he needs. He needs chuck. He hasn't got a broken heart. He's just got an empty stomach."

She walked toward the stove.

"Here's a red-hot place where I could grill a steak for him," she said. "Now, Bud, you trot out and whack me off a piece with plenty of fat on it. A young, tender chunk of caribou will put that fellow back on his feet. Jimmy, you rustle me up some bacon. Pete, you can get hold of the coffeepot and bring it in here with some water in it.

"Andy, there's no use in standing around, glaring. Hating me won't put Dean Carey back in trim. Button up that shirt of his and tuck the bedclothes up under his chin. Don't worry about him. He'll come to when the smoke of that burning steak gets to his nose. Ned, rustle some wood and jam it into the stove. Let's have a little action around here."

Action there was, accordingly. Every man in the room jumped to obey her orders. Only Andy Johnson, as he walked reluctantly toward the bed, turned his head and scowled at her over his shoulder. She merely waved at him as, with a piece of old newspaper, she scoured the top of the stove clean.

"Keep your temper, Andy," she said. "You know what happens when you lose your head in a fight. And this is a fight to get Dean Carey fixed up. Healing a broken heart is pretty tough work. But you just watch!"

Andy said nothing. But his look, it seemed to Windham, was a little silly as he sat on the edge of the bed and obeyed the instructions of the girl.

In the meantime, the other men had brought in the meat, the coffeepot, and the bacon. Almost at once, the steak was hissing upon the red-hot surface of the stove. The meal was quickly prepared. The great heat of the stove soon had the coffeepot simmering.

Larded with pieces of bacon, fried just enough but not dry, and with crackers flanking it, the girl carried the hot, steaming platter to the bedside. There she sat while Dean Carey, his eyes open now and his color much better, looked up at her with the puzzled, blank expression of a sick child.

"Try this, Dean," she said.

"Why, hullo, Julie," said Carey, and he smiled faintly at her. "By Jimmy, but it's good to lay eyes on your pretty face again!"

He had forgotten the scene that had gone before, at least, for the moment. "Try this," she repeated, cutting off a generous mouthful of the juicy steak, and holding it at his lips. "This is what you need, old son."

He let her feed him like a child. Between mouthfuls, his glance lifted from her hand to her face, and then dropped again.

"Seems like I'm as hollow as a cave," said he.

"Sure you are," answered Julie. "And we're going to fill up that cave, Dean. Hand me a cupful of that coffee, one of you. Take a sip of this, Dean. It's got just your amount of sugar in it. This'll fix you up, old-timer!"

He sipped the coffee. His color grew momentarily higher, until when the steak was half finished, he muttered: "I'm mighty sleepy, Julie. Want talk to you a lot. You'll be here when I wake up, won't you?"

"Of course, I will," said the girl. "You just drop off. When you wake up, there'll be a brand new steak for you, old son."

"Ah, Julie," said Carey. "I've been a terrible long distance away from the sound of your voice. Seems as though I've been—"

"Never you mind where you've been," said Julie. "You've had a fever. And you've had a lot of bad dreams. That's what you've had. You go to sleep, now, and I'll be right here when you wake up."

Instantly his eyes closed. He smiled, and a moment later he was breathing deeply and regularly.

"By thunder," whispered Bud Wagram, "you're a regular doctor, Julie. I never would've thought of feeding the poor guy that sort of chow."

"Yeah," replied the girl, nodding and speaking brightly, "there are a pile more people killed with kindness than with rough treatment, Bud. You write that down. You don't have to whisper, either. He'll sleep the clock round and never have a dream. He needs that much sleep to digest the steak that he has inside of him."

She stood up.

"What about some eats for us, Bud?" she asked. "When do we come in on the eating, I'd like to know? I could eat a whole herd of caribou myself, I'll have you know!"

Bud Wagram merely grinned at her.

"Julie," said he, "you've earned the best meal that I can turn out for you!"

"If she's bringing Dean around," said Andy Johnson, the words rumbling in his throat, "who was it that almost killed him? Answer me that? You're going to thank her for giving a hand to the fellow that she almost drowned, eh? That's the kind of a joke I don't laugh at. Not on both sides of my face at once!"

"You're sour, Andy," said the girl. "But you'll feel better when you see Dean Carey sitting up in bed and talking rough again."

"Tell me this," said Johnson. "Are you even sorry about what he's gone through? Do you give a rap about what he's suffered, on account of you?"

She replied evenly: "Listen to me, Andy. You've had your inning, and you've had a long one. You've driven me like a dog, and I've had to take it. As for what you think about me, I don't give a rap. As for what I think about Dean Carey, and what he went through, that's my business. As for what I think about you—well, I'll let you know what that is, before long, and it won't be with words! Put that idea in your pipe and smoke it for a while."

She turned from Johnson, and for the first time since Windham had joined the pair of them he saw Johnson stand, scowling and silent, at a loss for the proper words to speak.

At length the little man turned to Windham and murmured, as he came up to him:

"You see what she is, Ned. I hope you're cured."

"Cured?" said Windham. "I tell you, that I'm cured for life. She's not a woman at all," he went on, grasping vaguely at an idea. "She's in a class by herself—and what that class is I don't know, except that it's dangerous."

"Dangerous?" said Johnson. He laughed faintly.

"She's a snake. Where she breaks the skin, she leaves poison." He paused, and then he added: "She'll get me, too. I wonder how she'll go about it."

That question was soon to be answered!

# CHAPTER EIGHTEEN

After dinner, that night, they rented two rooms from Bud Wagram, whose place was half store and half hotel. Windham turned in and slept like a dead man, the round of the clock and something more. He was awakened in the morning by a whining in the next room. When he opened his eyes, he saw that his roommate, Andy Johnson, was already up and dressed.

"It's her," said Johnson, slowly. "She's got your wolf dog in there with her, talking baby talk to him, and teaching him to do tricks, I suppose."

Suddenly, from the next room, Windham heard soft, joyous barking, that wound up in a whimper of excitement.

"What can she be doing to him?" muttered Windham, jumping up from his bed.

"Aw, she's teaching him to jump through a hoop, I suppose," said Andy Johnson.

He buried his face in both hands and stared at the floor.

"What's the matter with you, Andy?" asked his friend. "You look mighty bad."

"I couldn't sleep all night," answered Johnson. "I kept thinking, all the while, how it was that she would get even with me—how she would sink the knife into me! I couldn't figure it out!"

"She'll never be able to do you any harm," said Windham. "Not while I'm up and around!"

Johnson put out a hand and gripped the great arm of the other.

"You're a friend, old son," said he. "You're a friend of the right cut, and I'm going to need you. Still, she'll find a way. She'll get at me, sooner or later. I knew it when I grabbed her and took her on this trip to Fort Yukon."

He stood up, with his fists clenched high above his head, but his voice was soft as he said: "Why doesn't someone put a bullet through her cursed, clever brain and end her forever? That's what I want to know!"

Windham shuddered as he looked into the contorted face of Johnson.

"You look here, Andy," he said with concern. "You lie down and try to get some of the sleep you've lost. You're letting your mind work on this girl too much. She can't harm you. I'll promise you that! Now I'm going to get out and take a run and get some fresh air into my lungs. This room is as close as a sealed barrel."

He heard the scratching of the lobo as the girl and the wolf passed down the hallway.

"Go on out and take your walk," said Johnson, gloomily. "I'd do the same thing, if I had any nerve left. But my nerve's gone. It's a funny thing how she can take the heart out of a man. Look at Dean Carey. Look at me!"

He shook his head, and the last that Windham saw of him that morning, Johnson was seated on the edge of the bed, his face buried in both hands.

For his own part, he ate a hearty breakfast, swallowed a quart of steaming hot coffee, while he ate half a loaf of bread heaped with vast mountains of apple jam. Then he strode forth to get his lungful of the open air.

He went down to the river bank, striding happily, his shoulders back, new vigor pouring through him with the knowledge that this day there would be no more marching than he chose. Yet he missed something. There had been a weird fascination in trekking forward, day after day, pushing along toward the goal.

He had thought it was the mere excitement of the march itself. Now he saw that he was wrong. It was not the excitement. It was the joy of conquering something from the iron white strength of this Northern kingdom.

94

A sharp halloo behind him made him turn, and there he saw the girl running along, pulling back on Chinook. He seemed to be charging headlong after his master, but when she spoke one word, he came to a halt and sat down, lolling his long tongue and watching Windham out of green-glimmering eyes.

"Hates me, doesn't he?" said Windham. "Look at the green in those eyes, will you?"

"You don't understand him, Ned," said she. "Some day you will, and then you'll get on with him."

"Tell me what there is to understand," said he, "and then I'll try real hard."

"You're afraid of him," she answered, with her level glance probing his.

He remembered, with shame and with inward cold, the day when he had striven vainly to master the eye of the wolf dog.

"It's true," he said. "I've been scared to death of him."

"That's why he hates you," said she.

"And not because I've beaten him to a pulp?" he asked her.

"Because a thing that's afraid of him was able to beat him. That's why he hates you," said she. "That's why he'll wait for years till he has a chance to slash your throat. And if you stay with him long enough, sooner or later, he'll certainly be the death of you, Ned."

"I'm not putting a price on him, however," said he, smiling at her.

She nodded.

"I wasn't trying to cheapen him, either," said she. "Even if I wanted him, I haven't the price that Andy Johnson would bid for him."

"I thought," said he, "that you knew a place where the gold is sticking its knees and elbows right out of the ground?"

"I know that place," said she. "Bert and I know it. We went out and worked it, too. There's a couple of thousand ounces lying there, sacked, right now. Done up in home-made caribou sacks. And we only skimmed the surface of that pot of milk, I tell you. We hardly made a dent in things."

95

"Then why don't you go out and haul in the ounces?" said he. "A couple of thousand ounces make over thirty thousand dollars of any man's money."

"Why is Dean Carey lying in there, about done in?" she asked.

"Why, the Indians, I suppose."

"The Indians just about did us in, too," said she. "We managed to pull out, but all that we took with us was light stuff for fast traveling. They followed us pretty hard, but we had seven good dogs, and they saw us through. We nearly starved, too, before we made it back to the Fort. They ran us within eyeshot of it, very nearly."

She snapped her mittened fingers.

"That was a run for you, Ned!"

And she laughed joyously at the terrible memory of it! She had surprised him so often, he seemed no longer able to wonder at her.

"Then what about your brother, Bert? Why doesn't he get the stuff, if he's so thick with the Indians?"

"What good would gold do him, out there?" she asked. "Gold doesn't buy you anything from those fellows. Besides, he's been afraid to come back. He thought that he was wanted for the killing of Tiny Doc Morris. That's why he ran away and joined up with the tribe. And it wasn't he who had killed Morris. It was Turk Sanderson. Turk confessed it before he died. He confessed it while the ice pack that had caught him was crushing him to death. Jock Fuller brought that story in to the Fort."

Windham listened to this grisly tale, so lightly told.

"But Dean Carey says that he found your brother and yet your brother is still out there."

"Dean Carey," replied the girl, grimly—one of her rare dark moments—"also said that Bert double-crossed him. That shows that Dean is either a fool or a liar. If Bert hasn't come in, it's because he can't come. Nothing in the world would keep him away from me, if he could break away from the tribe, and he knew that a hangman's noose wasn't waiting at this end of the line."

Windham grinned at her.

"Are you telling me the truth, Julie?" he said.

"Yes," she answered. "It doesn't pay to lie, most of the time. I usually tell the truth, Ned."

"You told me," said Windham, "when I first met you, that if I took you away from Andy, you'd show me where the gold was pouring out of the ground."

"That's true," said she.

"Except that the Indians would have cut me up for fish bait before I got away with the stuff. Is that the way of it?"

She merely shrugged her shoulders, totally unembarrassed.

"That's one way of looking at it," said she. "There's another angle," she went on. "You've seen Dean Carey stretched out in there. You know now what those Indians are capable of doing. How does that make you feel, Ned? Just tell me that."

"Feel? I'm mighty sorry about him. That was a bad sight, when he opened his shirt," said Windham.

"Did you give up the idea, when you saw those scars?" she asked him.

"What idea?" asked Windham, frowning down at her.

"Why, the idea that you had had before, about trying your own hand to get Bert in."

She planted her feet a little apart. There was a ring in her voice that made Chinook leap up and face his master, with a silent snarl.

"Who told you that I had that idea?" asked Windham.

She shrugged her shoulders and smiled at him.

"You know, Ned," said she. "You're not so very deceptive. I've seen you looking at me, on the march, now and then, as though you were telling yourself that the she-devil might be worth having, in spite of what Andy Johnson said!"

And she laughed a little, softly.

"Would you sell yourself, Julie?" asked Windham. "To a man?"

"For Bert?" cried the girl. "Why, I'd sell myself a thousand times over. I'd marry a Digger Indian, if he

97

could save Bert. You don't understand. He's my brother, my kid brother. My father told me to look after him, and I promised! And here's Bert, lost to me and lost to himself!"

# CHAPTER NINETEEN

Windham looked down at the girl quietly, with an odd numbness taking hold of his brain. Then he smiled at her, faintly. "I don't know about you, Julie," he said. "You may be right. Again, you may be wrong. But that doesn't seem to have much to do with it. You get what you want. Who am I to stand up against you? Only, we'll make no bargain. If I go out there to try my luck and get your brother—well, I simply try my luck. It might make us better friends and nothing more. We'll let it ride at that."

She slid her arm through his and began to walk along at his side, urging him forward, so that she was turned a little toward him, and laughed gaily up to him.

"None of the rest would ever have said that, Ned," she told him. "You're the biggest pair of shoulders; you're the biggest heart, too. I always guessed at that!"

"I'm a pretty dull fellow, Julie," he answered. "And you've guessed that, too!"

"I've guessed at that," she replied with her amazing frankness. "But I don't mind it. Cleverness you can find in a fox. But the lion leads a fatter life and so does the bear. Now tell me if you've really made up your mind?"

"I suppose I have," said Windham. "Don't crowd me about it, but I suppose that I'll do the thing if I can. I try to think that I'm not fool enough to tackle a job at which so many wiser dog-punchers have failed. Still, I'm fairly sure that in a day or so, I'll be getting ready to leave. That is, if I see your face now and then, Julie."

"I don't want to be a Delilah with you, Ned," said the girl.

He sighed.

"You can't help being what you are, Julie," he answered. "Any more than Chinook can help being what he is. You see, I'm a smaller and a weaker sort, except for mere muscles. I'm afraid of Chinook; I'm rather more afraid of you. But I'll go ahead like a fool attached to a lost cause. That's the way of it. Bad luck has found me out. A year ago, I was as secure as a gopher in a hole. Now I'm routed out and chucked up here in the North, to freeze, I suppose."

"Or to get rich, Ned," said the girl.

"Well, that's the other chance," said he. "But with me, it's like roulette. I'm putting my life on a single number, and thirty-five chances against me."

They went on in utter silence. It was more than an hour before they returned to Fort Yukon and the hotel-store of Bud Wagram. They had not spoken a word, but every minute the slender arm of the girl had been inside the arm of Windham; he had heard her breathing at his shoulder. Once she broke into song, softly, checking herself suddenly as though she did not wish to intrude upon the privacy of his thoughts.

When they came to the store, he had made his decision. He gave one long, farewell look at the girl and then marched inside, taking Chinook with him, the big brute bristling with hatred all up and down his back, his mane standing like the mane of a great black lion, multiplying his size.

In the inner room, Windham found Andy Johnson at the bedside of Dean Carey. The latter was already a changed man. His eyes were clear. The dreadful puckered look was gone from about the eyes and the mouth. In place of the gray-green color, there was an almost healthy, clear pallor.

He waved his hand feebly to Windham.

"Andy's told me how you helped him on the mush up here," said he. "I'm thanking you, big son! I've written it down where the writing won't rub out! Have you seen Julie this morning?"

"No," lied Windham instantly.

Johnson looked at him with relief in his eyes.

"I don't understand," muttered the sick man with irritation. "Don't understand why she's not around. Confounded strange girl, Andy, ain't she? Ain't I right?"

"Yes," replied Andy. "How's the weather outside, Ned?"

"Sharpish," said Windham. "But pretty good to breathe."

Now he went into the corner room, where he found Bud Wagram nursing a pipe, sleepily, and perusing a tattered newspaper, at least five months old.

He had spread before him a closely printed double page of want ads, and these he read with the utmost attention, one by one, here and there pausing to make a little mark with his thumb nail, like any lounger on a park bench in Manhattan. Now and then, also, he would give a small shake of his head or a nod, or raise his eyebrows with an expression of the utmost interest.

Windham watched him, unobserved, for a time with great amusement.

"Hullo, Wagram," he said at length.

Wagram marked his place with a sooty forefinger. Then he looked up.

"I want some advice," said Windham. "I want to ask you because you're an old-timer. I want to go out after Bert Fernal."

"There's only one kind of advice to give you," replied the storekeeper. "Go in and take another look at the body of poor Carey, and see just what the damned Chandalars did to him."

"Is that the name of the Indians?" asked Windham.

"That's their name," said Wagram.

"If you won't advise me," said Windham, "then I'll pick up a guide and go ahead on my own hook. Wagram, you could tell me enough to give me a start!"

"I'll tell you nothing," insisted Wagram. "I won't help you commit suicide! Get out of here."

But Windham waited, and said nothing.

"Will you get out?" asked Wagram, sullenly.

Windham shook his head.

"All right. I guess I gotta talk to you, you fool," said the storekeeper. "Sit down there. No, it's better that you should come out with me, and I'll show you what you want. How many dogs have you got?"

"One."

"One!"

"Yes, that's all."

"You'll need eleven more, or a dozen more. And a guide. What have you got?"

"Myself, one dog, and plenty of spare cash."

"I hope you rot!" exclaimed Wagram.

# CHAPTER TWENTY

For two weeks, steadily, Windham accumulated his equipment. First he bought eleven dogs. It was the idle season at Fort Yukon and dogs, therefore, were not overly expensive, considering how far in the post was. He got dogs with the look of travelers, dogs that their owners were willing to vouch for.

He bought single harness, to tail them out in a line, harness made of the strong, light webbing which is far stronger per ounce than any leather. And on this trip, ounces would count. From the first, Wagram had impressed that idea upon him.

They used to sit up until late every night, working out the details. Upon Wagram's advice, he did not buy woolen underwear, but linen, which was actually woven in mesh! As Wagram pointed out, that would allow evaporation.

"You're going to be out in forty below all the time," said Wagram. "It'll be a mighty warm and balmy day, when it gets up to thirty. There'll be wind, too. Don't let them tell you that zero temperatures kill the wind. Not up there on the tundra. No, sir! And a wind at fifty below, which is what you'll have more than one day, goes straight through to the bone. That's not all.

"It will hit sixty below, too, and maybe even lower. And that's death, as sure as bullets through the grain, unless you've got the right equipment.

"Even the dogs can hardly stand it. Even that big ugly brute of a leader of yours will hardly be able to make the grade!

"From the minute that you leave Fort Yukon, everything about you has to be right or you're a dead man. You're a dead man anyway, most likely, as soon as the Chandalars get their hands on you! Chief Little Knife will lick his lips when he sees that much white man all wrapped up in one skin. But I want to keep you in good condition, so's you'll get that far, at least!"

He grinned savagely, without humor, at Windham.

Siberian squirrel, for its weight, is as warm a fur as there is in the world. Of this his parka was made. The hood was faced with fox and wolverene. The wolverene was there because it is the only fur on which the moisture of the breath does not collect and freeze, putting an ice pack around the face! The hood was lined with silk, which enabled one to don it readily; also, it was light.

The lightest and warmest-footed animal in the wilds is the lynx, with its great, cotton-furred paws. Of those paws were the mittens made, cunning Indian work. The feet of the mukluks were moosehide, the tops were of caribou with the fur, of course, turned to the inside. Altogether, in spite of his size, the weight of that clothing, was hardly more than six and a half pounds!

Men hesitated to go out upon a New York street without a ten-pound overcoat weighting down their shoulders. But in those light and highly efficient garments, Windham would see seventy degrees below before ever, by the grace of fortune, he could come back to Fort Yukon again!

There are luxuries, too, such as extra light socks of caribou fur, the fur of the unborn caribou, the most delicate thing in the world. And there were other matters, too numerous to mention, worked up by the careful forethought of Wagram.

"You ought not to win," he said. "You ain't got a chance to win. Everybody knows that you ain't. If the folks around here was to guess where you aim to travel, they'd arrest you for a crazy man and send you outside in shackles. Only, you might have beginners' luck!"

A hundred pounds of big brown beans were cooked and frozen. There were paraffin bags to hold the flour, sugar, rice, and other provisions. There were axes, dog feed, stove, stovepipe, guns, medicine kit and sewing kit, besides other details, small in bulk but great in importance. Hardly less important than all the rest, were the sleds; perhaps they were the most important of all!

Wagram got from his storeroom three toboggans, each a few inches over nine feet in length. The carry-alls were of walrus hide, in good condition, which was an essential point for quick, secure packing. In addition, the working surfaces of the runners had to be gone over carefully with linseed oil, which was rubbed in again and again.

Now when these preparations were completed and the pile of luggage was stacked up, it was found that Ned Windham had nearly fifteen hundred pounds to be hauled by his twelve dogs!

Well, they would pull it. Chinook was as good as two or three in one. Although the going in many places might be hard, Wagram told him that it was better to have the dogs working hard, rather than to have extra mouths to eat up the food too rapidly.

In the end, Windham had reason to think that Wagram was wrong in this respect.

When the total outfit was assembled, Wagram swore that it was as well outfitted a pack as ever had left for the Far North. Windham himself felt a great sense of security and confidence when he looked over the dogs and saw what they would pull.

There was still the guide to find. Wagram got hold of a big, rawboned, wide-shouldered half-breed.

His mother herself had been a Chandalar. His father was a Scotchman named Aintree. Gus Aintree was the half-breed's name. He had been raised with the tribe. During those years they were occupying their pleasant southern range, long before they were crowded north by the rush of the gold diggers, before they had developed that passionate hatred of all things white.

Now Gus Aintree was a professional guide and dog-puncher.

Sullen of mouth and eye—how small and piglike were those eyes—he stood before Wagram and Windham, shifting his glance from one to the other.

"You know the way out to the Chandalars?" said Wagram.

"No," said the half-breed, and shook his head violently.

"You're a liar. You know damn well that you went out there on a trip, the last year or so," said the storekeeper. "You visited some of your red relatives. Don't you lie to me, Aintree."

The half-breed did not even blink.

"Well?" he said.

"This man wants to go out there," said Wagram.

Aintree failed to look at the giant.

"This man chechahco," he replied, gruffly.

"This man is fire on the trail," said Wagram. "You know Andy Johnson, run all week, never stop. This man, he run down Andy. He make Andy sick, he so tired. He nearly make Andy cry. Savvy?"

"Aintree think maybe Andy Johnson no cry," said the half-breed.

"Cut the talk short," said the trader. "You're going to go with Windham. How much you want a day?"

The breed held up both hands.

"Ten dollars a day?" said the trader. "Sure! That pretty cheap price for you and your father, his brother and young John. But this man want only you. What your price, Gus?"

Again both hands were raised, the ten fingers lifted stiffly.

Wagram grinned. "You talk like a fool, Gus," said he. "You never made that much money in your life."

Gus shrugged his shoulders.

"Chandalar very bad, now," said he.

And he whipped his forefinger across his throat, though his face retained its immobile expression.

"Too much. Ten dollars a day a lot too much," said the trader.

Gus, without farewell, turned about and strode to the door. Wagram made an angry gesture to Windham.

"He's an iron man on the trail. You've got to have him," he muttered.

As Gus reached the door, the trader called out: "Hold on, Gus!"

The half-breed turned slowly about. He showed no interest whatever.

"Look here," said Wagram. "You want lot of money, Gus."

Gus shrugged his shoulders, as much as to say that the job was worth much money.

"Well," said Wagram, "my friend want good man. He pay you money, then. He pay you a lot. One hundred dollars a month!"

The eyebrows of Gus lifted.

Windham was about to break into a laugh. One hundred dollars was offered in the place of the three hundred which the breed had demanded, but now he was amazed to hear the Chandalar reply: "All right. Gus go. Hundred dollars, eh?"

"Yeah. A whole hundred dollars a month," said the trader. "You're a lucky dog, Gus. You be ready tonight. You'll make early start. Savvy?"

"No. Not tonight. Gus want one more good drunk. Then he go," said Gus. "Tomorrow night lot better. Gus go then." He did not wait to discuss the matter, but stalked on out from the store.

When he was gone, Wagram sat down with a laugh.

"I don't want to cheat that fellow," said Windham.

"He's weak on arithmetic," said Wagram. "But that's his fault. He's had chances to learn. Now he'll have to pay through the nose for never opening a book. However, he's the man for you on the trail."

"He looks like a throat-cutter," said Windham.

"Sure he is," answered the other, carelessly. "But I think it'll take a bigger man than he is, to cut your throat, old son. You'll have no trouble with him, I guess. Take things easy. The time'll come, mark my words, when that ugly map of his will look better than an angel's to you. He'll never play out, unless you work those long legs of yours too fast the first few days out. If he gets ugly and tries to come back, knock him down and drag him along for a day. That'll put the fear in him, the half-breed dog!

"Never trust him behind your back! All the same he'll do his share of the work. He won't talk too much. And he knows every inch of the ground between Fort Yukon and the Chandalar village. He's the only man for you, so what more can you ask?"

Windham nodded. The ugly face and the uglier manner of the breed still stuck in his mind, as it were, like a bur. But he managed to nod his head.

"I'll try it with him," he said. "But it may not be a very pleasant companionship."

"What you think it'd be, anyway? A pink tea?" grunted Wagram. "You go in and sleep thirty-six hours. That's what you'd better do before you hit that trail. And don't let a soul know where you're going, or the boys are likely to lynch Julie Fernal. And I'd be the next one they'd string up!"

# CHAPTER TWENTY-ONE

In spite of the fact that he knew there was sound sense in the advice which he had just received, Windham preferred to go out into the open air.

So he went out into the street, and there he almost floundered against Murray, the half-breed. The dark-faced man did not try to escape. He stood there with a smile upon his ugly face and looked steadily at Windham.

The latter struck. He would have used the ball of his fist and thereby smashed in the face of the other; but he changed his mind at the last instant and used a mere backhand. Even this had ample weight enough to knock Murray flat.

The smaller man got up again. He wiped some blood from his mouth and faced the giant once more. The wan, strange smile was still upon his lips.

Then Windham collared him and thrust him into the store, to the big room, where many men were seated around the stove.

They looked up. A murmur went around the place. For Windham still had his hand in the neck of Murray's parka. Old Wagram came in, puffing at his pipe, scowling through the smoke he raised.

Julie Fernal came in, almost unobserved. Andy Johnson was there, also, and Chinook stood at the girl's back.

"This fellow," said Windham, "is the one that swiped Chinook from me, down there in California. I had to trail him all the way north. I had to run all the way clean on to Fort Yukon to save my neck, and keep Chinook. Now, in my part of the country, there's something done to horse thieves. What happens to dog thieves in this neck of the woods?"

He flung Murray from him. The man went staggering, close to the stove, before he recovered his balance. Then he straightened up and began to rub his neck, pushing back the hood of the parka.

The smile was still on his lips. It reminded Windham, with a sudden thrust of pain and disgust, of the smile of Julie Fernal herself.

"Let's have a look at this snitcher," said Wagram, approaching inside the muttering circle of men who stared at Murray.

Then he nodded. "I know him. He calls himself Murray. Tell me something, Murray. Are you a breed?"

Murray lifted a hand to his bleeding mouth and wiped it. It came away streaked with red before he answered:

"You look, and be damned! That's all I answer you when you ask me if I'm a breed!"

"I'll break your head for you," said Wagram, who had a violent temper. "You dirty sneakin' thief, you!"

"Hold on," said Blondy Grey, a man much respected

107

all through the North. "Hold on, there. Murray, talk up like a he-man. Let's hear what he's got to say for himself. What have you got to say, Murray. Did you really steal the dog?"

Perhaps lies shot through the mind of Murray, but he discarded them, unused. It was too plain that the people knew and respected the great Windham. Andy Johnson, that fierce and famous dog-puncher, had worked over to the side of the giant and was glaring at the stranger.

"Yeah. I swiped Chinook," said he. "What's more, if I got a chance, I'd swipe him again. What other one of you would have the nerve even to try to swipe that brute—from that man!"

He pointed at Chinook, first, and then at Windham.

Chinook lay down at the feet of Julie and looked adoringly up at her face. Then he dropped his head upon his paws and closed his eyes, feigning sleep.

Every man in the room was looking at the wolf dog.

"You take Windham, there," said Murray, in the same matter-of-fact tone of confession. "I swiped his dog, and he oughta be glad of it. He was living like a gopher in a hole. But he followed my trail until he learned how to be a man. He's a man now, leadin' a man's life. Should I be ashamed that I led him up North? Well, I'm not. All I regret is that he got Chinook back from me."

Wagram, when he heard the end of this speech, broke out into hearty laughter.

"You look here, Windham," he said. "You go and take him and turn him over to the authorities. That's the best thing to do with him. Speakin' real personal, though, I wouldn't hold no grudge agin' a thug that was willin' to talk right out like this about his thuggery."

Windham said nothing. He saw that most of the others in the room appeared to agree with Wagram. Numbers were against him.

Murray went on: "I see that Chinook has picked up a decoration since I last seen him. Is he your dog, now, ma'am?"

"I don't talk to thieves and dog-snatchers," said Julie, looking the half-breed deliberately in the face. And she left the room, with Chinook gliding behind her.

108

That smutched the triumph of Murray. The rascal immediately slunk away. Wagram called after him: "Whatever you do, don't come back in here, Murray. Windham may be too dog-gone good-natured to lay a hand on you, but some of the rest of us has got tempers of our own!"

Murray went out and disappeared in the whirl of snow which the wind was raising in the street.

This left Windham rather staggered. For he had promised himself a thousand times, during the long, wild journey he had made from California and during the flight toward Fort Yukon, that he would one day have it all out with Murray, hand to hand. He had gripped his fingers against his palms with force enough to crush bones. One day he would crush the thief in just that manner.

But now Murray had appeared and disappeared safely, like some grim, grinning spirit of Eskimo legend.

Windham went out and found Julie in the storm. It was not really a blizzard. It was simply a mild, rapid dance of the newly fallen snow, which the wind was throwing into a thousand smoky images and half-guessed-at forms.

He found her by following the rapidly dissolving, great footprints of Chinook. She ordered the dog back from her when he came up; and Chinook obeyed, half-blotted out by the falling throngs of the snow.

"I'm going to turn in and have my last warm sleep before I hit the trail," he said to her. "I'm saying good-by and taking Chinook."

"Here's the lead," said the girl. "Only, about Chinook—"

"What about him?"

"You think that you're safe with him? I know the chances that you've taken in the past, but suppose on this trip that you're burned up. Suppose you get giddy, some day, and slip in the snow. One slip, if he's near you, and it'll be the end of Ned Windham!"

"I know that you're right. I've figured out the thing the same way," said Windham. "But there's where I'll need him more than I'm apt ever to need him again. Out there in that white hell, you know—that's the sort of a place where a devil would be useful, Julie."

109

"You're going tonight?" she asked him, dismissing the other question with a gesture.

"No. I'm going to sleep twenty-four hours, eat and then start."

"You've got a guide?"

"Yes."

"Well, good luck, Ned."

"Thanks. Good-by, Julie."

She stepped suddenly inside his arms and held up her face. But Windham shook his head.

"That won't help me any," he declared. "It won't even help me to remember you. I'll be thinking enough about you all the way. And besides, it wouldn't mean anything from you—now. Not from you, Julie."

He saw the pucker of a frown. For the first time since he knew her she seemed baffled by a thing he had done, but his brain turned slowly upon such matters, and he was back at the store before a possible solution presented itself to him.

Even to this he did not give much thought. Only, as he was falling asleep, he remembered that he had made no bargain whatever with the girl. He was to make this stride out into the unknown not even for gold, but to discover an unknown man and drag him back to civilization, willing or unwilling.

As he thought of this, he smiled. He was a fool; indeed, he was a madman.

But, after all, had he not achieved the impossible already, in Wind Valley? Had they not laughed at him and his "valley of rocks" when he first went up into the place? He was attempting a greater and more dangerous thing, now, but he knew that if one patiently, bravely adds day to day, a great total will at last be achieved.

Then he slept for twelve hours, awoke, ate five pounds of caribou meat, drank a quart of scalding black coffee and returned to sleep fifteen hours more.

Then he got up, dressed, paid his bill to Wagram—a big one it was, leaving him with little money in his wallet! —and went out to harness his team in the night. It was already harnessed!

Gus Aintree was there with eleven dogs in harness and

the sleds loaded and in line. Only Chinook was not in place, and Windham quickly put him there.

He said: "You savvy that dog, Gus? Bad medicine!"

Gus Aintree grunted.

"Gus and Chinook, they understand," said he.

This enigmatic statement was all that he would make.

A lantern came blinking through the snowstorm. Wagram stood beside them.

"It's a bad night for a start," he said. "This soft snow—"

"Any time is a bad time for starting this trip," said Windham. "But this will have to do for us."

"So long, then, old son," said the trader.

"So long, Bud," said Windham with determination.

He leaned his weight on the gee pole of the leading sled. He called. Chinook took up the slack with a jerk. The others swayed forward. With a crackling sound the sled came clear of the incrustations along its runners, and they were on their way toward the distant Chandalars, and Chief Little Knife, and Bert Fernal, the vanished man.

# CHAPTER TWENTY-TWO

From the very start, it was the bitterest sort of hard slugging. Windham, striding ahead of the dogs to make trail, told himself that a bad beginning made a good ending. Then he almost laughed at himself and his childish folly.

For something spoke in his inner ear, saying that the end of this, no matter what it was, could not be entirely good. Just as one feels the coming of disaster from the raising of the curtain upon a tragedy, so he felt horror in the future.

A few hours out from Fort Yukon, there was a change in the weather and the wind. The snow stopped falling. The mists were blown presently from before the face of the stars, and the long electric flags of the aurora borealis began to stream across the sky. There seemed to be joy in the heavens; yet never did Windham feel so far removed from happiness.

Underfoot, the snow was bad. The toboggans were overloaded. They traveled for twelve hours, and at the end of that time they were not more than eighteen miles from Fort Yukon!

Then they made camp.

Gus Aintree moved about with his jaw set hard and his nostrils flaring. He was far spent, but he did not want to admit it. Suddenly, from time to time, he fixed Windham with a side glance. The latter had broken trail every inch of those terrible miles, yet he was fresher at the end of the run than was the hardened half-breed. Of course, Gus Aintree was recovering from the effects of too much alcohol. He would do better later on.

They were on the march the next day long before daylight. Aintree plotted the way, from landmark to landmark, and Windham broke the trail as on the first day. They went on for two hours, and then Aintree came up and, silently, took his place before the white man.

Windham understood, and glad he was to discover some pride in the heart of Aintree. Most men on the march like to match themselves against other men. And Aintree, it appeared, was willing to meet the test, breaking trail all of that day. But they covered even fewer miles than on the first day.

When they were drinking tea, after supper that night, Aintree spoke, almost his first words of the day:

"Too damned much weight on those sleds!"

"I know they're heavy," explained Windham. "But we've got to keep everything. When we get out on the tundra, it will be worse going. We need every pound of supplies that we're carrying. No use whining about it, now. We've got to go on. Later on, we'll be able to start making caches, every few marches. That will lighten the sleds a good deal. Believe me, Aintree, if what Wagram

112

tells me is true, we'll need everything that we have with us, before we see Fort Yukon again!"

"We won't see Fort Yukon again!" said Aintree.

"What d'you mean by that?" asked Windham.

There was no answer. Aintree looked steadily down into his cup as though he had not heard the question, and Windham forebore to press him, for a moment.

At last he asked:

"Do you mean that we're both cooked?"

"Both cooked," said Gus.

"Why don't you turn back, then?" demanded Windham. "You're free to go back to the Fort, if you want to."

Aintree looked up with a start. His face was fierce with an angry scowl.

"Gus Aintree never turn back," he said. "White devil or black devil, Gus break trail with him to the moon!"

And he straightaway turned in and refused to speak again. Yet, what he had said was a great comfort to Windham. He knew that muscles will give way and tendons sag, but a great pride will sustain the failing body.

They slogged on through the broken country. The days were short, beginning at nine and ending at three, or thereabout. They were much in the black of dusk, feeling their way, as it were, toward their distant goal.

Aintree was always shaking his head and saying that they must go faster and farther during each day's march.

"Gotta fly! Gotta fly!" he used to mutter under his breath.

"We're not birds!" exclaimed Windham once, impatiently.

The other laughed suddenly, harshly, and would speak no more; and his eyes were fastened upon Windham with an evil light.

It was plain that he felt no love for the big white man. It mattered not that Windham was always eager to do more than his share of the work, whether it were making camp or breaking trail. In the latter work, his size of foot, his weight, his tremendous endurance made him preeminent. Still there was neither praise nor gratitude forthcoming from the half-breed.

They went through a low country, cut by sloughs,

marshy, with lakes here and there and a dotting of scrub spruce and brush. They had plenty of wood for their camps; that was one comfort. But the roughness of the way more than made up for any such advantage.

It took them three days to reach the locality where they could make their first cache. That was about fifty miles from Fort Yukon, and every fifty miles from there to the end of the journey they would make similar caches. Ideally, they should reach the Chandalars with empty bellies and empty sleds—empty of food, that is to say. Then on the return dash, they could pick up the caches that they had left on the way.

It was a perilous prospect. Various things might happen to break up those caches, and if two of them in a row were missing, it was probable death and destruction for the dogs and the men.

Usually such caches were safe. Well covered against wind and storm, the bundles were hitched into a tree at a height that secured them from the leaps of hungry animals. Of course, they were in full sight of all human travelers, but to break into a cache in Alaska is the last sin. It is far worse, even, than the sin of horse stealing in the West, for it may mean life or death to the man who has established the cache.

He who violates the cache of another may plead, as an excuse, some extreme need. And his way of atoning for the crime is to rush back down the trail, where he can secure supplies and thus replace those which he has taken.

If he is too poor to buy such provisions, the community at large will never fail to make a sacrifice to replace all that has been borrowed. In Alaska, as a rule, outlawry never reaches the trail.

On this subject, Windham had no doubts whatsoever. He secured the caches and carefully hoisted them into the trees.

The weather fell colder. It hit forty below, and there was a pale, gray mist, pooled chiefly in the hollows. To descend into those foggy low places was like dipping into icy water.

But Windham steeled himself against this torment. He knew, from what Wagram had said, that they would constantly be passing through temperatures the mildest of which would be far worse than the damp, icy hollows through which they were now dipping.

They slogged on.

They came to a stretch where the snow covered the small shrubs almost to the tops of the branches, and upon the ends of the brush the feet of the dogs were cruelly wounded.

They made five miles. The dogs began to leave trails of blood, and that day's march was ended. All the rest of that day was spent in making foot-gear. As the half-breed, with expert speed, made the moccasins, he constantly shook his head and mumbled to himself.

Windham shut his ears against the noise. In spite of himself, he was growing more and more upset by the persistent gloom of his companion.

They rarely exchanged words, and the white man began to fear that they were falling into that arctic silence which first freezes up the tongue of a man, and then leads to a cruel, silent, deeply submerged hatred, never voiced, but ending in a murder by night, perhaps!

In the marshes, they found many muskrat nests. There were rabbits, also, and these replenished the larder, for both Windham and the half-breed could clip a bullet through a rabbit's head, and the creatures were so stupid that they often offered good close shots. Then, a few days later, they found moose tracks.

They made camp. Windham did the work, fed the dogs, and cooked the supper. The half-breed, on his own insistence, went off to get the moose.

Six hours later he came back and sank down in the shelter, exhausted and silent, but with a monstrous ear in his hand which he threw down upon the snow. He carried with him, also, two vast moose steaks. He had found his game!

While Windham ate that delicious fresh meat, it seemed to him that there was actually someting angelic about the sullen half-breed! Ideals fall low on the arctic trails; belly needs are greater than the requirements of a starving soul!

The moose meat they froze and loaded down the sleds

115

with it. The next day, they gorged the dogs with it, when they drove to the carcass, and the half-breed showed the white man how he had hunted down the trail, continually making excursions to this side and that, so that his course was like a vast snake's, winding continually back and forth across the trail of the moose. For the habit of the moose is to leave the trail, cut back from it, and hide its monstrous bulk with a magic skill in some patch of brush or woods.

From such a cover, Gus Aintree had startled the monster and brought it down with his second shot!

The moose meat put heart into both men and dogs, and they were glad to struggle with the additional weight. They would lighten it by eating, fast enough, to be sure!

And the very next day Julie Fernal joined them on the trail!

# CHAPTER TWENTY-THREE

They were going through overflows, down the side of Champagne River—what a name for a stream in that wilderness! The going was very stiff, for the ice was caked thick upon the runners. They had stopped to free the runners somewhat, when the half-breed straightened and pointed behind them.

There Windham saw a single sled drawn by four running dogs, and at the gee pole a small figure swinging along with an easy lilt.

They waited to give a greeting to the stranger and, as the traveler came up, Windham heard the mellow voice of Julie Fernal crying out to him and saw the wave of her mittened hand. He was dumb with amazement.

"What the devil brought you here, Julie?" he asked,

without any further greeting. "And how could you follow our trail as far as this?"

"I didn't follow your trail," she answered. "But I knew that you'd hit the Champagne River and follow it north. So I headed straight for the river. I hit it thirty miles above and followed down."

"When did you start?" asked he.

"Four days after you."

"And caught up with us, eh?"

"Oh, you fellows are freighters," said Julie Fernal. "Hello, Gus. You look as sour as ever. Smile for me, Gus, will you?"

Gus Aintree, in fact, favored her with the broadest of grins. Windham was amazed to see the first flash of good nature on the face of the half-breed.

"What in thunder brought you out?" asked Windham.

"That sneaking devil, that Murray," she answered. "He's got together the slickest dog team that ever ran out of Fort Yukon."

"He has? I thought Wagram got the pick for me," said Windham.

"Whitey Mott and Champ Tolliver came in the morning after you left," said the girl, "and their teams are full of champions. Murray got the pick of 'em all."

"He did?"

"Yes. He paid for 'em. He paid up to the hilt. He got to playing poker with Bud Wagram. That's where he got his stake. He got nine dogs and two toboggans. He has two men with him. There's a full-blooded Indian by the name of Jim Martin. You know him, Gus?"

"I know him pretty good," said Gus. "He takes long steps to follow."

"You bet he does," said the girl. "The other is a thug by the name of Peg Roos. He ought to have been strung up a long time ago. If he has any luck, he'll hang before long, anyway. He's killed enough. He's a breed, like Gus, here, an outcross from the Chandalars, like Gus. You know Peg, too, don't you, Aintree?"

Gus scowled.

"Plenty bad!" said Gus.

"Yeah. Now, then, two days after you pulled out, Murray pulled out, too, and said he was going to start for Circle City. That's the direction he went. But I got to thinking that it was a mighty strange thing that he'd shy at white men and take to breeds for guides and mushers, when he was only driving for Circle City. So I just dropped down his trail a ways, old son, and eight miles out, he doubled back and headed east. You know what that means, I guess!"

"I don't know," said Windham. "I don't know what he wants to do in this direction."

"Don't you?" said the girl, her eyes narrowing. "Are you as big a woodenhead as all that? Can't you put two and two together, now and then, and hit a million?"

"What million?" asked Windham.

"To cut your throat—that's all Murray wants to do, big fellow!"

"Why should he want to do that?" muttered Windham. "He's the fellow who's wronged me. I've never harmed him, really."

The girl laughed, ironically.

"You've whacked him over the mouth, haven't you?" she asked him.

"Why, I hardly tapped him," said Windham.

"You gave him the taste of his own blood, though," said the girl. "What more do you want? Choke him with it? A better thing for you if you had, Ned! Because now he'll never leave your trail until he gets at you. Then, there's Chinook. Hello, there!"

She waved her hand to the big leader and Chinook stood up, bristling with excitement.

"Look! Look!" cried the girl.

Windham obediently looked and saw that the tail of Chinook was waving slowly from side to side.

"He's wagging his tail!" said the girl. "Why, he's a lamb, that man-killer is!"

She ran up to the harnessed leader and dropped on her knees and threw her arms around his throat.

Gus Aintree had seen something of the ways of Chinook, by this time. He said nothing. He simply caught up the rifle but Windham held his hand.

"She knows his language," said Windham. "She's the only person in the world that does. He won't touch her. Look!"

Chinook was making such moaning sounds of joy as Windham never had heard before from any throat, animal or human. And the tail wagged more decidedly than ever!

"That makes the dog come out in him," said the breed, soberly, as he watched.

Then he added: "She always make so. Wolves, men, she makes them into dogs!"

But the thought did not seem to offend him. He merely laughed, again, as he ended.

The girl came back to them, panting. And the great wolf dog actually sat down in the snow and began to howl dismally after her. Windham watched with steady bewilderment.

"This fellow Murray," said Windham, as the girl returned, "what could he do, after all? If he tries to stick us up on the trail, we've got rifles. We can shoot as well as he can!"

"He's got a flying team. He's loaded light. He's loaded for a one-way trip, it looks to me, and he's bound for the Chandalars!"

"What makes you think that he wants to be skinned by the Chandalars?" asked Windham.

"Skinned by them?" cried the girl. "He's a breed himself. He's got a red man and another breed with him. The Chandalars will never harm those fellows! But they can help the Chandalars hurt you!"

Windham grunted. The blow had struck home fairly.

The girl went on: "He'll be with the Indians days and days before you can possibly get there. You're chewing off only twenty-five miles a day. Murray and his crew will be doing forty, at least! He's an old dog puncher. He knows his stuff!"

"All right, Julie," said Windham. "What do you think I should do?"

"You go straight back to Fort Yukon," she answered.

"Go back to Fort Yukon?" exclaimed Windham.

"Of course. You only had one chance in ten of doing anything with the murdering Chandalars. Now you have only one chance in a thousand. You ought to be able to see that!"

He rubbed his huge hands together; they were cold inside of the lynx-skin mittens.

"Turn back, eh?" said he.

"Of course, you'll turn back," said Julie, impatiently. "I had you on my mind anyway. I've had enough things laid at my door. I didn't want your death laid there, too. Not that I give a rap what other people think, but I care what I think myself! No, Ned! The thing for you to do is turn straight back to Fort Yukon. I'll go back with you— for company!"

He sighed, as he listened to her.

The temptation was very great. The woman for whose sake he had undertaken the adventure was now commanding him to give it up.

"What about your brother?" he asked.

"Well," said the girl, "he seems to have dug himself in pretty securely with the Chandalars. According to Dean Carey, Bert didn't want to leave the tribe at all."

"Did you believe all that Dean Carey said?" asked Windham.

"Most of it," answered the girl, nodding her head. "Didn't you?"

"No," said Windham, feeling his way carefully. "I think Carey's all right, mind you. But I guess he's a little hysterical. He was there at the fort. He was fooling himself, until you came along and braced him up. He might have been hysterical when he was with the Chandalars, too!"

"Maybe," said the girl. "But the fact is, he saw Bert then he got away, but Bert didn't come away with him!"

Windham agreed. That was the knotty part of the problem. "However," he suggested, "I could throw Bert on a sled and break away with him, I suppose. I could do that."

"Chuck the whole thing out of your mind," answered the girl. "What you've got to do is to get back to Fort Yukon. Forget about Bert, at least this season. Next year if you're still around—"

Windham pointed south. "I've got a home down there,"

he said. "There may not be another year up here for me. No, if it's done at all, it has to be done now."

"Then it can't be done at all—by you," replied the girl, firmly. "Ned, don't get that bull look in your eyes, please. Come out of it!"

He put one of his vast hands on her shoulder.

"You're a good girl, Julie," said he. "You can talk against your own heart. But in spite of what you've said, I'm going to go on to the Chandalars."

"Ned!" gasped the girl. Then she added hastily: "But you can't. Gus Aintree won't budge a step, now! You won't have a guide!"

"I'll feel my way in the dark, then," said Windham.

"You?" muttered the girl, moving back from him a little. "You won't turn back, Ned?"

He shrugged his wide shoulders.

"You know how it is, Julie," he said. "A broken trail is a rotten thing to have on your record."

"A broken neck is worse!" she cried.

"Well, I'll take that little chance," said he. "Nobody lives forever. And there's Chinook, out there, that I'm still not acquainted with!"

# CHAPTER TWENTY-FOUR

They camped where they were. In the morning, when they lined out the dogs, the girl harnessed her own string to her own sled. Then, instead of saying good-by, drove straight past the larger outfit and down the river side. The snow was so firmly packed that there was no need of trail-breaking before her.

Windham hurried on after her.

"What's this, Julie?" he shouted from a distance.

She did not answer until he had run up beside her. He

was breaking through the snow crust with his great weight upon the snowshoes.

"If you go on to the Chandalars, I'm going, too," said she.

He caught at her arm, protesting as he did so.

"You're scaring the dogs with your bull's voice," she said. "Let me alone, Ned. They'll run away and wreck my outfit."

He ran on beside her until she recovered the gee pole.

Then he halted the team.

"Let them go on," said Julie. "We haven't any time to waste. Every hour you delay now is an hour out of your provisions coming back. Every hour you pause now, Ned, is an hour of starvation added to the trek to Fort Yukon!"

He held her by the shoulders.

"Is this your way of forcing me to turn back?" he asked her, scowling.

"I'm not forcing you back. I'm going on with you. I can be useful. I can talk the lingo of the Chandalars," she told him. "I can punch a team of dogs. I can use a rifle, too. I'll kill a moose before you do, old son, and I'll shoot my rabbits on the run, too. You won't find me a weight on your hands. I travel light and I travel fast!"

"Suppose that something happens—to you!" said he.

"I'm taking my chances," said she. "And I'm taking them for my own blood. Bert Fernal is no kin of yours! Let me alone!"

Slipping from his grip, she gave the word to the dogs, and sped with them down the white, curving line of the river.

He looked after her, for a moment, grimly realizing that he could not handle her. He had size, strength of muscles, but she was at least his equal in the might of will and mind.

Then he saw that the breed was bringing on the team with the toboggans and he fell in beside Aintree. The latter favored him with the broadest of grins.

"One devil!" said Aintree, pointing ahead toward the small form of the girl and the line of her dogs, now swinging around a sharp bend.

"One devil!" agreed Windham.

So they forged ahead, day after day.

The girl was always leading. Even when there was trail to be broken, she did the mushing in the lead, and her dogs with their much lighter burden followed along after her at a pace more rapid than the bigger outfit could maintain.

She gauged nicely the distance which the men could cover with their bulkier freight, and when they came up, at the day's march, when the dogs had done all that could be expected of them, she already would have picked out the best camp, her shelter tent would be up, and the sound of her ax was ringing among the trees. Sometimes she cut all the wood that was burned at the camp. Always she appeared to have an excess of nervous and physical power which she could tap for an emergency.

She did not burn out and grow hollow-eyed and lean upon the trail, as Windham and the breed were doing. The arctic cold was now fifty below, day after day. Sometimes a slight wind would increase the effect of the icy atmosphere. That cold, of course, burned up like a fiery sun every particle of fat in the bodies of the men. They grew gaunt, hard as iron. But the girl was not so affected. She remained sleek, rosy of face. Nor was her disposition drained of charm. Her laughter and good nature filled up the day.

Two things were notable at that stage of the journey. The one was that Chinook mourned every moment that he was away from the girl; the other was that, during the evening when they were sitting together, Gus Aintree never took his eyes for one instant from the face of Julie Fernal.

Windham spoke to her about it.

"I don't like the way that dirty breed eyes you," he said. "What shall I do about it?"

"He's getting poisoned," she answered. "There's nothing that you can do about it except to pretend that you don't notice."

"What do you mean when you say he's getting poisoned?" asked Windham.

"Look at me, Ned," she replied.

He looked and could not help smiling at her beauty.

"That's it," answered the girl, gravely. "It's the face that does it. It's because I was made with a pretty face. Also, because I can't help smiling back. I feel good. I'm strong and well. That's what makes me happy. I'm happy on this trail. I don't know why. I guess there'll be hell at the end of it. But I'm happy now. That makes me smile, and the smile makes the breed think that he's part of my happiness or else he wants to be. No, there's nothing that you can do about him. Just let him go. If he needs a word to bring him up short, I'm equal to the occasion. Don't you worry!"

He let it go at that, as she suggested. Still, he was worried.

It was a little later that they struck the first Chandalar village. There were threescore of well-built log houses, there was a big log building for public worship, since the tribe were Christians. All of the structures were in good repair, except where storms had pried off a roof, here and there. But there was not a soul in the entire place. There had not been for many a year. Where doors were open, rooms were found blown almost full of snow.

"Look! What more would anybody want?" said the practical-minded Windham. "Look at those woods, all around! There's building material and there's game, too, I warrant. There's firewood to keep the tribe warm to eternity. Besides, there's the river, for fishing. What more would the tribe want, this far north? I'd call this place a perfect home for 'em."

"That's what they thought," answered Gus Aintree, speaking up suddenly, unexpectedly. "But you know how white man come, red man go! Always! White man come here. Chief Little Knife move on. Long time ago, Chandalar far south. Gold far south, too. White man find him; Indian come here. White man come here, Indian go north and north. Always that way. But, pretty soon, Indian come to sea. Then he must stop! White man come there, too. Then, good-by, red man!"

He spoke without emotion, cheerfully, if anything.

But Ned Windham watched him darkly.

"I'm sorry for those Indians, too," said he. "This is a

mighty neat little village. It's a pity they had to move out from here!"

"No sorry for Chandalar—Gus," said the guide. "They not know much. Plenty fool! Stupid men, he always starve. Smart man wears furs, eat plenty moose meat!"

He grinned broadly at his companion, his brown cheeks puffing out. At this point Windham caught the eye of the girl and saw that she was winking broadly at him and nodding, for she was behind the back of the half-breed.

Afterward she said: "You know, Ned, dark blood is stronger than white blood. That half-breed is more of an Indian than he is a white. We've got to watch him, or he'll surely be the finish of us. He's got reasons for wanting it that way."

"What reasons?" asked Windham. "I've treated him pretty well, right from the start. I've done more than my share of the work all the way from Fort Yukon."

She shook her head. "You can't make up," she declared. "You're only one white man. And you have to carry on your shoulders all the dirty work of all the other white fortune hunters who have been up here. Indians don't understand the idea of personal responsibility. It's the tribe that shares the kill, if a moose goes down. It's the tribe that shares the blame of a killing. Clan spirit, you see. They do the same with whites. You're already tarred all over with the work that other whites have done this far north. You can't get out from under and carry only your own pack. You have the whole white race on your shoulders. Never forget that! And take my word for it, our friend Gus Aintree never forgets, either."

Windham brooded long on that speech. Gradually, he could understand. Chief Little Knife had become a Christian and led his entire people to the same faith, thinking that this would prove a shield between them and the onward, crushing advance of the whites. But he had been wrong. The whites kept on coming, and the Indians had been driven from post to post. The empty log village spoke more clearly than a million words of cursing and of execration.

That night they slept warmly for the first time since

they had left the fort, for they had a big cabin to themselves, all the wood, well-seasoned, that they chose to burn, and they took off their heavy clothes and basked in the artificial sunshine.

They remained in the Chandalar village the next day. It was a delay, but the rest would do them good, both men and dogs. That night, like a commentary upon the words of the girl, Windham noticed the half-breed seated beside the fire, slowly sharpening his hunting knives upon a smooth stone which he had dug out of the ice on the bank of the river.

He worked with his head tilted a little to one side, a slight smile on his lips. As he drew the knife back and forth across the stone, he kept time to the movements with a weird, discordant song, like the whistling of the winter wind.

Again Windham thought of the girl's words of warning. He thought of something else, too, unbidden by her, while he watched the man there by the fire, naked to the waist basking in the hot firelight, and working over his knives. It was the smile of the half-breed, the strange, faint, unwitting smile of physical content. Suddenly a chill shot through him as he was reminded of another smile, it blood brother, which he had often seen upon the face of Julie Fernal.

# CHAPTER TWENTY-FIVE

The hills loomed beyond, the foothills of the mountains, which stretched vastly upward through the mist dull, gray outlines in the distance.

From that moment the slogging north became desperately harder. Twenty white men, it was said, had reached the confines of the Chandalars. Of them all, only Dean Carey had come back to tell the tale. And what a tale he told from the smoky remnants of his memory, distorted to a nightmare thing by his sufferings, his hysteria!

Well, it was only a wonder to Windham that so many men had been able to endure across the frozen spaces! Twenty men! He remembered hearing sailors back from the sea tell of the terrible perils of reefing and furling in a gale, perhaps south of the Horn, when the canvas was coated thick with ice that had to be beaten off with the naked, bleeding hands, while the masts swayed dizzily across the sky. It had seemed beyond human courage, until he was able to remember that a dozen other sailors were at the time on the yard!

So in this journey through the bleak, white North, he looked back with wonder, and yet with a vague comfort, to the thought of the twenty who had preceded him. They had managed to complete the dreadful march.

For now there was the slogging over the hills that made the toil across the plains an almost playful labor!

It was down slopes, braking every inch of the way, and then up long inclines, sometimes with all the sixteen dogs hitched to a single sled, and great Chinook straining and laboring far in the lead. He seemed to have a man's instinct for what was to be done; he seemed to have the generous heart of a man to pour into his work, and never did he stint! Level or uphill, he gave what was in him, and they swore, all the three who watched him, that he lugged as much as any three of the other dogs.

Yet, for all of his apparent devotion to his task, his attitude toward Ned Windham remained unchanged. There was proof of this the third day of their struggle through the hills. For the toboggans ran away down a slope, and the dogs fled madly before it, until one of them at the wheel stumbled.

The sled struck his body, and swerving against that obstacle, tumbled over and over down the slope. The dogs were thrown into confusion, tumbling one against the other, and Windham, with a yell of alarm, threw himself among them.

He knew very well what would happen. It would be a ripping and slashing of teeth. The half-wild beasts tearing at one another.

Heedless of danger, as the toboggans came to a halt in the next hollow, the big man was there. He caught two dogs by the scruffs of the neck and tore them apart. Another, throttling his leading mate, he stunned with a heavy blow. Two more he kicked apart, and so came on the place where Chinook, bathed with crimson over head and shoulders, stood up, leaving a quivering, lifeless body before him on the snows. One stroke of his fangs had been enough.

Windham, lurching toward the spot, at that instant tripped over a trace of strong webbing and plunged head foremost into the snow. The next moment the parka was ripped away from his head and he was gashed across the back of the neck.

He looked up and saw the dreadful, grinning mask of the leader as Chinook shook away the clinging tatters of the hood and drove again at the throat which he had so narrowly missed. Half blindly, Windham thrust up both his hands and, by the grace of chance, he locked them both just under the jaws of the brute.

One furious second the wolf dog struggled and strove gnashing his white teeth, already filmed with blood. But he could not gain play for his death-dealing head. The grip was too tremendous. The digging finger tips of the man reached to the nerve centers and numbed the whole body of Chinook. Besides, he had known that grip before and now he stood patiently, still.

Windham got to his feet. He untied the monster and Chinook stood calmly before him, licking his bloody lips staring upward at his master with the same unquenchable hatred, the same unconquerable eyes with which he had glared at Windham a long time ago in the cabin in California.

Windham was shaking now. It was not fear because of the wound he had received. But it was the feeling that he had just crossed the threshold of hell!

There was something about this even more strange than Chinook's furious attack. This was that when the breed and the girl came up they offered to Windham not one word of consolation, not one syllable of praise for the work he had done in prying the dogs apart before they slaughtered one another.

There was a single casualty. There might have been death for half of the team. As it was Windham should have received the credit. But he got not a word.

Instead, he noted that the two were silent. Only, they exchanged grim looks as they noted, first of all, Windham and then the huge dog that had just attacked him.

The breed started to work repairing harness and straightening out the dogs. The girl busied herself with the repair of the torn hood, which she accomplished with wonderful expedition.

It was not until two days later that she said to him, quietly, one evening when they were pitching camp:

"I've been talking it over with Gus, Ned. We both agree. If you're not the death of Chinook, he'll be the death of you."

Windham turned on her angrily.

"You've been talking it over with the half-breed, have you? What's there between you and Aintree? Will you tell me? What's he to you, and what in the devil is his opinion worth?"

Her poise was generally an unshakable thing, but now she looked at the big man in amazement. Never before had he spoken to her like this.

"Now, what do you mean by that, Ned?" she asked him. "I'm telling you that Aintree feels something coming between you and the wolf dog. So do I. Instincts don't lie, old-timer. I'm telling you that the best way is to kill that dog before he kills you. I don't like to say this. You know I love Chinook, and he loves me!"

"Whatever you and Aintree may feel about it," he answered, in the same ugly humor, "please let me alone. I can take care of Chinook. I don't need any half-breed opinions on the subject."

He expected that she would fly into a fury, as she could so easily do. Instead, she turned as gray as a stone, looked at him for a single long moment, then turned and walked away.

He remained where he was standing, sick at heart. The thing that he had suspected now seemed indubitably true. She was a half-breed!

Perhaps other men had guessed the thing. Perhaps it was even knowledge so common that no man had thought to tell him. Perhaps that was the reason that she herself had adopted such a careless attitude toward others. Julie Fernal!

Well, there was undoubtedly a French accent in the name, and are not the French famous for the quick manner in which they mix with the natives of any country, adopt their manners, take their women for wives?

Julie Fernal, a half-breed. Then he snapped his fingers in disgusted certainty.

No darker eyes than hers ever glowed in an Indian's face. Her skin was translucent, to be sure; nevertheless, it was a deep olive. Was there not a coppery tint in it, also? Was there not red-copper in what he had always thought the mere glow of healthful blood, gleaming through?

Slowly, like a man half-numbed with cold, he went about the rest of his work that evening.

When it came time to eat the supper which the breed had cooked, Julie was as gay, as light-hearted, as full of comfortable talk as ever. But Windham looked down to the ground.

The soul was dead in him; he was risking his life to tame a wolf dog, and to rescue a half-breed, Bert Fernal!

She and Aintree, of course, they had something in common!

He broke out, in the midst of the meal, with a thunderous laughter, so that the breed started up in his place, greatly alarmed.

"Oh, it's all right," said Windham. "I was just thinking."

He went after the girl when she started for her tent. Across the door of it, the wolf dog was already lying, waiting for his mistress. That, too, seemed to Windham a sinister sign.

He thought of that worn maxim: "It takes a thief to catch a thief!" Why not, also: "It takes the wild to master the wild!"

That was the secret, then, of her power over the wolf dog!

When she heard the heavy crunch of his snowshoe, she turned about to him. "Well, Ned," she said. "Something's grinding you. What is it?"

He took her beneath the chin with a careless roughness in his grip.

"Tell me the truth," he said.

"You're breaking my jaw," she murmured.

He did not alter his grip. He pressed harder.

"Tell me the truth!" he commanded.

"I'll tell the truth," she said.

"Did you think that I knew?" he said. "Did you think that I knew about you all the time?"

"Knew what?" asked the girl.

"What I found out today."

"What did you find out today?" she demanded.

"What a fool you think I am!" cried Windham. "And I am a fool! The damnedest in the history of the world!"

With that, he threw her away from him so violently that she staggered and almost fell into the snow.

He watched her, staggering, as she recovered her balance.

Then he waited for a torrent of words from her. Instead, she put up her hand, where the pressure of his fingers had hurt her and went with a bowed head, submissively, toward her tent!

# CHAPTER TWENTY-SIX

What kept Windham going for the rest of the toilsome journey through the hills, he never was to understand. He used to say to himself that he was venturing his existence for the sake of three half-breeds. One was Chinook, crossed between wolf and dog. One was Bert Fernal. One was Julie.

Yet he kept on the trail. It was true that he avoided her face, that he never spoke with her, that he could hardly speak to the breed, Gus Aintree. Still he kept on the trail.

Every day he told himself that he had gone far enough and that now, in all common sense, he must turn back. Still he went on.

Then they came to the end of the woods and looked down upon sheets of white fog. Here and there, through the top of the mist, the round heads of hills appeared, each like the other.

When he saw this white dreariness, the heart of Windham shrank within him! If only he had had a cause in which he could invest a touch of that passion for grandeur which is in every man's soul! But there was no such element in the cause to which he was devoting himself, it seemed.

For half-breeds he was laying down his life!

"That tundra," said Gus Aintree, pointing across the waste of the white fog and the shadowy hills. "That tundra. Plenty no good!"

He shuddered, and, gradually, carefully, he explained. It was true that much the shortest route to the Chandalars lay across the tundra, but it was better to dodge that hellish cold waste of a hundred miles and take the more circuitous route down the valley, where timber could be found.

Yonder on the tundra, there was no life, except the tundra moss itself—the frozen moss between ice-hard earth and the compact snows. There were no shrubs, no bushes, no trees, however stunted. There were no birds, no rabbits, even. The very caribou, which seem to live wherever they can cut away snow and come to green things, even to moss, shunned this strip of white desolation!

Bannocks were the only food for that crossing.

Then Windham sat down to the fire and began to cook bannocks, one after another, bannocks in heaps and piles, bannocks which must feed them all the way to their destination! The soggy, cold thought of such food was enough

132

to turn even the hardened stomach of a dog-puncher. But Windham had made up his mind.

Even the girl protested, when she saw his preparations.

"It'll be worse than hell, out there," she said, calmly. "You don't want to talk to me, Windham. I know that you hate the sight of my face. I don't quite know what turned you, but I know that that's the fact. Well, out yonder is tundra, old son. And on that tundra the wind is king. When I say wind, you think you know what I mean. But you don't. The wind out there, it hops straight down from the North Pole. It has a running start, and it takes a broad jump and plants both heels in your face. You don't want any of that in your business, Ned."

He looked up at her, after a moment. "I guess that we ought to eat these bannocks," was all he said.

In spite of his sneer, she seemed disposed to pause and argue for a moment, but then she turned about and left him, her head down, as he often saw it during these days.

A few hours later he told Aintree to put the dogs in the harness.

"What trail?" asked Aintree, sullenly, looking at the last of the bannocks, as his employer wrapped them up.

"Tundra," said the big man, tersely.

"I no go," answered Aintree. "I go back. I go too far, already. I no go!"

Windham rose to his feet. He made one light step forward and struck. Aintree fell and rolled a dozen feet away.

He got up with a gun in his hand. Windham was unarmed.

"Aintree," he said, "you drop that gun. If you shoot, you will put a bullet through me, all right, but that won't stop me, unless you nick me clean through the brain or the heart. If I once get to you, I'll break you open like tinned fish. You hear me? I'll break you open and give you to the dogs!"

Aintree, crouched above his revolver, his face working, stared bitterly at the giant. Then he lowered the revolver. Turning slowly about, he put away the gun and started harnessing the dogs. Windham returned calmly to the final touches in preparing the packages of bannocks.

There were three parcels. In each parcel was all that one human being would eat on the way across the tundra. Life was suddenly made simpler. Even the simple fare which he had cooked for himself on the farm way back in California was a king's banquet compared to this bitter diet.

Then he saw that the girl already had harnessed her team. She was there, leaning on a staff, watching. He knew, suddenly, that she had been watching all the while, during his scene with the breed. He went up to her.

"Why do you try to go across the tundra?" he asked. "We don't want you. You're no help. D'you simply want to be a dead weight on our hands? Go back to Fort Yukon. That's the place for you, or as far south as your skin will let you go!"

She met his glare with her usual calm.

"You think you're a man," she said. "I understand, now. But you're only a hulk. That's all! I'm about the only thing with wit enough to steer you through what's coming. Don't talk to me about being a weight! Before the finish, I'll have to tie you to the sled and pull you in by your long legs. That's what I think of you, Windham!"

He was not offended. He was almost rejoiced and he laughed in her face. At least, peace was ended between them.

Then they struck across the tundra; they entered the white hell. There were no words for it. Half a day out, the wind of which the girl had spoken swept down on them. It came with a scream. It tore the white fog to pieces. It filled the air with level driving snow that cut the skin as with knives.

To face that hurricane and march on was impossible. Even to stand, when it was at its height, was a vast trouble. One wavered in the air currents like a bit of empty cloth! When one strove to speak, a fist of ice was thrust through the parted lips and into the aching hollow of the cheek.

Dogs and all, they lay down in a heap in the lee of the sleds. They huddled close. Chinook lay beside the girl. The other dogs swarmed close about the two men.

Even with the protection of that animal heat, they al-

134

most froze to death. Five hours they lay there. Every hour brought them nearer to death. When Windham looked at the breed, he saw that the face of the man was purple. They had to bury their faces in the fur of the dogs to drive away the frostbite.

Then, just as it had come, the wind leaped away to an infinite distance, the snow stopped swirling. For a moment they saw the grim sky, the color of dark steel. Then the white fog shifted over them again before they could get under way.

They mushed on. When they had marched to the limit of the dogs' endurance, lightened though the sleds were, they put down robes on the ground. Tarpaulins were spread and under the tarpaulins crawled the three human beings and the fifteen dogs, in one tangled heap.

There they ate the one meal of the day. They lighted candles and thawed the icy bannocks with the flames which softened the frightful food, to be sure, but also coated it with soot.

That strangely horrible taste would remain in their throats forever, it seemed then. Likewise the smell of those close quarters. The dogs lay there, chewing usually at the rock-hard frozen fish which was given to them, and as they lay, entangled, they began to steam. The air grew close. It was choking. Sleep came only in snatches, a few moments at a time. But it was sleep, at least. And the dogs, it was true, seemed to get on very well for the first day or so.

Afterward, they, too, suffered terribly. The wind was never away from them. It shrieked in their faces. It beat them with peltings of snow, like hard-flung stones. It threatened to bowl them over, or to whip their feet from under them. Yet the dogs kept on, and the men kept on, too.

They were going to the end of the world. That seemed plain to Windham. For the sake of a half-breed, they were accomplishing what Xenophon's ten thousand never had done, never could have done. Of the three, gradually Windham came to see, the girl was suffering the least of all.

It was true, now and then, that she had to ride for a

short distance on her sled. But she never asked for help and her load was so light that her four dogs seemed well able to endure the burden of her lesser weight.

Otherwise, she was constantly jogging at the side of her sled or running ahead to break trail. Now and then, she would insist on taking her turn to break trail for the bigger team, though generally Windham or the breed did that work and she followed over the compact snow.

Day after day, the going was ghastly hard and harder, as the dogs began to weaken, their heads and tails sagging. Every day there was almost incessant wind. Every day, for at least an hour or more, they had to stop because of a freezing hurricane. Still they slogged on! Still they mushed the dogs forward.

The climax of distress came when they found, one day, that the girl, in the lead, had gone wrong, and doughty Chinook had faithfully followed her. They had spent half of the day going through a smoke-white fog in a circle—a fog so dense that the swing dog could hardly be seen from the sled!

But the trail problem was worked out. The breed did that. Then they straightened away on the true course, and a scant hour later they had their reward.

It was as though a door had opened in a dark room. The fog and the mist parted before them, and they found themselves looking down a valley and toward a distant patch of silver.

"The lake!" shouted the breed. "Look! The lake! Him Chandalar there! There him Chandalar!"

He began to wave his arms, to dance back and forth like a madman, still laughing, still shouting.

But Windham stood as one turned to stone. They had come to the end of the journey. They were almost in the presence of the Chandalars. Would it not be like jumping from the frying pan into the fire?

136

# CHAPTER TWENTY-SEVEN

There was no question of weakness and weariness, now, either among the dogs or the men. All were revivified. Down the slope they went at a racing gait, big Chinook setting such a long-stroking pace that the dogs behind him staggered with the speed.

Onward they shot. At last the speed of the toboggans slackened somewhat, and they found themselves on the level lake side.

Somewhere, on the verge of that lake, Chief Little Knife and his Chandalars were posted. But that was not, for the moment, of prime importance. What mostly counted was the fact that they were near wood; and wood meant the necessary heat with which they could cook their food!

Feverishly they gathered the wood, therefore. Feverishly they heaped it up. While the breed was at a little distance, taking up armfuls, Windham kindled the fire, heaped brush upon it, stood back and laughed with joy to see the flames shooting upward.

The girl came and stood with her hands on her hips, laughing also, so that they glanced one to another, and their laughter interchanged, as it were, with the ugly thoughts left from their journey mutually buried, for the moment.

Then came the breed with a big clamor and started to scatter the wood as it flamed, kicking straight into the blaze, reckless of his mukluks.

"What's the matter, you woodenhead?" shouted the girl.

"No matter me! Matter with him!" yelled the excited

breed. "Why him make white man fire, Julie? Bring all Chandalars quick!"

"That's true," said the girl. "I'm such a fool that I forgot about it, too, Ned. If the Chandalars see the smoke from a fire of this size, they'll know right off that white men made it, and they'll come sneaking up in a swarm!"

"I want them to know that we're here," said Windham.

"*Want* them to know?" cried the breed, totally bewildered.

"Of course, I want them to know," insisted Windham. "Why not? Because if they're all around the lake, how are we going to sneak up on them with fifteen dogs and three people? They're not blind and they're not deaf, if they're like other Indians that I've come across. The more we try to play the part of sneaks, the more certain we are to get into trouble with the Chandalars, and trouble with them is just what we want to avoid."

The half-breed quit disturbing the fire, at this, but he stood back, shaking his head and muttering in rapid, discordant gutturals.

"What's the fellow saying?" asked Windham.

"He's saying," answered the girl, "that it's a foolish business to pay too much attention to the truth when you're dealing with people who have dark skins."

Suddenly she raised her hand to her own face. Color flamed in her cheeks. Her eyes widened.

Windham looked hastily away from her. "Stop it, Julie!" he commanded. "Damn it, don't act like that, will you?"

"All right," replied the girl.

"Maybe there's something in what Gus says," went on Windham. "But I can't put much stock in it."

"What do you intend to do?" asked she.

"If I can see Little Knife, I intend to tell him the truth about everything," said Windham.

"What!"

"Yes. That's what I intend to do."

"And what do you think will come of it?"

"Well, we'll be able to make a bargain, perhaps."

"What sort of a bargain?" snapped the girl.

138

"He'll give us your brother. That's one part of the bargain."

"Very well. He gives us my brother—and we give him thanks! Is that the way of it?"

"No," replied Windham. "We make him and his entire tribe rich, in return."

The girl gaped at him.

Then she said: "Go on, Ned. We'll make the whole tribe rich then, if you say so."

"I'm not batty, either," replied he. "We'll make them rich, all right, unless you've been lying to me!"

"Lying to you?"

"You told me that you knew where the gold was sticking its knees and elbows out of the ground."

"Great Scott!" exclaimed Julie Fernal. "And we're to show that place to the Chandalars?"

"That's my idea. Unless you'd rather have the gold than your brother. What about it?"

"You think I'm pretty low, big fellow, don't you?" asked the girl.

"Yes," he said, bitterly. "I think you're pretty low. But there's no use arguing about that. We're here to do a certain job. Let's get it done—if you're willing to give up the gold strike. Otherwise, I'll have to find another way of tackling the thing."

"Give up the gold?" said the girl.

Suddenly she laughed. The sound was so hysterical that it seemed like the cry of a sea bird, that screams against the wind.

"I'd give it up a thousand times over if the ground were covered with diamonds," she exclaimed. "Give it up for Bert? Oh, Ned, what have I been dreaming and praying for these years except a way to get him back? And perhaps it's a way. They say that Little Knife knows the value of money. He might take the thing as an exchange."

Then her voice changed. She faced him squarely.

"What do you get out of the business, then?" she asked. "You were to get that gold. You could have me, Ned. But heaven knows you don't want me."

"No, I don't want you," he replied, brutally. "And I'll get on without the money."

"You get nothing then. What under heaven has made you stick to the business, then, from the time you began to despise me?" she asked.

"I don't know," he answered her, with a more than equal frankness. "But when one starts, one just keeps slogging on. I don't know why. You stick to the trail because you want to get to the end of it, no matter where it leads. That's the only explanation that I can give you, Julie."

She made not another comment. In a moment more, both she and the breed appeared to have forgotten any danger that might be threatening. They were busily cooking at the fire, and the odor of tea boiling presently spread like a blessing to the nostrils of Windham himself.

Food, cooked food, to rub out of his palate and out of his throat the sooty flavor of the bannocks!

They began to grin, all three of them, and presently they were eating with the appetite which the horrible tundra had built up in them during those days of exposure and semi-starvation. The dogs ate, too, and wolfed down their rations.

Then the half-breed leaped to his feet and pointed. Windham and the girl rose up, likewise. Still, almost regardless of whatever danger might be about them, they held out their hands toward the fire. It was almost more than a religion to them, this glorious heat which, streaming out, penetrated their bodies as joyous thoughts penetrate the mind.

Now they saw enough to fill the eye. Standing in a circle but removed some little distance from the three of them, appeared a dozen muffled forms of Indians.

"The Chandalars!" said the girl, quietly, to Windham. "Now we're in their hands, and I hope your idea will work. It's about the only thing that will work in this pinch, Ned!"

They were big fellows, these Indians, but one of them exceeded all the rest in bulk and height. He was seen nearer than the rest, with what seemed an excellent rifle tucked under his arm. Now he came striding toward the fire.

When he was close by, he halted, raised his arm, and uttered a guttural greeting: "How!" That word did not accurately reproduce the sound, but it was as near as Windham could come to the spelling of it.

What the Indian said was of little importance just then. It was his size that dominated the mind of the white man. For the first time in his existence, he felt himself over matched by sheer physical proportions!

He had met, long before this, men who outtopped him; but in every case their clumsy physical mechanism was nothing to compare with his own glorious, quick moving, nervously compact body.

This was a different case. The monstrous Indian was not four fingers short of seven feet in height and he was faultlessly proportioned. One hardly needed to watch the swing and grace of his stride as he walked. His strength was only too evident.

Windham wanted, instinctively, to draw back a stride or two, so that he could measure the fellow with more consummate care, so that he himself would not appear dwarfed by the comparison. But in every detail he was outdone. In breadth of shoulders, in deepness of chest, he could not compare with this colossus.

"Chief Little Knife!" breathed Gus Aintree, now crowding close to Windham, as though for protection.

The chief, standing close to the fire, spoke again in those deep, guttural accents but, as before, it was a single syllable. Without answer, hastily, like a frightened dog when its master speaks, the breed bowed his head and walked rapidly out from the circle about the fire, going straight toward the ring of waiting Indians. When he reached them, two men took him by the arms and held him prisoner.

The chief followed this maneuver with a single glance. Then he turned back to Windham, and smiled.

"What shall I do?" asked Windham, briefly, of the girl. "Shall I start shooting?"

Then, instead of waiting for an answer, he called: "Gus, I'll start the fight to get you back right now, if you like. Are you afraid?"

But the lips of Aintree were sealed. The courage, the manhood, the strength had drained out of this breed, who had been such a powerful and courageous musher through the long leagues of the march.

# CHAPTER TWENTY-EIGHT

Small things may lead to great results. Windham felt the quiet, studious eye of Julie Fernal upon him, as the chief approached, and he knew what was in her mind. Instantly he stepped forward to meet the Indian.

The closer he approached, the more awe he felt. The features of even the best favored Indians are likely to be bluntly chiseled in one respect or another, but those of Little Knife were of a Grecian distinction. He had the jaw and the judicious, the spacious brow of a thinker. His dark color made him, to be sure, a statue in bronze, but a statue he was.

When they were close together, he could feel the Indian measuring him. Then Little Knife turned to the girl and spoke rapidly to her in the Chandalar tongue. She answered, more briefly, and then said to Windham: "He wants to know what has brought you up here to the Far North?"

"Tell him," said Windham, "that I've come here to get Bert Fernal, the white man they've been holding here."

The chief broke in, with his rich, bass voice. "That is a lie, my friend!"

He spoke in perfect English, with the intonation of a cultivated man.

"It is not a lie," said Windham, as he recovered from his surprise. "I'm telling the truth."

"Why should you come here to take back the white

man?" asked Little Knife, his eyes never leaving the face of Windham.

"Because I said that I would do just that," responded Windham.

"And what you said made you do it? What caused you to say it?"

Windham pointed to the girl.

"She did," he replied.

The chief regarded her for a moment.

"I know," he said, "that a pretty squaw is enough to turn the brain of a warrior and a wise man. You are not of the blood of the man who lives with us?"

"No," said Windham.

"Did you think," said the chief, "that we would give him to you?"

"I came to buy him," said Windham.

The chief stamped violently upon the ground. Then, as though regretting this almost childish sign of impatience, he drew himself to the full of his imposing height, and made Windham seem foolishly small.

"You come to buy!" said the chief. "You have bought our land. You have bought our clothes, our weapons, our dogs. Now you come to buy men?"

"I've never bought another thing from the Indians," said Windham.

"You or some of the others," said the chief. "That makes no difference. What is gained by one white man, the other man enjoys afterward. Where one white man comes, a hundred follow. We shall be hunted out of our last home!"

"Well," said Windham, "for my own part, I want Fernal, and nothing else."

"So they all say. I have heard them lie ten thousand times," replied the chief. "In the days when my father was the chief of the Chandalars, it was the same. Why don't you leave us alone?"

He controlled his passion, keeping his voice low, but he reared his head still higher at the close and he stared at Windham, waiting for the answer.

"You," said Windham, "are a chief. I'm only a single

143

white man. I can't answer for what other white men have done to you. At least, they've taught you our language perfectly."

"I paid for it," said the warrior. "I saw when I was a young man that the ways of the white man should be studied and, therefore, I went to live among you. I studied in your schools. I learned your ways. I learned your laws, also, and saw that you have laws only to help one another, to crush the red men. Then I came back to my own kind.

"After that the white man came, searching for gold and I did not wish my poor Chandalars to give their own blood to stain the snows. So we left our well-built cabins and came to the verge of this lake. Here there is brush from which we can make our fires. But our homes we have had to make of the cut tundra and the ice in the winter. There is not much game. We have to chop holes in the ice and catch the fish there. It is a wretched life. Many times we almost starved.

"Peace is ended. The white man's hunger is never satisfied. A little meat in the pot and we are contented, but the white man must fill his mind, too. And the mind can never be satisfied.

"Now you say that you are offering us a price for a man. What will you pay down? Tell me that, and it may be well between us."

Windham had listened with the greatest attention. He was impressed. The wrongs of an entire race were pouring from the lips of this dignified chief.

"Let me ask you something," said Windham. "If you don't want the whites, why do you keep this man?"

"When I asked you for a reason," said the chief, "you pointed to a woman. When you ask me for a reason, I must point to a woman, also."

"Ah!" said Windham. "Has he a wife, up here among you?"

"He has no wife," said the chief. "But he will have a wife before many days have passed. We have been patient long enough with him."

Windham looked at the girl. Her color had not altered.

"He has promised to marry some one of them," said

the girl, "and then he's tried to change his mind and they won't let him. Is that the way of it?"

"That is the truth. My sister's daughter pleased him," said the tall chief. "He offered to marry her. She gave him her heart. But when he learned that our marriages are also performed as among the white Christians, then his heart changed. He did not want a wife to love. He wanted only a wife to live with. But when a Chandalar has given his heart, he gives it forever; and when a Chandalar woman loves, she loves once and for all time. My niece has given her heart to the white man. How can she take it back? It is no longer hers!"

"Very well," said Windham. "We are going to offer you a price great enough to make up for whatever wrong he's done to any one of your tribe."

"What is the price?" asked the chief, running his eye over the slender packs of the sleds. "Have you brought bright cloth, knives, axes, spearheads, rifles and ammunition for us? We have plenty of all those things. We get them from the traders on the ships. They are glad to sell everything very cheaply for the sake of the furs which we bring with us. You cannot give us more rifles than we can hold in our hands."

"I tell you," said Windham, "I'm going to bring you to a place where the gold is sticking its elbows and knees out of the top of the ground. I'm going to give the place to you!"

"Gold!" cried the chief. "What is gold to me? What will gold buy? More useless rifles! All things are useless, when there are no longer men to wield them. More than enough is folly. Keep your gold, then, because I know that the white man has a belly which gold never can fill."

"You talk," said Windham, quietly, "like a man who never knew that gold will buy nearly everything that the white man has, except his honor."

"I have seen the white man's honor for sale, also," said the chief, with a faint sneer.

"That may be," answered Windham. "There are bad people in every race. But I have heard you complaining because you have lost the big woodlands, where game was plentiful, and the trees were big enough to build log

145

houses with them. Now, then, with that river of gold which I'll show to you, you can buy square leagues of the best woodland. You will find moose and deer again. You can go still farther south where the winter is only six months long. There you will find the big elk, also. You will find rivers filled with all sorts of fish. If you scratch the ground, the corn you plant will grow twice as high as your head. You will all be happy there in hunting grounds which you have bought, which are registered in your names according to our law, and then the law will never let you be driven out. What you have bought with money is yours forever, unless you are foolish. That is what you can do with the gold I can lead you to. Answer me, Little Knife!"

# CHAPTER TWENTY-NINE

The chief, when Windham made his pause, regarded the white man for a long moment. What he had heard seemed to impress him, seemed actually to make him wonder. At last he said:

"The man you want to buy is no kin of yours?"

"No," said Windham.

"No cousin, even?"

"No."

"It is only for the sake of the woman that you offer to give the Chandalars this?"

"Yes."

"But gold can buy many women among your people," said the chief. "Or is it because you have given your heart to this one woman forever?"

Windham, as he heard this, turned toward the girl. He was surprised to see that she was looking downward, a faint frown upon her smooth forehead. Never before had she failed to meet any eye that was cast upon her. And Windham smiled a little.

At last he said to the chief: "Whatever is in my mind, Little Knife, is of no consequence to you. I offer you a bargain. I offer to strike a trade. There is gold, which means land. I offer you this in exchange for the man. Will you give me your hand?"

"Not for the bargain, but to welcome you as a stranger to the Chandalars," said the chief, "I give you my hand, for this day!"

He put a certain accent upon the last three words, an accent which Windham was to remember later on.

Then he offered his grip and Windham accepted it gladly. Instantly he found that his fingers were seized in a vise behind which the lever seemed to be turning powerfully.

"A strong heart has a strong hand," said the chief, with a pretended calm, which could hardly disguise the fact that he was putting forth all of his power in that hand. "I hope that the heart of the stranger is good and strong also!"

The sweat, in spite of the cold in the air, was oozing out on the forehead of Windham. Sheer pain had done it. His heart leaped with fear. Yet he threw back his head and made himself smile straight into the face of the chief. After all, he had met the yellow hatred in the eyes of Chinook and he had faced the mysterious glance of the girl. Compared with them, even the huge Chandalar was hardly formidable, except for the agony of his grip.

Little by little, Windham began to secure a better position for his hand. He could curl in the tips of his fingers a little, now, and the thumb from the first was free to press like a powerful lever against the back of the Indian's hand.

That grip of Windham's had been practised not in idle wrestling contests, not in holding a rifle, reining a fierce horse, or wielding a slim fishing spear, but tugging and lugging at the rocks of Wind Valley, day after day for six mortal years, had ribbed his forearm with muscles like tough shreds of iron.

He was not unregarded. A flick of his eyes to the side,

caused by the pain he was enduring showed him the girl as she stood close by, calmly observing, watchful, detached, as it were, from the scene which she was witnessing. There were others. The Chandalars who had stood aloof at the beginning were now pressing closer and closer. From the width of their grins, from the manner in which they looked at one another, softly chattering, it was clear that the handgrip of their chieftain was a famous thing among that tribe.

Then pride stood up like a wild stallion in the heart of the white man. His hand was numb, to be sure, but somewhere in his arm he found an added well of strength into which he could dip in the time of his need, and in it he dipped. His whole purpose was concentrated in the effort, while still, his head high, veiling his eyes a little so that the bulging of the eyeballs might be less noticeable, he looked the chief steadily in the face.

Wonder flashed for one instant over the features of the bronze giant. It came, and it was gone. Then the nostrils flared in an instant's passion; his eyes glared; and a terrible pressure met that which Windham was exerting.

Their arms quivered, not an ordinary trembling, but such a shudder as electricity sends through the body.

The face of the chief was also wet. It was a comfort to Windham beyond anything that words could express. In place of despair, a hot wave of confidence surged through him. Once more, in a frantic effort, he put forth the might of his arm, and suddenly the hand of the chief collapsed in his own.

He could, he felt, have crushed the bones with his unsatiated power. But the instant that he felt the resistance give way, he withdrew his own grip and let his hand fall.

"We shall be happy here, Little Knife!" said Windham.

"This day," said Little Knife, "everything in our village is yours, to use as you wish to use it. Come with me to our homes. You are welcome, my friend."

He spoke with a little pause between his words, which the white man well could guess was to disguise his panting breath.

Straightway turning, the Chandalar made off with great strides down the side of the lake.

Ned Windham, watching him go, guessed at once that he could not match paces with that light-footed hunter. For the great Indian stepped as a panther steps, lightly and swiftly.

Instead, Windham followed more slowly behind and the girl beside him. The Chandalars were harnessing the dogs to the white strangers' sleds. Chinook, of course, followed at the heels of Julie.

Now a sort of exultant joy maddened the brain of Windham. He could have sung. He smiled as a sick man smiles, when for the first day in many, he comes from the house, and feels the purity of the outer air upon his face, the life-giving warmth of the sun upon his body.

"Yes," said the quiet, musical voice of Julie Fernal beside him, "that time you won. And the Chandalars don't know what to make of it. They're muttering and shaking their heads like a lot of gossiping old women. But you know, Ned, that you can't ask a cat to do what the dog does."

"What d'you mean by that?" he asked her, frowning down into her calm face.

"You told me how Chinook killed the mountain lion," said the girl. "Well, isn't that something like your meeting with Little Knife? He wasn't at his best, you know. He was a long distance from his best. But if you were to run into him when he was in action, on the move, he might be a different fellow to handle, eh?"

"I don't expect to have a fight with him," said Windham. "He's a big fellow and he steps like a cat. I can see that. I don't want to fight anyway. I'm a peaceable man, Julie. You forget that!"

She muttered to him, softly: "Great Scott, Ned, you don't think that you'll be able to get away from the Chandalars before you've had it out with the chief, do you?"

"Why not?" he answered.

She stopped short, and gripped his arm. "Look at me, Ned, and tell me that you're a grown man. Didn't you shame him before his own pack of warriors?"

"I didn't shame him," said Windham. "I didn't keep the thing up, after his hand wilted. I could have smashed

149

the bones in it!" he added, with a touch of savage power in his voice.

"I know that," said the girl. "And the braves knew it. And the chief mighty well understands, by this time, that the braves knew it. Why, Ned, everything was as plain as electric light in that big open face of yours. When you smiled at him and all the while you were sweating with the pain of his grip, don't you think that was clear to everyone? Do you think that you were fooling us? Don't be as simple as that!"

She actually laughed at him and Windham grunted in the height of his displeasure.

"In the end," she went on, "when you put on the pressure, and finally he collapsed, couldn't we all see his arm relax and his shoulder sink in?"

"What makes you think he'll tackle me again?" asked Windham, curiously.

"His face, his walk, the way he holds his head," she replied. "Everything forces me to know what he'll do. He'd rather fight and die ten times over than to allow any other man in the world to be called a greater fighter than he is. Look at his shoulder-swing. Why, man, don't you see 'champion of the world' written all over him? But he's not beaten. Right now he's beginning to get a thirst for your lifeblood. By thunder, Ned, I think that I begin to see the one possible way out of this trouble for you and me and poor old Bert!"

"What way?" asked Windham.

"Your way," said the girl. "Your way with your great big hands. Your fighting way, Ned!"

She looked up to him with a flare of her nostrils. A loud series of explosive words came from behind them.

Windham saw behind him half a dozen warriors, motioning to them.

"They want us to get ahead," said the girl.

"We're invited by the chief," said Windham. "We're not under guard."

"Aren't we?" said she. "Use your eyes, old son. Try to break through that line of bucks, Ned, and they'll take you apart and see what makes you tick!"

# CHAPTER THIRTY

There were no trees of any size in the vicinity of the Chandalar village, and yet there was one good-sized log cabin. It was the dwelling of the chief and into it the visitors were escorted. The wood for the structure, it was apparent, must have been dragged by men and dog teams from a great distance. But all the rest was as wretched as an Eskimo village—more wretched even, for the work was not so perfectly done, nor did the people seem so wholly in tune with their surroundings. There was an air, as it seemed to Windham, of melancholy on all the faces of the Indians.

When they entered the log house, they found the interior cut up into several rooms, to one of which they were conducted.

It was furnished and arranged like an old Indian tepee, with divisions like stalls, running around the walls, and big flaps of skin that could be pulled across the foot of the stall and so give privacy to the occupant. But in the center of the room, instead of the usual open fire, there was a small stove, which connected with the roof through a length of crooked stove piping.

In this room there were already two men, occupants, who were playing cards on a tarpaulin spread down near the stove. They raised their heads when the girl and Windham entered. And they saw, with astonishment, that one was their quondam guide, Gus Aintree, and the other, none other than Murray. The two half-breeds did not rise. They merely grinned at the in-coming pair.

"Here we are at the end of the trail," said Murray to Windham. "Glad that you've got Chinook still with you. I'll be needing him, before long, when I start back!"

151

Windham, pulling off his mittens, stood with his legs widely spraddled. He made no reply.

The girl walked up and down the apartment, examining the individual stalls. As she did so, she threw a few words at the pair. The latter had continued their game of twenty-one.

"You fellows," she said, "seem to think that you're wearing our scalps already. But you're not. You think you can deal them to us from the bottom of the pack, but you can't. This is a tight game, but Windham never does anything but win. You ought to have noticed that, Murray. He's beaten you. No matter what happens to him, he's made Alaska too hot for you. Murray, the dog thief. That's what they call you."

"You lie!" shouted Murray angrily, flinging his cards down on the table.

He sprang up. His face was convulsed. She walked over to him and stood before him, laughing in his face.

"Don't talk so loud, Murray," she said, "or the big fellow may hear you and break your neck for you. You and Mr. Double-Cross Aintree, yonder. You poor fools! You must want to spend the rest of your lives with the Chandalars. Because if you ever get outside again and leave us two behind you, your name will be mud!"

Murray was about to answer, when Aintree reached over and plucked at his leg. Murray looked down, nodded, and suddenly resumed his place at the card game. He was even smiling in a smirking content a moment later, as Aintree leaned over and whispered to him.

The girl came back to Windham. "What's on your mind?"

"Bert," said he.

"Nothing about how you're going to get out of this mess?"

He shook his head.

"Bert, first," said he. "After that, we can worry about how we get away."

Here a squaw came in, a wide, waddling creature, carrying a basket of newly caught fish. She put down the gift, eyed the pair of whites with little, cruelly bright eyes and went out again in silence.

"She's an appetizer, isn't she, that old girl?" said Julie. "Wait till I slip those fish into a frying pan, though. I could eat 'em raw, I think. Fresh fish, Ned!"

Windham grinned at her.

Then he went over to Aintree and stirred him with the toe of his boot.

The half-breed turned as a cat turns; a drawn knife took the place of needle-sharp teeth, but he changed his mind. Windham took him by the hair of the head and lifted him to his feet. Gus Aintree, cursing like the sound of escaping steam, let the knife drop to the floor.

"Go tell your chief, Little Knife, that I want to see Bert here, in this lodge, will you?" said Windham.

"Run your own errands," said Aintree. "Damn you, I've always hated you. Plenty big, plenty fool. Pah, you pig!"

His face writhed as he looked at the giant. "Open the door," said Windham to the girl.

She obeyed, silently, without excitement in her eyes, and watched thoughtfully as Windham took the breed by the scruff of the neck and the trousers seat, and hurled him out into the snow. He struck a drift and the loose snow blew up around him like an exploding shell.

Through this white mist, still flying about him, still shining in the air, Aintree rose and stumbled forward. He was screaming with rage, like a child or a woman, when the girl closed the door.

"That was pretty foolish," said she. "That may make the Chandalars pretty hot."

"Maybe it will," said Windham. "Only, I'll tell you something, Julie. I'm too tired of the game to be afraid any longer. They go and put that pair in the room with us. Apparently they think that we'll let Murray and the other rat spy on us. That's just a little too simple."

Murray stood up.

"So I'm ordered out, am I?" said he.

"Some people would take it that way," said Windham.

Murray paused by Chinook, who lay near the stove, his giant head resting upon his paws. "You've got more in you than I guessed, Windham," said the thief. "But you ain't got enough. You're a gone goose."

Windham watched him through the door. Then he faced the girl.

"You've made a declaration of war by throwing out that pair," said the girl.

"All right," answered Windham. "At least, I'm out in the open. That's what I like. No more fencing around for me. If there's to be fighting, let's begin now. Besides, we won't be any better off if we show that we're afraid of them. I couldn't be polite to that hired Chandalar, that Aintree."

"Well," said the girl. "We'll soon know. If Bert comes here, it's well and good. If he doesn't we'll get a message from bullets, instead. That's perfectly clear."

"Of course, it's clear," said Windham. "Now, how about some fried fish?"

The fish had already been cleaned by the squaw who brought them, and they found cooking utensils near the stove. In a few moments, the fish were hissing in the pan and smoke and steam began to roll through the room.

Windham sat down to watch. All at once he was tired. It was a weariness as much of the soul as of the body. The bleakness, the dirt lay about him. A rising wind was beginning to whistle mournfully; and Windham's spirits began to go down.

He wanted to relax, to give up. And relax he did. Out of the haze of his thoughts he wakened a little to see the girl coming to him with a great plate of fish and a steaming bowl of tea. He looked at the stuff with a lackluster eye.

"You eat, Julie," he said. "I'm not hungry."

The next instant, her hand struck his cheek sharply. He started up, enraged, but she stood her ground calmly before him.

"You great big four-flusher," she said. "Are you going to curl up like a yellow dog, just when you could be some use to yourself and everybody else? You get your appetite back and eat that fish or the Chandalars will get you—and grill you, first, the way they grilled Dean Carey!"

He answered nothing, but sat down to his food, and silently, sullenly forced down the morsels. At last he looked up and felt her serene and critical eye cast upon him.

He met it and suddenly he smiled.

"You're all right, Julie!" he said. "Dead right, this time. Thanks!"

She did not have time to answer, for the door to the room was pushed open, here, and a man entered, pulling the door shut behind him.

He was such a man as Windham never had seen before. His skin was like the white belly of a fish. His cheeks were sunken. The skin upon his fine, wide forehead seemed to be withering like old parchment. And under his brows his eyes were lost in dark caverns. Vaguely he looked about him.

"Bert!" cried the girl, springing to him.

The stranger caught her with one hand and held her away from him.

"Who are you?" he demanded harshly.

She seemed to wilt at the touch of his hand. All the strength went out of her, and she began to whimper.

"Look at me again, Bert," she said. "Don't you know Julie?"

"You lie," said he. "Julie's dead. She died and left me here in hell."

#### CHAPTER THIRTY-ONE

That was the great scene of welcome between the long-parted brother and sister. The brains and the intelligence had been stolen from the eyes of Bert Fernal. He was still, in outline, a big and imposing man but, when one came close, the outline was seen to lack filling. He was a wreck, a suggestion of what he once must have been. Still, in the haggard outlines of his face, a resemblance of beautiful Julie Fernal remained.

After the first shock, Julie collected herself, rapidly.

"Sit down, Bert," she invited.

"I don't want to sit down," said the brother. "You know, I don't want to sit down with a liar, like you. I'm going out again."

He went toward the door and the girl did not strive to prevent it, but when he pushed the door open a wide-shouldered Chandalar brave stood filling the entrance. He flung in a roll of blankets that flopped heavily upon the floor, and spoke three or four sharp words of command to Bert Fernal.

The latter winced as though he had been struck by a whip! That was too much for Windham. He dropped his head and stared at the floor. His brain spun.

They not only had stolen the wits of Fernal, but they had broken his heart, as well. He was no better than a street cur, kicked by many a boot!

Apparently, the brave had said that Bert was to remain in the room with the other two, and he evidently did not dare to appeal against the order.

Straightway, in a dull and awkward manner, like a sleepy child, he began to haul at the roll of bedding, which he took to one of the stalls along the wall. There he unrolled the coverings upon a good willow bed.

It took him half an hour of feeling about to accomplish what an ordinary man could have done in two minutes. Once he sat down and seriously, helplessly pondered a knot which resisted the first efforts of his fingers!

Windham, as has been said, could not watch the movements of the ruined man. But Julie Fernal, to whom the sight must have been tenfold more terrible, never shifted her glance from Bert. In her face, as in a dim mirror, Windham could watch the misery of the broken man, her brother.

For the last disguise was snatched from Julie now. What Windham saw in her was sheer agony of heart and sheer blazing for revenge.

Finally, she started over to her brother, stood before him, and thrust back the heavy cowl from his head. As the thing fell clear, Windham saw that the whole throat of the man was dreadfully mottled. It was marked as the breast of Dan Carey had been scarred by the tortures of the Chandalars.

Windham leaned back against the wall, half fainting.

He was roused by the deadly silence in the room. When he looked again at the girl only, avoiding Bert Fernal, he saw that she was cleaning a rifle, working the bolt of it smoothly back and forth.

"Well, Julie?" he asked her, suddenly.

"I'm praying, Ned," said the girl. "Don't bother me."

"Praying for what, Julie?" he demanded again.

"That I may get Little Knife," said the girl. "I don't ask much. I only want to get him. Then I'm ready to die!"

Windham went over to her and took the gun from her hands.

"Look at me!" he said.

She looked up, obediently; her eyes were so blazing, he shuddered as he met them.

"You'd better wash your face with snow," he told her. "There's no good in going crazy. Not in your going crazy, too."

Some of her passion went out of her, and she rested her head against the wall behind her.

"I know, Ned," she said. "It's not much good, what I can do. I don't suppose that I can do anything. But— God help me! I didn't expect this."

She added, with a gasp: "He was a lion. There was no backing up in him. Now he takes orders from a dirty, greasy Chandalar."

"Steady, Julie!" said Windham.

"Yes. Steady!" said the girl. "I won't go mad, if I can help it. Only—he doesn't know me, Ned. He doesn't know his Julie!"

She began to cry. It was an odd and horrible thing to watch her. For she was striving to control the sound of the sobbing, as though she wished to keep the noise from reaching the ear of her brother.

"Julie," said Windham, "you're the man, you're the brains of this party. If you go smash, where will we all end up?"

157

She snapped her fingers several times. Then she mastered herself.

"I'm going to be all right, now, old son," she assured him. "Only, it was a sock in the eye, seeing Bert like that. But I won't sink."

"No. I know you won't," said Windham.

He was watching her with the most intense, the most anxious interest. "How is it now?" he asked her.

"I'm all right again. Let's go on and eat. Bert, will you eat with us?"

Bert was loading an old, blackened pipe with tea leaves. He lighted them, carefully, and turned his blank eyes only then upon the girl. But he made no answer. He simply stared at her.

She carried some of the fried fish to him. He picked up a piece of it, smelled it, tasted it, ate a little, and then threw it down on the floor.

Chinook scooped it up with a flash of teeth, and it was gone. Bert Fernal went on with his smoking, tamping down the tea leaves with an insensitive forefinger, now and again.

The girl and Windham spoke not at all together. They ate their own food, choking down the mouthfuls, until, once more, the door of the room was thrown open.

The great chief, Little Knife, entered, bowing his lofty head to pass beneath the lintel.

He paused and leaned a little on the massive walking staff which he was carrying. One end of it was shod with steel, hammered to a fine point. It might have served him to steady his way when passing over hard, slippery ice. Or it might have been used as a spear, in case of need.

At any rate, it was a formidable weapon in that mighty hand.

The chief, having looked about him, settled his eyes for an instant upon the figure of Bert Fernal. The young fellow shrank back among the shadows of the stall, actually curling himself up sidewise upon the blankets.

Little Knife, with a slight twisting of his mouth, turned to Windham. "You have seen him," he said. "You may have him, if you wish to have him. We don't care very

158

much about that. Here with the Chandalars, he runs about harmlessly. He is even useful for a little work, now and then. You still want him, Windham?"

Windham moistened his lips. He felt the keen eye of the girl upon him, drilling to the very depth of his soul.

"Yes," he said. "I still want him."

"You may have him, then," said the chief. "And not an ounce of gold to pay for him, either."

He smiled again, that same humorless twisting of his mouth.

Then he went on: "The other matter is not so easy. You hear?"

He took his staff and with it knocked open the door. From the distance, Windham could hear a muffled chanting that sounded to his unfamiliar ear like a hymn. Then he remembered the Chandalars had been converted to Christianity, after some manner or other.

"They are praying, all of my people," said the chief. "They are praying for guidance and for wisdom. They want to know what they should do with you and with the young squaw. For they say that when such a big man and such a young girl can march all the way to the Chandalars, we must cut them off so that they cannot go back and tell other whites how easy the trail is!"

He made his pause; he was still sneering as he continued.

"You know, Windham, that I'm only the chief, and the chief is only the servant of the tribe. I cannot knock all of their heads together. But this is what I can do; go to them and tell them about your offer of the gold mine. Then some of them could go with us and we'll see the place. When it's found, if it's as rich as you say, I've no doubt that the braves will be willing to let you all go freely home again. That's what I've come here to ask you. If you agree, I'll go to my people and try to persuade them. But they have stubborn brains! First, give me your answer!"

Said Ned Windham: "First, we show you our secret, the gold. After you've seen it, it's yours; no matter what you do to us. It's more yours, if we're dead. Is that a bargain to ask from a sensible man?"

"No," said the chief. "I understand that. But the Indians don't lie. Not unless they've learned the ways of the white men better than I think they have."

Julie broke in: "Why don't you make an honest bargain, Little Knife? We're in your hands, but we're not fools."

"Why should I make a bargain?" asked the chief, coldly. "You are here. You are in the hands of my people."

"We are," said the girl. "But we have rifles in our hands, too. You know, Little Knife, that white men shoot straight. And I shoot straight, too. Don't doubt that! Well, you would lose some braves before you could rush this house, believe me. In the finish, we could set fire to the house and use our last bullets on ourselves. That would be the end of us and the end of your log house, too. I think it's the only one that you have, just now?"

The chief nodded at her. "A good squaw always has a sharp tongue," he declared. "Therefore, I am not surprised to hear you talk in this way. But what does the white chief say?"

He looked suddenly at Windham. "I agree with her," answered Windham. "Go tell your braves. You don't think, Little Knife, that we're going to trust ourselves in your hands and be turned into—that?"

He pointed toward the shadow where Fernal lay curled and cowering. The chief shrugged his great shoulders.

"I shall talk to my people," he said. "Perhaps I can change their minds. What words can do, I shall try."

And straightway he left them.

# CHAPTER THIRTY-TWO

When the chief had gone, Julie began to walk rapidly up and down the room. Now and then she cast a glance at big Windham, but her eye was half vacant with thoughts of other things, matters in which he could be no help to her. He realized that her mind was far away from him and, somewhat as a child, he continued to watch her, troubled, ill at ease. But he felt that there was in her some great and overmatching power that might be able to extricate them even from this difficult situation.

She said to him, suddenly, not looking into his face but at the floor:

"Ned, what do you think?"

"I'm letting you do the thinking," he answered.

"I know that," said the girl. "You're waiting for the pinch to come, for action. But that's what I want to dodge as long as I can. When the action starts, we're all dead! Oh, it isn't the dying that bothers me so much. It's the wastage of the two of us!"

And she made a gesture toward the spot where her brother lay.

"It's hard to have to see," admitted Windham. "But we've got everything coming to us that the chief wants to deal out."

"Why?" asked Julie.

"Do you remember the last Chandalar village that we looked at? It was a lot different from this lay-out of ice and misery. They blame the white man, and some day they'll try to make the white man pay up. The three of us —we're just tidbits to the stomach they have for revenge."

161

She was turned a little away from him, but she faced about sharply, when she heard this, and stared at him.

"What sort of fellow are you, Windham?" she snapped at him, in that sharp, almost fierce way she sometimes had.

"Well, I'm not an Indian," he reminded her, grinning a little.

"No," she answered, "but I didn't guess that you were that white!"

He was a good deal bewildered by this remark. Under the sting of her manner he could not help guessing that she was trying to pay him a compliment; for she continued to look at him with a gathered frown of appraisal.

Her brother began to whimper, raising his head from the shadow.

"Is he gone?" he asked, faintly.

The girl tried to answer, but suddenly she sickened and looked to Windham for help.

"Yes, he's gone," said Windham.

"I'm glad," said the broken man in the corner.

Then a very odd thing happened.

Big Chinook stood up, crossed the floor, and stood just before the crouched figure. Suddenly he licked the face of Bert Fernal. Both Windham and the girl, stupefied, stared at one another, but before they could make any comment on the miracle, back came the huge chief of the Chandalars.

He stood in the entrance to the room like a tower. "I have talked to the old men among my people," he said. "After one sleep, we start with you to find the gold." He left them like that, and straightway they prepared to take advantage of the priceless opportunity of rest in a warm room. The cold of the tundra was still gnawing their bones, and weariness was eating their brains, that sort of fatigue that comes only from long treks through the friendless arctic, where the cold is the only bedfellow and with its icy fingers keeps probing the body, waking or half waking the tortured sleeper a hundred times in a night.

But now they could relax. Their sleeping bags were almost too warm!

162

"And what about the door?" said the girl.

"There's Chinook for that," said Windham, and they agreed that the problem of watching against a treacherous attack could be left safely to the wolf dog.

Then they slept, not a little sleep, but the round of the clock.

They wakened to the noise of Bert Fernal rattling at the stove as he began to prepare food. Both Windham and the girl sat up and watched the starved, gaunt, pain-bowed figure of the poor fellow for a time. Then they looked at one another. But neither found for the other an answer to the great question.

And the question was this: No matter if all went smoothly, and the Chandalars kept their agreement after seeing the gold, there would lie before the returning travelers a voyage across the snows sufficiently grim. And how could they manage this weak, cringing, spiritless hulk of a man?

Windham saw the girl suddenly set her jaw and he knew that the iron had reached her soul.

As he pulled on his mukluks, he began to wonder about her for the millionth time. She had been strange enough from the first, but never so strange as during the past day. For she was a man and a superman; and, with-al, she was woman and superwoman. If one thing was clear in her life, it was her love for her brother. Yet, she was able to look into the whining face of this wreck without blanching.

They had a hearty breakfast, still yawning throughout the meal until the strong tea began to take effect upon them, for the luxury of real relaxation only slowly passed out of their nerves and their long-taut muscles.

They were still eating when the girl said to Windham: "You've got to remember, Ned, that when Little Knife said that he and his tribe would march with us, he didn't add that they would make any agreement."

"He didn't need to," said Windham. "He's honest. I can feel that. If he agrees to play the game with us at all, he'll play it fair and square."

"You're an optimist," said the girl. "But, anyway,

there's nothing that we can do except to bump our heads against a stone wall. So we'll have to go!"

Out they went, when the time came, to find that preparations were already complete. The white man's toboggans had been loaded by the Indians and the dogs hitched. Only the place for Chinook remained, of course, vacant.

Besides the Ned Windham string, there were three other outfits prepared and ready, with three men to an outfit. And every man looked a chosen musher. The dogs, too, were big, powerful animals, and it was plain that the chief was putting his best foot forward in the dash for the gold fields.

"Look at those faces!" said the girl to Windham. They were as black as night, scowling and puckering at the strangers.

Trouble started at once, but not among the men. There were two mighty Huskies near the outer door of the big log house and, when Chinook came out with his master, they took exception to the stranger. They must have been blood brothers, members of a single team, for they attacked like trained wolfish fighters, one from either side. Chinook, however, came off victorious and Windham was now free to put the dog in its proper place as leader.

Close by, a voice spoke to him. It was Murray, wrapped in the outfit of a Chandalar.

"You start him out," said Murray. "But I'll do the bringing of him back, big fellow."

"Are you going on this trip with the rest of the Chandalars?" asked Windham.

"Of course, I am," said Murray, grinning. "I'm your shadow from now right to the finish and heaven help you!"

He finished off his grin with a laugh. Windham made no answer. He had a sick foreknowledge that there must be something in the vaunt of Murray—some inside understanding of what was to take place before the inland voyage was ended.

Then the start was made. No greater courtesy could have been shown to Windham. He had the biggest and

164

the best team, by far. His load was not very heavy either. But still the sleds of the chief took the lead, those of Murray followed, and Gus Aintree was third.

It was a well-packed trail that was left to Windham, and after the long labors of their tundra march and all the marches that lay behind it, they loafed along this trail as though it were a joke to them all.

It was a good day. The temperature was neither cold enough to make the snow bite at the runners, nor was the snow so soft that they crushed through the upper crust. The sky was a pale gray, and there was only enough wind to toss up small vaporous clouds of the snow particles.

It was such weather, in short, as would have shrunk the heart of a New Englander; but for the arctic it was mild.

Fernal kept up well enough for the first two hours. Then Windham looked back and saw that he had fallen to his knees in the snow and that the girl was trying to lift her brother to his feet.

So Windham stopped the team and returned. He folded the exhausted man over his arm, carried him back to the sled, wrapped him in a great robe and actually tied him in place.

For Bert sat like a mound of flesh, rather than a man. His chin rested on his chest, his weak arms hung at his sides, while his eyes hunted vaguely toward the round, gray horizon. He said not a word of thanks. In fact, he had not spoken since this day began!

Windham told himself that it was the beginning of the end.

# CHAPTER THIRTY-THREE

A rousing hurricane struck them the next day and they were stopped for forty-eight hours as by a stone wall. When they started on again, the surface of the snow was a terrible thing. Each team had to take its turn in breaking trail. And Windham did treble duty, mushing in the lead, because his great weight enabled him to break trail better than any other man except the chief.

As for Little Knife, he made no difference between himself and the other braves who accompanied him. He seemed particularly cheerful, as the days went on. Sometimes he actually spared a smile for Windham, as the latter went up to the lead to break trail through the roughly crusted snow.

But even Little Knife was of small interest to Windham and the girl, compared with the progress of Bert Fernal.

For the first three days he steadily sickened. On the third day, Windham fed him by hand.

"He'll die tomorrow," said Windham to the girl, brutally.

On the fourth day, she undertook the feeding. She pushed the fur hood back from the head of her brother, caught him by the hair of the head, jerked him upright, and struck his face with the flat of her hand.

"Eat, you!" she shouted.

Her brother looked at her with a faint glimmer in his eyes. Windham, horrified as he was, could not tell whether it were anger or fear that illumined the glance of poor Bert. But the certainty was that, without a spoken word, he obeyed orders, sat up, and ate with twice as much appetite as he had shown the day before.

The day that followed, it was Julie, again, who pulled her brother off the sled and promised to lash him with a dog whip unless he attempted to walk. This time, plain hatred glared from the brightened eyes of Bert Fernal. But he marched that day for a while. Windham tried to interfere.

"You'll kill him!" he declared.

The face of Julie was set as iron.

"He'll die anyway, unless I brace him up," she answered.

Windham actually was afraid to argue the point. He merely waited to see Fernal fall, but for a drunkenly staggering mile, Bert kept his feet; then Julie ordered him back onto the sled.

To the amazement of Windham, the young man refused to go. His jaw was locked. He looked, for the moment, astonishingly like his sister, if not in his wasted features, in his expression, at least. He would not speak, as usual, but he grimly shook his head and refused to get on the sled. Windham had to put him there by force.

But every day, after that, Bert Fernal improved. He maintained his silence. He seemed as wasted as ever. But he walked with an even lighter stride and his head was carried higher.

"Once I get his shoulders back, like a man, you'll see the Fernal blood take charge of the situation," said the girl, as she studied him one day.

Before the end of that march, the young man actually mushed all day, without a spell on the sled. And there was coming into his gait some of that graceful lightness characteristic of Julie's step.

Windham was almost sorry, in an odd sense, to see the young fellow so recovered. It had been a mind-filling drama to watch the struggle of the vital spirit in Bert hour after hour, to see the sinking of his weak body counteracted by the growing strength of his will.

But now it seemed definite that Bert was on the way to health of body, at least. The mind was still in a cloud. The animal part of it was awakening, the brute, blind will, the instinct to fight for life. But the human intellect was still sleeping in silence.

167

"Chinook will bring him on, though," said the girl once to Windham.

That was at the end of a day's mushing, when Chinook took up his place in the snow, at the feet of Bert, and the young fellow sat up to pat the great head of the dog before he lay back in the sleeping bag.

"Oh, look!" whispered the girl. "Bert smiled that time. His brain will be working soon. Wait and see!"

Chinook had adopted the brother as he had adopted the girl before him. It was a bewildering thing for Windham to watch. Perhaps there was something in the blood of these people that reacted upon Chinook. Perhaps there was in them an essential wildness that exactly matched the nature of the big beast.

But he, Windham, remained forever excluded, thrust out from the circle of the dog's attention. Only, from time to time, a thrill would run up the back of the man and then he knew, even before he turned, that Chinook was coming toward him over the snows, silently as a cotton-footed lynx. Every time the dogs were unharnessed, that duel of danger began between him and the stalking wolf dog.

Yet not Chinook nor the strangeness of the Fernals could keep his attention after the trek was a few days old. For it seemed to Windham that he was bound on such a journey as the Norse myths describe, when the gods of Valhalla wandered far north to the misty region of ice and clouds where giants reigned and spirits of evil. Then, all the bright heroes of Valhalla would strive against the giants of the darkness, and the gods would fall, one by one, and the world be wrapped in coldness and gloom forever.

And so it was, he daydreamed, on this journey they had undertaken. The dreadful cold and bleakness of the tundra took them with a hand of white iron at the beginning of the trip. That was the worst of all. Afterward, they struck a river valley. It was a shallow depression fringed with small, dark-lying brush. But the brush increased in size from day to day. It grew into small trees, and the fires every evening were built larger and larger.

The sight of them gave Windham greater heart. Sometimes he began to feel actual hope that the adventure would not end in blood and disaster!

If only Little Knife would speak. But the Chandalar was as silent as Bert Fernal. Only, from time to time, in passing, there was a look or a gesture. That was all.

"You remember," Julie said twice more on the march, "that Little Knife really never made a promise! He simply ordered us out on the trail."

And at last she said:

"Tomorrow we'll come to the place, Ned. But it's my idea that the devil is in Little Knife's head. I've half a mind that it would be best for us to slip away some night, after camping, and make a run to get in the clear."

"They have a watcher out every night," said Windham.

"Strangle him, then, just as any of those watchers would strangle us!" said Julie.

Windham sighed as he looked at her. Then he shook his head.

"You're too soft," said the girl, angrily. "You think that it's a virtue, but you're wrong. You're too good to live this far north. You won't believe me and I know it won't change you but, just the same, I'm right and you're wrong."

"Look here, Julie," said Windham. "If we killed the watcher at night and slipped away, as you say, we'd soon starve to death. We have a mighty long trail before we come to the place where we made our line of caches. You know that. We have to get food from the Chandalars before we can ever get back."

"We'll steal food before we start," said the girl. "That's the best way. Would you do that?"

"I never stole in my life," said Windham. "It's pretty late for me to start in learning that sort of work."

"Well," said the girl, "I can steal like a cat from a pantry shelf. I know all about stealing. Leave that part to me, if you'll take the man off! Will you do that?"

He made no answer. He was sitting with his chin in his mittened hand, staring down, thinking not of her words, but of the whole picture of the girl as he knew her. It was a riddle to which he still had found no answer.

She loved her brother, true. One other touch of affection, and she would seem almost a human being. But now she remained like the very heart of the northland, aloof, cold, grim, unapproachable.

When he looked up from his thinking, he saw that she had gone away from him as softly as ever that big, deadly shadow, Chinook, could move.

The next day they made their last march to the promised land. They saw three hills to the south and the east of them, the dark streak of the river's trees winding toward them.

"Right at the foot of the middle one!" said the girl. "That's the place!"

Windham looked at it with a start of excitement. "Julie," he said, "you don't answer many questions."

"What's the use? Questions are just wind and words, and so are the answers. Words go hang. It's what you do that counts, not what you talk!" she replied.

He could not help nodding.

"But," she said, with a sudden change of voice, "what is it that you want, Ned?"

"I want to know how you ever got out there, to the end of the world. Will you tell me that?"

"I'll tell you that," she said. "How could you guess?"

"Why, you might have hitched on a pair of wings you'd borrowed from a sea eagle. You're likely to have done about anything, Julie."

She chuckled.

"I trekked out there with my father," she said. "He had the idea. I don't remember whether it was some iron-headed old trapper or an Indian legend about the three hills of ice. Look at 'em and see 'em shine. They're hills of ice, all right."

"Yes, or steel," said Windham, noting the glimmer of the rocky, frozen sides of the hills.

"We got to them, all right, and we found the stuff. Tons of it. Then we started back to get a big outfit and a lot of dogs and return. We just panned enough to pay for what we'd need. Then we started out."

"Well?" said Windham.

"Oh, an old story. Dad got pneumonia. He went west

170

couple of the dogs died. I ran short of grub. I chucked the gold dust and mushed on, and I managed to get out. That's all."

# CHAPTER THIRTY-FOUR

That was the story that rang through the mind of Windham as they mushed the rest of the way to the base of the Three Hills. What manner of man was that elder Fernal, to have taken a young girl with him through the heart of Alaska? Why had he done it, why exposed her?

Well, there was one class of men who would do such a thing, and that was the half-breed. That would be the explanation! And again the thrill of horror went through the brain of Windham.

It diminished, as he strode on with the dogs. For, at a stroke, she had explained much to him that had been the deepest mystery before. If she were hard-tempered, reckless, half-wild, what was to be expected of a young man who had accomplished what she already had done in Alaska? Her father dead, and she had seen him die—the horrible death by strangulation, in the helpless cold of the trail. And she had gone on, lost dogs, thrown away the treasure which she was carrying with her and finally she had got out from the grip of death.

Well, he could imagine the walking skeleton which had emerged. Yet she had been willing to enter the wilderness again and fight the same battle over again, not for her own sake but for the sake of young Bert Fernal! For had she not been willing to pay the whole of the gold strike to the Chandalars or to any white man capable of bringing out her brother from the Indians!

If evil and good are to be judged by actions alone, then

171

she was almost above criticism, so far as her relations her family were concerned. And he remembered, no that among Indians, among all primitive peoples, the c of blood, the call of clan, are imperative and far overri all sense of duty to mankind.

Once again she was fixed in his mind as a person mixed bloods, which to Windham was tainted blood!

The word had passed up the line that the desired pla had almost been attained. Suddenly the dogs were put a run; there was a general shout; and the whole proce sion shot forward.

Windham, covering the ground with his tremendo stride, looked back and made sure of Fernal. He saw th the young man was running lightly, easily. His head w high to make breathing easier, and the depth of h breathing was forcing his shoulders back.

Well, that was the thing that the girl wanted, and he it was!

The Three Hills, now that they were close under t feet of them, appeared rather more mountains than hil They glimmered still with a faint, dull sheen, more as ste than as ice-covered rock.

The teams were halted. The spot had been reached.

It was a point where the river, dropping down ca cades, broadened its course suddenly as it reached t level and swung in a broad, easy curve. Of course, t surface water was now frozen in a great sheet. On t curve, the ice was translucent. But over the cascades hung in long stalactites.

Perhaps the spot was sheltered by the height of t frozen hills, so that in the summer, during the brief seas of the long, warm days, the wind was shut away and t sun cupped. At any rate, this was a district where t trees grew to a very respectable height. Snow-laden a stark, they now looked grim enough, but they gave pleasant promise for the spring days.

Straightway, after the arrival, the preparations we made. While some of the men felled shrubs and sm trees and made a vast fire on the verge of the strear Windham and the girl set about the construction of a cr dle in which to wash the soil when it was thawed.

The fire burned wildly, in the meantime, throwing up ast yellow arms and casting a glow into the white mist hat was gathering through the trees. So strongly did it urn, that by the time the pan was completed the embers f fire could be raked away and the film of the surface soil was scraped away, a few inches deep.

The pan was then loaded. Heated water was poured over it. And the cradling began. A silence came over the men. Even the dogs seemed to feel that a moment of importance had been reached. With silence followed motionlessness, and with motionlessness, the arctic chill crept through the blood. To Windham, it was like the cold of a premonition, that he had had more than once.

The surface, lighter soil was now washed away. More water was added. Julie herself did the cradling, moving the water about with an expert motion, while the steam of the hot water rose up in a cloud about her face.

She seemed to Windham like some priestess performing an obscure rite. And from what rite had more misery sprung into the world than the taking of gold from Mother Earth?

They were crowded closely about her, when she made a sudden wave of her hand, commanding them back; and all obeyed, except the gigantic form of Little Knife.

He, however, remained standing fast. Suddenly the girl emptied the pan. She stood up. Into the hands of the chief she poured a stream that looked like liquid sunshine.

Windham glared in his amazement. He heard a sound like the whine of a dog in the throat of Murray, who was standing close beside him. Gus Aintree grunted, like a man who has received a blow.

As for the Chandalars, they paid little or no attention, except to the face of their chief. But Windham, ignorant as he was of such things, knew that the sight he was watching was a little natural miracle.

For he had heard of the days when men ventured their lives to live in Circle City and wash out, there, fifty cents' worth of gold in a pan. Then there had come tales from the Klondike of dirt that washed fifty dollars, a hundred dollars a pan. But those were tales hardly to be believed. What was true was that the hand of the chief now con-

tained a little bright mound of the yellow treasure, th
heaviest of metals. There must have been several ounces
and those ounces were worth seventeen dollars each!

In spite of himself, Windham looked out into the futur
possibility of the treasure. A man might wash out here
working alone, an independent fortune in the course of
single summer. Or he might with help of hired laborer
wash enough in a year to make himself and all of hi
family rich.

Down there in the southland, in California, were th
fertile acres of Wind Valley. But how did they compar
with this single strip of shore at the bend of an arcti
river?

The price of land, like the price of virtue, is ever chea
and sinking, whereas the price of gold and sin is alway
high and varies little through the centuries.

At the yellow heap in his hand, Little Knife stared fo
a long moment. Then, without a word to the girl, h
turned upon his heel and strode off up the river and wa
presently lost among the trees and the white mist tha
drowned them.

The Indians he left behind him glared at one another i
wonder. But the girl and Windham drew close together.

"What on earth does he mean by doing that?" aske
Windham.

"You never can tell about an Indian's brain," sai
Julie, frowning as she looked in the direction of the chie
"There might be anything from murder down, in his wit
just now. I couldn't tell. I looked right up into his fac
when he got the gold. But his face was stone."

She added, with a ring of enthusiasm in her voice suc
as he never had heard there before: "There's somethin
great in him. By thunder, Ned, there's a man who stand
by himself! He'd conquer the world, if he had a whit
skin!"

He looked down at her, waiting for another word, bu
she moved impatiently away from him.

In the meantime, the rest of the party had begun t
make camp.

It would be a most comfortable one, with this store c
excellent fodder for fire all about them, but their move

ments were slow, stilted, unenthusiastic. The disappear-
ance of the chief seemed to have taken the spirit out of
them.

Windham noted that the half-breed, Murray and Gus
Aintree, were close together, talking earnestly, with ges-
iculations. Some deviltry must be in the air, or the pair of
them would not speak with such an enthusiasm!

The camps were made, the wood felled, the fires blazing, the food for dogs and men cooking, before Little
Knife came striding into view again through the pale dim-
ness of the woods.

He went not to his own men, but came straight to the
fire of the three whites. Beside it he paused and uttered
for a greeting his deep-throated: "How!"


# CHAPTER THIRTY-FIVE


The climax, as Windham very well knew, had come.
Life or death would now be awarded to him, to the girl,
to poor Bert Fernal, by the events of the next few moments, the next few hours, at the most.

The dark solemnity of the chief's face was enough to
make them prepare for the worst.

"How!" said Windham, as he pointed out a place
where the chief could sit. "We camp here tonight," he
went on. "After that, we'll start back toward Fort Yukon.
You have seen the gold that was promised to you, Little
Knife, and now I suppose that we're free to take this
other man with us?"

Little Knife answered:

"Tell me, friend, what will happen after you have
gone?"

"What will happen?" said Windham. "Why, you know
what will happen. You'll bring up the rest of your tribe

175

here, I suppose, and you'll thaw the banks all winter, an
in the spring you'll already have tons of gold out of th
ground. After that, you'll have the spring and summe
thaws to help you. Along about the middle of the sum
mer, you'll take a million in gold dust, and you'll star
south. You'll go south until you've found the good tim
berland that you and your tribe dream about. And you'
begin to buy. You'll buy land where you find goo
streams, big trees, moose and caribou or other deer,
you want that sort of game."

"Will it be that way?" asked Little Knife, with the sug
gestion of a sneer in his voice.

"That's the way of it, of course," answered Windham
with a great deal more cheerfulness than he was real
feeling at the moment. "You'll have other convoys of gol
following you to the navigation head of the nearest rive
where a steamboat can be found. On the first steamer tha
comes along, you'll have the rest of the loot loaded, an
down that money will go to an honest bank, so that yo
can buy more land and more land still. So that the Char
dalars will be rich to the end of time!"

"And what will come of you three?" asked the chie
still with a manifest reserve in his voice.

"We'll go to Fort Yukon, and from there we'll proba
bly get straight out of the country."

"You have seen the gold that came out of the rive
bank, nevertheless," remarked the chief.

"Of course, we saw that."

"And when you go back to Fort Yukon, you'll tal
about it."

"I see what you mean," said Windham. "You're afrai
that when we get to Fort Yukon we'll give them suc
news it will start another gold rush in this direction?"

"Perhaps it would be so," said Little Knife.

"Friend," said Windham, seriously, "we're honorabl
people. If we give our words, we won't talk. You ca
have the promise of each of us. How does that do fo
you?"

"Your promise would be very good. It would be a
strong as the steel of a strong knife," said Little Knife
instantly. "But this is a woman!"

176

He pointed suddenly at the girl.

"She'll keep her promises like a man," said Windham, nodding his head.

"Look at me, my friend," said the Chandalar.

"I am," answered Windham. And he looked into the full, bright eye of the other.

"Now tell me, still looking into my eyes, that you do not think this woman would lie."

The assurance arose in the throat of Windham. But suddenly he could not speak. His head sank forward a little. He sighed as he stared at the feet of the chief.

"You fool!" he heard the angry snarl of the girl's voice, as she got the words out through her locked teeth.

The vibration of her tone went sharply through him. He shrugged his shoulders.

"I say the thing that I think," said Windham. "I can't say any more, Julie."

"Even," said the chief, "if the girl would not talk, how could I take a promise from this thing?"

And he nodded calmly at Bert Fernal. There was something incredibly gruesome about the very thought. The devilish handiwork of his own tribe was responsible for the loss of poor Fernal's wits. And now the chief looked at the blank face of the young fellow and reproached him for his folly and weakness!

Windham, seeing all things in a sudden blur of red, doubled his fists. The girl leaped suddenly between him and the chief.

"No, let him strike," said the chief. "Once before, I was shamed before you all and my people by this man. Now it is time that I should shame him or die. In my life there is only one shame, and it must be taken away!"

Said the girl: "Now, Little Knife, listen to me carefully. Will you?"

"I listen," said Little Knife, "as I would listen if a bird opened its throat and spoke a human language. Speak, because I know that you are wise."

She actually flushed under the taunt.

Then she said: "We could be kept here with your tribe until the summer comes. By that time, you'll have had a chance to loot the cream of these diggings. At least, you'll

177

have the surface off, and that surface will buy your whole tribe more than it ever dreamed of having. After that, even supposing that we went back to Fort Yukon and word of the strike got whispered around, you would have what you want for your tribe!"

"What do I want for my tribe?" asked the chief.

"Land! You've said that before. Land and game and fishing grounds," she exclaimed impatiently.

"Will gold get us those things?" he asked her.

"Of course, it will!" she exclaimed.

"Tell me what gold gets for the white man?" asked the chief.

"Wealth," said the girl. "Homes, farms, houses in the cities, everything that his heart desires."

The chief merely smiled. "I have seen what the gold they dig out of the ground gets for the white men," he answered her. "It gets them death from drinking whisky, or from starving on the trail, or a knife thrust in the back, or a bullet through the head. The young man who comes here for gold is old in five years. He is worse than a fox and a wolf. He drinks much whisky. His brain rots. Now you tell me that the Indians will be wiser than the white men and turn their gold into wild forests?"

He paused.

"You can drive 'em to it!" urged the girl. "I've seen chiefs before, Little Knife, but I've never seen one like you. You can take your tribe in the hollow of your hand and put 'em where you wish to put 'em!"

Little Knife, it seemed to Windham, stood somewhat straighter as he heard the encomium. A flash came into his eye and darkened there again.

But presently he shook his big, handsome head.

"Madmen cannot be driven," said Little Knife. "Men who are drunk with whisky are mad. They hear no reason. Men who are drunk with gold also are mad and cannot listen. They seem to speak, but there is no sense in what they say. Whisky is worse for the red man than for the white. He does not understand the poison as well. And if gold is bad for the white man, who always has had some of it, what will it be for the red man, who never has possessed it?"

"Little Knife," said the girl, desperately, for she seemed to feel that the last chance was in this appeal, "you don't know your own strength. You can keep all of your people in hand!"

"Can I keep myself?" said the chief.

He pointed up the stream, in the direction in which he had disappeared.

"When I took the gold in my hand," he said, "I thought, suddenly, of the houses and the lands of the white men, the soft ways of living, the horses, the many kinds of pleasant food, and the white man's way of talk which makes winter of summer and summer of winter. Now, when I thought of those things, I wondered if Little Knife would be better there than here in the North, leading a lost people, in a lost cause? All at once, I wished to be rich, and in the Southern land."

His breast heaved once and was still. Then he added: "So I threw that bright poison out of my hand and into the snow. I wish never to see it again. I never shall. My duty is here. This is where I must live. My blood calls me here. The call of the blood is, indeed, a strong call."

The girl, suddenly silent, stepped away. She left the two men confronting one another. "What's to be done, then?" asked Windham.

"I am thinking," said the chief.

"And what makes you think," said Windham, "that if white men come to this place, they'll ruin the Chandalars? There's a good bit of hard going between this and your tribe!"

"Now," nodded the chief, "there is a hard journey between. But when the ice goes out and the river runs, a canoe comes swiftly and sweetly down the stream. The paddle dips a few times and again the white men are among the Chandalars. Again, there are diseases of all kinds which our medicine men do not know. There is whisky to numb our brains. There is cunning talk, robbery, hatred, shooting, murder! When the Indians kill one white man, a hundred Indians must die for it! We, the Chandalars, have killed whites. When the word goes back to Fort Yukon, soldiers will come. Not this year, perhaps, but next year, or the next, and then we'll be taken like sheep, our throats cut. And the name of the Chandalars is lost. It flies down the wind like a dead leaf and is lost forever!"

Windham could give only one answer:

"You made a promise," he said.

"I made no promise," said Little Knife. "But I told you that the journey was prepared. And you hoped, and came out with us. That is all."

"You know, Little Knife," said Windham, as soon as he could speak again, "that there is honor between men. You've spoken of that, before. You have your honor, Little Knife. I can see it in your face. That's what I appeal to, now."

"You appeal to the honor of one man," said the Chandalar, "and I appeal to the future and the happiness of all my people. Which is the stronger appeal, friend?"

"Murder," said Windham bitterly. "You speak of murder, Little Knife. Is that it?"

"For you," said the chief, "I speak of a fair fight, first of all. If you die, it will be by my hand!"

"Good," said the white man. "I knew that there was still some honor in you. I knew it before! But what of the other two—the young man, and the white girl?"

"As for the boy," said the chief, "he is dead already. When the mind is dead, there is less life in the body of a man than in the body of a dog. Now, he is no more than a dog."

A gasp of rage came from the lips of Julie, instantly muffled.

But Windham made no objection. Objections could be made in detail when the full mind of this man was known. So he went on with his questions.

"And what of the girl, Little Knife?"

"The girl?" said the chief. "The white men drive the red men. The white brain is quicker. It comes and goes, turns and twists like a snake. The Chandalars must have in the tribe more of the brains of the white man. And here is a white squaw for some Chandalar brave."

"A squaw?" said Ned Windham, hoarsely.

"I myself would take her." Little Knife spoke gravely, without, apparently, any sense of injustice in his words.

"She would be the wife of a chief. Our marriages are as binding as the white man's marriages, you know!"

Windham looked helplessly about him. His eye lighted upon the face of Bert Fernal, who was watching the great chief with a curiously placid interest, like a child that sees some half-remembered thing, once familiar in the past but now forgotten. The fear had gone out of his eyes.

He looked in turn at Julie. There was black murder in her face as she regarded the chief.

# CHAPTER THIRTY-SIX

Why should there be such an explosion of hatred on her part, when only a few moments before she had expressed the most intense admiration of the great Chandalar? Why, above all, if there were Indian blood in her?

He said to her, directly: "Julie, you see how it is. I'm to have it out with the chief, and you and Bert are to stay behind. Is there any possible way that you can better that deal?"

She was in a rage. But she merely glanced from the ground to the sky and back again. It seemed to Windham that it must have been the first time in all her life that she was thoroughly baffled.

At last she said in her sharp, clear way: "Suppose, Little Knife, that Ned Windham beats you when you fight?"

"Suppose that he—" began the chief. He paused, interrupted by his own astonishment at the suggestion. Then he went on: "Well, of course, you would be free, then, if you wished to go."

He said it so simply that the sense of his speech did not come home at once to the mind of Windham. Before he fully understood, the chief had gone back to the other Chandalars. He began to talk to them, and the deep, ringing tones of his voice floated clearly across to them. Julie Fernal listened, entranced. She translated in a soft, quick voice.

"He's telling them to load up our sleds with the best provisions they have. He's telling them that you and he are going to take a walk into the woods to discuss some little things. And if you come back alone, Ned, they're to let you go off with the dog team, with Bert and me! Can you beat that, Ned? Can you even begin to understand it? Of course, I see what he means. If he is beaten in a fair fight by another man, he doesn't care to be seen again so long as he lives—if he does live! If he dies, I suppose he thinks that the Chandalars can get along pretty well with what has been shown to them on the river bank here today. There's only one thing that baffles me completely. Why did he ever bring the two half-breeds along? I know that he never could trust them but—"

She stopped short and then resumed again, in a different tone:

"What have you with you? A knife and a revolver?"

"Yes," said Windham, dully.

"Are they both in good shape?"

"I suppose so."

"When did you look at the revolver last?"

"Oh, a few days ago."

"Look at it again, this minute!" said the girl. "You know how the oil congeals in this temperature."

"The gun will do well enough," answered Windham.

She stamped her foot, as she faced him.

"What's the matter with you? Are you sick?" she demanded.

"A little, I guess."

"Sick with fear?" she snapped.

"That's it," said Windham. "I'm about scared to death."

"Then he'll eat you alive! You've only got a fair fighting chance, anyway," said the girl. "You weak-nerved, you dullwit, you—"

She paused, breathless. Changing suddenly, once more, she came close to him, murmuring: "Ned, if you pull through, I'm anything that you want me to be the rest of my life and yours. I'm your servant, your cook, your

182

scrub woman. I'll slave for you, Ned! I'll love the ground that you walk on, if you get Bert out of this!"

He answered her:

"Down in my part of the world, Julie, white men don't live with breeds! I'll do my best with the big chief. But you can't bully me and you can't put dynamite into me by promising me yourself. I'm a little sick, all right. I'm sick to think that I've come this distance, only to find that the chief is more than half right, after all. He's the best that he can be, according to his lights. But you and Bert—bah!"

He snapped his fingers. He turned on his heel. As the chief came stalking up, Windham fell in at his side and they walked together toward the woods.

He regretted that he had joined the lofty Chandalar in that manner. For the staglike tread of the Indian made his own seem a blundering and earth-bound pace. He was again like a work horse beside a thoroughbred.

He could only console himself with the knowledge that in his hands, at least, there was a trifle more of strength than there was in the hands of the Indian.

Little Knife, without speaking, led straight into the trees.

Within the range of them all was a murky, silvery twilight, dimmed by the thin, hanging mist. Sometimes it gathered among the branches into ghostly forms. Sometimes it seemed that grotesquely shaped and goblin creatures were sitting there before them, grinning with obscure features.

With each step that they took farther among the trees, the obscurity became a little greater, so that Windham began to strain his eyes, in order to accustom them to the difficult light.

Presently he stumbled over a root which thrust its hard-frozen knee above the surface of the ground.

He fell upon hands and knees and started up suddenly, for perhaps the Indian might take advantage of his stumbling; such things were quite usual in the red man's warfare.

But when he leaped up, he was amazed to find himself alone!

183

There was no sign of the Chandalar and suddenly h understood. It was to be a fair fight, but a fair fight alon; the lines which the red man chose. It was to be a mutua stalking match!

To that match, he himself could bring some craft, bu he knew that the Chandalar must have an infinite advan tage over him. The entire life of the Indian had bee: spent largely among just such frozen woods as these, wit! the crunching snow underfoot and the icy, brittle brush which snapped with a report like that of a small calibe pistol.

But whatever happened, he must not stand where h was. He made a long leap to the side and crouched be hind a treetrunk. There he waited, his heart hammering i: his throat, his eyes blurring with terror. But he had sens( enough not to draw the revolver clear of his clothes. Th( handles were already warmed by his body. He could b thankful for that. He slipped off his right hand glove, let ting the heavy mitten dangle loosely by the string tha passed up around his neck. The bare fingers and the re volver within their grasp, he thrust up inside of his park: hood, keeping the hand close to the base of his throat.

It was not a bad position for a weapon in case of nee( for a quick draw but, even there, sheltered as it was, h found his hand rapidly growing cold. He had to keep flexing it in order to be sure of a proper circulation of th( blood.

In the meantime, all of his senses crystallized into th( intensity of accurate listening. But he heard not a sound.

Yes, there was a slight rustling, exactly behind him. H turned, inch by inch, until he was sure that he was facin; exactly toward it. Then, ready as a tiger for the kill, h( waited. The rustling, indeed, increased. There was a sligh rushing sound, almost as if some great object were hur tling violently against the wind.

He thought that he saw a human shadow disentangl( itself from among the gray and indistinct shapes among the trees.

Half rising, he snatched out the revolver and fired.

It was a miss, he knew, but before he could shoot agai: the figure that he thought he had seen disappeared.

The very next instant he heard the solid, crunching shock of a large body of snow against the frozen ground.

That rustling had simply been the beginning of the slide of a mass of snow from the sloping branch on which it had hitherto been supported!

But the noise his gun had made must surely have exposed him to redoubled danger. It would act as a shining light to guide the soft-footed Chandalar straight to him!

Well, he hardly regretted that. The sooner the shock of the battle came, the better. For another thing, the strain of the recent excitement and the boom of his own gun in his ears had acted to relieve the tension of all his nerves. His body felt warmer. He breathed more easily.

Now was the time for deadly keenness of muscles and mind!

He knew all of this, and yet he found his mind wandering in flashes. He saw Chinook, once more, standing over the body of the slaughtered bull. He heard the terrible voice of Chinook through the night. He faced Chinook once more with the rubber-padded club.

Well, what would come to Chinook, up here in the northland, among the Indians?

Perhaps he would found a new strain. A new breed of gigantic Huskies would appear among the Chandalars and, like all good things, they would gradually find their way into the hands of the white men. If that were the case, then many a lonely musher through the arctic would owe an unconceived debt to him who had come from the south and died in this lonely forest.

He met, again, the pretty face of Julie on the trail. Suddenly the thought of her wrung his heart. Was it the twist and pain of love that he felt? He only wished that he had parted from her in kindness, with gentle words; but her own reproaches and her stinging insults had maddened him. Suppose, after all, that he conquered in the fight?

The wolf itself may be killed by the bulldog, if the bulldog gets the grip!

The thought was a wonderful comfort to him.

For the first time in his life, he blessed the ponderous rocks which he had ripped out of the face of Wind Valley.

They had forced him to have hands of steel. Only let those hands now grip the throat of the Indian.

Something breathed close by. It was a sound he did not actually hear, but rather felt. He had heard no approach, but all at once he knew that the danger was close upon him.

Stealthily he turned, but as he did so, the glinting shadow of danger darted toward him from the opposite, the least guarded side!

There was no time to jerk about. It had been the sweeping motion with which a gun is raised to the shoulder.

So Windham dropped for the ground without turning at all and the roar of the gun seemed in his very ear. He felt the red-hot slash of the bullet along his side, at the same moment!

# CHAPTER THIRTY-SEVEN

He did not fall like a log. Instead he twisted himself about, and the swerving of his body undoubtedly saved him from the second shot; he felt the twitch of it at his hip as he swung about. His feet drove against the shins of the giant, and, as he struggled to gain a better position, he saw the mass of man plunging straight down at him!

He had his revolver out with a jerk and raised it in time to parry a stroke that would have battered out his brains, for the Indian smote out with the heavy barrel of his revolver as he dropped. As it was, the double shock knocked both weapons out of their hands.

The Chandalar grunted, and Windham had time to remember that there was a resonance in that grunt like the voice of a pig in the farmyard of his childhood. Then he

186

saw the knife of the chief come out in a dull, silver streak. He reached for that knife, and by the grace of fortune, his fingers closed over the wrist of the man.

One hand of the chief was imprisoned, for that moment, at least. The other fist he dashed into the face of the white man, and a dark blur blotted out all things before the eyes of Windham.

He was merely groping vaguely with his right hand, trying to strike an effective blow, and succeeding, merely, in effectually pommeling the body of the Indian.

Then a terrible blow struck him in the pit of the stomach. Little Knife, like a practiced rough-and-tumble fighter, had jerked his knees up against the body of his enemy, and Windham's breath was knocked out of him.

He would have liked to writhe and gasp for breath. But he knew that one instant of that writhing would be his last. Already the knife wrist of the red man was twisting and jerking like a mighty snake striving for freedom.

The eyes of Windham cleared a little. He had no room for effective action with his right. With it, however, he hammered at the face of the giant, and felt as though he were tapping at a mountain of rock. In retaliation he received a blow that seemed to spring all the bones on the right side of his head. So he cast his right arm around the body of the Indian and strove to crush the man in a bear hug.

In his ears he heard the short, panting, snarling laughter of Little Knife. At that moment the knife was almost jerked clear.

As for Windham's own knife, he could not get at it. It was behind his hip, with the weight of both bodies grinding it against his back.

He released his right arm from around the huge body of the other. And the free hand of Little Knife instantly throttled him.

He tore at that grip, seizing the hand by the wrist. He seemed to be tearing out his own windpipe, but the grip held true. He felt the fingers tearing the flesh as he tugged!

That way would not do. The weight of the giant's body

187

was pressing home his throttling hand! The head Windham spun. Death, he knew, was close at him. He fe the terrible outthrust of his tongue, cut by his own teeth.

There was one thing left. He thrust his right han elbow turned out, between him and the face of the India close above. Still that snarling laughter was at his ear he jerked the arm back again.

The laughter stopped. It seemed to Windham that I had shattered his elbow bone against a rock. The shootir pains numbed his entire arm. But the impact of the blc had been irresistible. It must have landed on the side Little Knife's head, and it rolled him sidelong, over a over. His knife hand tore from the grip of Windham, b the knife itself was dropped by the numbed fingers ar fell to the snow. Windham, as he lurched to his fee swept it up.

He was armed, now, and the Indian was free-hande —free-handed, and rising slowly, with a stagger.

Fear passed suddenly from Windham. He threw tl knife away. He drew out his own and cast it also to tl side. Then, striding close to the wavering bulk of tl stunned warrior, he said:

"Little Knife, you've had your try at me with guns ar knives. You've had the thing your own way, and yc weren't man enough to get me. Now I have no advantag And I'm going to get you without a weapon. I could ha slid a knife between your ribs, but I'm not going t You've already nicked me. The blood's running down n side. But there's still strength enough left to me. I'm goir to get you with no more weapons than God gave me. Te me when your head is clear and we'll start again. Or el there's the forest behind you. Get out and run for yo life like a scared rabbit. You're too fast in the feet fe me!"

The answer of the chief was a great groan of rage ar despair. Then he came in as a bull comes, charging de perately, caring little whether it lives or dies.

Windham was no expert boxer, and the light was ba But the target was large, and he had sufficient distance make ready. He balanced himself, his weight back on h right foot. His naked right fist, heavy and hard as a roc

e poised. Then, swaying his bulk forward, he smote with
all his might.

It was a solid shock. He felt, he thought, the face of the
Indian sag under the terrible weight of it. Hard against
him struck the body of the rushing brave, but it was a
loose, ungathered bulk. Then Little Knife dropped upon
his face.

Windham jerked him over on his back. He leaned
close, one hand ready to throttle the giant, but as he
brought his eyes close to the face of the fallen giant, what
he saw made him recoil with a shudder.

The Chandalar would live, no doubt. But one thing was
certain. Windham would be able to walk out of the woods
alone!

He stood up.

Once on his feet, he wavered a little. All the blood of
his body seemed to be rushing into his head; a song as of
the ocean was in his ears. But, breathing hard, he fought
the spell of faintness away. He gathered himself; he
pressed back his shoulders; he filled his great lungs.

All at once he was laughing a little, deep in his throat,
a rumble of triumph. So he strode on. His right hand was
almost frozen before he remembered to thrust it back into
its mitten. His head was almost frozen before he drew the
hood back over it.

But now his stride was long and certain. He was even
sure of the way, though he had paid no heed to it, so far
as he knew, when they had entered the woods.

In another moment he had come from the trees, with
the mists wreathing away from his body as he stepped out
into the brighter light beyond.

That light the high-headed flame of the fires increased,
and about the fires he saw the dark silhouettes of the
watchers, all turned his way, all facing toward the woods
to see which one of the two men would come striding out.

He laughed again.

His lip was cut. He was tasting his own blood. But that
was as nothing. The triumph was his! He could have
shouted!

Indian eyes are keener than the white man's. From the
watching Indians, familiar with the noble outline and the

deerlike stride of their chief, first came a deep-throated groan from every man.

Next he heard a high, shrill, but musical call. It was Julie, shouting: "Ned! Ned! Ned!"

And here she was, running swiftly out to him, light as a boy, an athlete, unhindered by the bulk of her arctic clothing. She came dancing around him. She caught his arm.

"What happened?" she said. "We heard the two shots! And yours was the first one!"

"No; he did the shooting," said Windham.

"He did the shooting! You mean that he fired both the shots?"

"Yeah. He did that."

"Ned, for heaven's sake, what happened? Are you hurt?"

"Nope. Not at all. Get that dog team started." They had advanced now until the light of the fires flickered more clearly over him. She stopped him, gripping at his arm, shaking it.

"Ned!" she gasped. "One side of your face is smashed."

In fact, when he talked it had to be from one side of his mouth now. And he felt that his right eye was closing rapidly, so that things blurred before him, as though he were growing faint.

"It's all right." he said. "It's not the side of Little Knife's face that's smashed in. Let's get on, Julie. Let's get Chinook, there, into the harness. You get him in. I'm a little short on eyesight, just now, and I don't want him to smell my blood. But let's get going before the damn Chandalars and those two sneaking breeds see that I'm a mess. Hurry, Julie, d'you hear me?"

"I hear you, Ned. I'll do it!"

She ran toward the waiting dog team. Even as she ran she turned and looked back toward him now and again. She spy-hopped like a rabbit in the childish exaltation of her joy.

"Bert! Bert!" she was crying out.

And the form of Bert appeared, with Chinook beside him, Bert striding forward with an easy, graceful step.

Suddenly the whole adventure seemed good, seemed sweet to Windham. For what is there in the world really worth having unless one works for it; best of all, works for it in a far country, a country far, far from home?

Well, he had won. Those Chandalars yonder, they knew about it, too!

He shifted his position, and suddenly he staggered a little. The whole of his side was wet, and the wet was beginning to freeze against the outer clothes.

Besides, his knees were giving and always that song was in his ears, sometimes loud, and sometimes softer than the hum of bees.

The sled came up almost on the run. He got to the gee pole and brushed the girl away. He needed that support, for he knew that he was failing fast.

"Ned, what's up?" murmured the girl. "What's the matter? Oh, don't tell me that he really got you!"

"He didn't," said Windham. "But let's get on. Stay close to me. That's all. Things are a little dusky, aren't they? Don't worry."

"Ned, you're dying!" rang her voice in his ears.

"Don't talk like a fool," he told her roughly. "But I'll be dying mighty soon if those Chandalar wolves see the moose stagger and look at his blood in the snow. Julie, get the team on! Not fast, but steady! I think our work on this job is only beginning!"


# CHAPTER THIRTY-EIGHT


The fast-gathering gloom of the fog soon shut them off from the eyes of the Chandalars. Then the girl wished to make a stop, but still Windham would not permit it until they had driven on a considerable distance through the woods up the river.

When at last he consented to the halt, his head wa spinning. He could not help with the making of camp, bu to keep off the cold, kept moving around in a staggerin circle, blundering against the trees here and there.

One thing amazed him. He could hear the quick, shar voice of Julie Fernal through the mists and the blacknes of his mind, uttering commands to her brother. Thos commands were not repeated often.

It was as though Bert Fernal had understood and wa working according to what he was bidden to. Hitherto, h had sat like a lump at every camp.

But in a short time the fire was blazing generously, tarpaulin was on the snow, and Windham was stretche on it with a sleeping bag over him.

Even though his wounded side was turned toward th fire, when the skin was bared, the cold seemed to bit through him like the thrusting of a sword. He muttered little. Looking up—for his eyes had been closed in some thing like sleep—he saw above him a wild staring mask c horror, the face of Bert Fernal, and the lips of Bert wer parted, gibbering: "How did it happen, Julie? It couldn happen! He was too big! It couldn't happen!"

And the young man stretched out his hand as if t touch the bloody side. But Julie struck it fiercely away.

"It happened for you and me!" she said. "Push tha kettle deeper in the fire."

Windham could see her, also. She was not like Ber Her face was set, grim, determined, with her lips presse together, and a scowl above her deep-set eyes.

"Poor Julie!" said Windham. "I guess there's not muc use. They've sagged me. There's not much use. Just wra me up and keep the fire going a while."

"Be still!" commanded the girl. "Keep quiet. I don want to hear your foolish chatter!"

Then a long flexible, iron-hard arm went around hir and ground together the lips of his wound, pressing th pain straight into his heart. He gasped and found that hi breathing was cut short by the bandage.

"Lie still," said Julie.

"It's no good," said Windham. "Loosen the thing Julie. You know it's no good."

"You're a great, whimpering, helpless baby," said the girl. "I always knew it. Lie still, or I'll despise you more than ever before. Lie still or I'll make you."

"All right," said Windham. "I'm a little too far spent. Only, before I die, I want to tell you something, you half-breed."

His mind went blank. When he came to again there was a shelter tent over him. Outside the great fire was burning. He could see the yellow outline and tremor of it through the translucent canvas. Inside the tent the stove was burning, also. And yet he wondered at the cold that was in him.

Ever since they left Fort Yukon there had been cold enough on the outside, but this was within. There seemed to be a cold hand gripping his vitals. That inward cold flowed upward into his throat.

"I'm going to die," said Windham to himself. "I've never felt like this before."

He thought that he had spoken to himself, but the heavy snarl of Chinook answered him instantly, and so he knew that he had murmured aloud.

Afterward came the hard voice of the girl:

"You're going to die because you're a quitter. You're going to die because you're a coward. Otherwise, you'd live, if you were a man. You want to die so as to wring our hearts."

"Your hearts!" whispered Windham. "The heart of a breed and a half-witted breed brother."

Someone groaned.

"Steady, Bert!" he heard the girl mutter. "He's half out of his head. And the other half is crazy anyway. Crazy, or he never would have taken this mush on his hands. Steady, boy! You're coming out of the woods. We'll get him out of the woods, too!"

She leaned over Windham.

"Look here, Ned," she said in her fierce, decisive way, "how do you feel now?"

"Snug as can be," he answered.

"I want you to eat some of this."

She put a hand under his head and lifted it a little. She put the food close to his face.

A sudden revulsion stiffened him. He thrust the prof
fered food away.

"I don't want it," said Windham. "Take the filthy stuf
away, Julie, will you?"

There was a moment of pause. She allowed his head to
sink again.

"Oh," moaned the voice of Bert, "he won't eat! That'
the finish if he won't eat."

"Stop your whining," she commanded. "You, listen to
me!"

Her face thrust close to that of Windham.

"You know why you won't eat? Because you've given
up, like a whipped puppy. That's why. But you've got to
eat."

"I can't," said Windham. "You're only bothering me.
won't eat. Leave me in peace, Julie. That's the only favo
that I've ever asked of you!"

Bert began to sob. "Get out of the tent!" Julie com
manded him. "You make me sick. Two of you at once i
more than I can handle. Get out and sit by the fire—
you!"

There was the sound of Bert leaving the tent. Then sh
leaned over Windham again.

"Let me tell you something, you great, oversize
puppy; you're going to eat."

"Am I?" said Windham.

Anger began to warm him a little. The ringing in hi
head stopped. It had been like the beating of distant bell
He had told himself that when the sound ended his lif
would end, too. But now the bells were still, and his lif
remained to him.

The grim face of Julie was still close to him. How ut
terly and bitterly he detested her!

"You're going to eat," she said, "if I have to jam th
muzzle of a gun between your teeth and force the foo
down your mouth."

He moved his hand suddenly and caught both of he
hands in his.

She smiled. He increased the pressure a little an
smiled. "You'll be breaking the bones in a moment,
that's any pleasure to you," she said calmly.

He released her at once.

"You talk of making me do everything!" he explained briefly.

"I don't have to make you, now," said the girl. "You've got your appetite back hating me."

"No," said he. "I don't want anything."

"It's your fool pride that makes you say it," said the girl. "Because you didn't want it before; you want to be consistent. Here's something to put under your head. Try this tea, Ned. You can drink tea, no matter how hard it is to swallow. Try it, will you?"

He looked blankly at the top of the tent. Smoke and mist were crowded and clouded there. It was true, all that she had said. He had the appetite of a wolf now, but pride stopped his throat.

Suddenly her voice altered. "Ned," she said, "I've asked a lot of things of you before. I've asked you for your life, practically, and it seems that I'm going to get it. Now I'm begging one thing more. Try to eat a little of this. I'll go away so you won't have to see me. I know you hate me. Only, try to eat a little!"

"Listen, Julie," said he. "I hate you, I suppose. But you're right. I've been acting like a cur. You don't have to leave, Julie. Stay here. No matter what I feel about you, you're something to look at that gives a lift to the heart."

He rested his head upon the roll of furs which she had placed, and he began to eat and drink, while she remained close by, with the wolf dog crouched at her feet.

She had her chin in her hand, watching the smoke wreaths that sometimes curled upward through cracks of the warped and crazy stove; and sometimes her glance moved to Windham, and she smiled and nodded encouragingly, like a mother at a child.

"You'll feel the difference," she said. "You'll be on the trail tomorrow."

"Yeah," said Windham, "I'll be on the trail to-morrow, or else we'll all be dead."

"Why?" asked the girl.

"Because the Chandalars will come after us like devils after they've seen the face of their chief, Julie!"

"Yes?"

"Send that damn wolf out of the tent!"

He cried it out in horror.

For big Chinook lay there with his head high and with his yellow eyes blazing at the face of the man with invincible hatred, with the ardent longing to destroy. That longing might be translated into one lancelike thrust of the whole big body. Then a single long stroke of the fang would put an end to Windham.

Now, as he saw the picture, it seemed to him fate from the beginning. He had taken the creature out of the wilderness. Now, in the wilderness, Chinook would destroy him.

Julie, without a word, rose and obediently led the dog outside.

Without a word she had done as he asked, and yet Windham felt in the very constraint of her silence that she despised him more than ever.

He was not surprised. The greatness of body which enabled him to perform difficult feats was no match for what he felt in her—the greatness of an iron soul.

# CHAPTER THIRTY-NINE

Windham slept, for the food had warmed him. He wakened to find the others deep in slumber. He raised his head to look at them. Dizziness struck him down again.

As he lay there he turned the problem accurately and calmly in his mind. And he could see that in his present weakness lay the destruction of them all. If it made him dizzy even to lift his head, what would it be when he strove to take his place with the dogs and mush ahead?

This much was clear, that the girl and her brother could probably win through. At the least, they had a golden chance to do so. If he remained with them, how ever, he would not save his own life even. He would merely prolong his misery and bring death, at the last, upon all three.

Then he thought of Julie and the stinging words which she had spoken to him the day before. Well, what he was about to do now would confirm her in her idea of him. He would be to her the weakling. Would enable her to turn her back upon his body, if it were found, and to go more cheerfully on her way.

She, the half-breed, what should he care for her opinions this way or that? Yet he knew that she loomed larger than anyone else in his horizon. Whatever her blood, she made all other human beings as nothing in his eyes. Compared to her strength, what was the strength of any man?

He got up from the sleeping bag and, inch by inch, lest he wake the sleepers, he made his way out of the tent.

As he passed he saw the girl turn suddenly with a groan. It stopped him, but he saw that she slept again, and so he went on. The cold cut of the air and the purity of it entering his lungs had given a delusion of strength. But when he got to his feet the delusion entirely vanished.

He staggered against the wind which was blowing. It was not a strong breeze, but at that temperature the slightest gust passed through his clothes and found his body, thrusting a sword through the ready passage of his wound.

So he went straight up the wind, leaning a little against it. Three times he thought that he must fall, but each time he recovered himself and saw the dim, gray trees drift slowly past him.

Then, at last, when his knees were buckling, he struck a drift of snow and floundered into it. He tried to rise. His brain spun into darkness, and the softness of the snow received him like a feather bed.

So he lay still, his mind clearing. It was better in this way. After a little, men said, came drowsiness, and after that, deep sleep, from which there is no awakening.

The deep-throated snarl of a beast just beside him scattered the calmness of these thoughts. Horror flooded his soul. It was Chinook!

Why had he not thought of that, as he had thought the day before? Some weapon against that brute—but now his hands were empty! There was no gun, no knife, no club to beat the monster away.

And now full into the drift Chinook hurled himself.

His forefeet planted themselves with the weight of heavy fists upon the breast of Windham. Dimly he stood above the fallen master, and Windham could see through the gray gloom and the yellow gleaming of the wolf eyes, and the white flash of the fangs.

He started to lift his arms to guard his throat. Then, with a strong effort of the will, he abandoned the thought. For it was better to have the futile contest ended quickly, to let the stroke fall like the edge of the guillotine, where life would burst out most quickly.

Down dropped the head of the monster. Right against his face was the grinning mask of the teeth and the snarling lips, and out of the throat of Chinook poured a rumbling thunder of hatred and of triumph.

But still he did not strike home. Perhaps, like the cat with the mouse, he would play a moment with his helpless victim. Well, that was all the better, for then the cold would have anaesthetized Windham wholly or in part.

Still the blow did not come. Sinking down on shuddering haunches, all his body on the body of the man, Chinook lifted his huge head and lifted to the sky close above him the long, terrible wail of a wolf.

No wonder, hearing it, that people told tales of werewolves; for there was something human in it, like the howling of lost souls in a windstorm.

The cry trembled and died away.

"He's telling of his kill!" said Windham to himself.

The wolf dog leaped suddenly away, out of the range of the man's eyes.

"He'll come again with a side attack," said Windham to himself.

He closed his eyes. Life was a queer thing. It was a great and continued war to maintain it. But to lose it, how simple! Like dropping a golden coin into the dark sea!

The cold began to strike through him. He tried to move his fingers, and found there was no feeling in them. Only

198

through the wound in his side, concentrated torment was pouring, burning and scalding him. Otherwise he would have sunk to sleep more swiftly.

Even so, he was growing drowsy when something suddenly leaned above him.

"Chinook," he said through his stiffening lips, "you're a slow murderer."

A strong hand smote him full in the face.

"Wake up!" shouted the voice of Julie Fernal.

Julie Fernal! He would rather have faced a thousand devils than that fiend of a girl. If she had shamed him before, how would she shame him now?

"Julie, listen to me. The thing's done now," he said. "Let me be here. It's better for me alone to snuff out than all three of us. You know how it is. If you get through to Fort Yukon with him, you've finished the job that I started. Go on. Let me stay. The pain's almost ended."

"Get him on that side, Bert," said the girl. "I'll take this arm. Now lift!"

They tugged with all their might. They could not budge the enormous bulk of the man.

"Ned, will you try to help us?" shouted Julie in his face.

She struck him again, brutally.

"Will you try, you coward, you quitter?"

"I'll try, if you won't leave me alone."

He tried then, but it was no good. He was as helpless as a log.

He settled back with a faint groan, and at the sound of this Chinook came with a bound, stood over him, licked his face, and whined!

"What's happened, Julie?" exclaimed Windham.

She cried out at him. Her voice was stifled, as though she were coughing; not sobbing, though. There would be no tears from Julie Fernal to the end of the trail. Surely not!

"I have it, I think," said Bert Fernal. "Put Chinook on the job. Let him take hold."

"That's the idea, Bert," said Julie. "Chinook! Here, old fellow!"

She laid a fold of Windham's strong parka in the teeth of the wolf dog.

"Back! Back, Chinook!" she cried.

As the beast drew back, slowly at first, then more and more strongly—mouthing that garment so skillfully that hardly a toothmark was found in it afterward!—the girl and Bert lifted at the armpits of the fallen giant.

Slowly they raised him now!

Were these murmurs of thanksgiving that Windham heard from the lips of the girl? He put forth a great effort and managed to gather his feet under him a little.

So he was standing at last, supported.

Chinook no longer pulled. But he ran back and forth before them, hastening them with whines and incidentally beating down a trail toward the camp.

"Chinook! Chinook!" Windham kept muttering through his chattering teeth. "Look! He came back to me at last. I didn't win—he only gave it up! Chinook, old-timer!"

Strongly the girl and Bert supported him, reaching up, thrusting beneath his loose shoulders.

He stiffened them a little. That helped the work. He bent his whole will upon lifting and moving his legs, and slowly, stumblingly, they responded.

"Keep fighting!" panted the girl's voice. "Keep fighting, big fellow!"

"Yes," said he. "I've got to now. Chinook—he came back! Chinook!"

He wanted to laugh. The chattering and beating together of his teeth prevented this. But more strength flowed into him. Suddenly he saw the glow of the fire before him and the tent gleaming in that light.

Then he was inside, he hardly knew how, and they were drawing the sleeping bag over him.

The girl built up the fire outside so that it roared like a flaming tower; she started the stove roaring, too, until it was red-hot all over.

In the meantime, as she brewed hot tea, Bert Fernald was industriously pommeling the feet, the legs, the arms of the half-frozen body.

The circulation began again. Ten thousand pangs shot through the body of Windham, but he knew that the life was being revived in him.

Hands lifted his head. Above him the faces of Bert Fernal and the girl were pressed close together, looking down at him. He drank deep of the scalding tea that was proffered.

Beside him was a heavy breathing. It was Chinook, panting, lolling his long- red tongue, sniffing cautiously now and again at the face of the master; then, at the hands which ministered to him, as though the brute suspected that some harm might be done.

"It's all right, Chinook," said Julie Fernal.

In response to her voice, which he had loved so well, Chinook growled!

The marvel of it passed in waves through the brain of Windham. It possessed and enchanted him, for he saw, after that long and fierce duel between them, that Chinook had indeed become a one-man dog, and he was the one man!

# CHAPTER FORTY

Time became to Windham like a flowing river which a boy watches from the verge of the bank until he is hypnotized by the slow tangling and disentangling of the currents, the green-brown sliding mystery.

He ate, he slept, he wakened; ate, slept again.

The keenest moments of consciousness were when the wound was dressed—at first a burning misery, afterward less and less important.

At last, on a morning, he sat up suddenly. His head was light. He felt that his knees were not very strong even before he put his weight upon them, but he knew that he was breathing easily.

All of the days behind him were a haze; but at his feet lay Chinook, head erect, eyes fixed full upon him. There was this difference in the stare of the wolf dog—that the yellow glare was gone from the eyes!

Deeply, in wonder, Windham looked straight down into the face of the dog, and suddenly the glance of Chinook wavered! Yes, that fixed and blazing eye, now so softened, turned to the side!

It came to Windham's face. Cruelly the man persisted in his stare, and now Chinook abased his great head upon the feet of his master, which he was warming with his own body, his eyes quite closed, the ears twitched down a little, and the long, wolfish brush of a tail slowly swept from side to side.

"Old son!" said the man, and stretched forth his hand.

Chinook whined with joy and licked that hand which had been to him so terrible an enemy.

"Old Chinook, old fellow!" said Windham, wonderfully moved.

Straightway the great dog was beside him, lying close, his head lifted high, his tail still wagging, and in his eyes a fond light of absolute possession.

Julie came in and found them so. She stood at the entrance flap and smiled down at the picture.

"We mush today," said Windham.

"All right," said the girl.

"I won't be able to make many miles, but we can start in."

"All right," said she.

It reminded him of the calm submission which she had shown to Andy Johnson, that formidable trailer.

"You better call Chinook outside," said he. "I want to get up, and he about fills the tent."

"I'll try," she answered.

"Here, Chinook!" she said.

He turned his head, regarded her, and snarled with formidable depth and malevolence.

"You see?" said the girl, and smiled at Windham again.

He took a great breath.

"I'm trying to believe it," he said. "Chinook, you go outside for a while."

Chinook instantly arose. He cocked his head and regarded his master, as though to make sure that the cruel order was intended. A gesture reassured him, and turning, Chinook left the tent with head down and tail much abased.

"Look!" whispered Windham, and pointed.

She nodded at him, as quiet and cheerful as before.

"He loves you," she said. "He always wanted to love you, I suppose. You always were the man for him. Only you wouldn't let him."

He shook his head.

"Sit down here, Julie," he said. "You explain the thing to me, will you?"

"It's easy to explain," she answered.

"You fought him. And, you see, he's half wolf and half dog, or something like that!"

"Well, what does that have to do with it?"

"A lot. While you fought him you kept the wolf in him on top. You see, when he met me, I didn't fight him. I wasn't afraid of him, even. Because, just about then, I was already too desperate to be very much afraid of anything new, dog, or man. You know how it can be! But most of all, I was pretty helpless. I mean, compared with you two men. And I suppose that I looked to Chinook rather small and useless, and needing protection, out there in the wilderness. So the wolf in him went down, and the dog came right to the surface. He started in taking care of me, as you remember."

"I remember," he nodded. "And poor Bert, too—I suppose it was the same with him?"

"Why, of course it was." She nodded.

"You could have told me before, Julie," he complained to her. "I think that you might have given me the hint."

"Tell you to be helpless before the wolf dog?" she replied. "Why, it was a toss-up as to what he'd do in such a case. He'd hated you so long that he might cut your throat before he had a chance to think. He's able to cut throats, as you know. But when at last he found you flattened in the snow, it didn't take him long to realize the truth. He saw that you needed him. As long as he's sure that you need him, he's your slave. Mind what I say—your slave for life!"

"No slave to me," said Windham, shaking his head. "But a friend, rather. We've been through enough together, Chinook and I. I've nearly killed him. He's nearly killed me. And all the while it only needed—"

He paused to find a fitting phrase, and the girl found it for him.

"Call it the strength of weakness, Ned."

He sighed.

"You have all the ideas, all the strength. What a man you would have made, Julie!"

She smiled again in this peculiar new way which gave her a beauty he never before had seen in her face.

"I'm content to be as I am," she said. "I'm not ambitious any longer."

"Hey, Julie!" called a ringing voice out of the distance.

"Who's that?" exclaimed Windham, for the voice was utterly new to him.

The girl spoke with a slight attempt at carelessness. "That?" she said. "Oh, I'm not surprised that you don't remember. That's the man you brought back from hell. It's Bert!"

She went suddenly out of the tent.

Windham, shaking his head at the marvels he had seen and heard, thrust back the sleeping bag, crawled out of it, and began to dress. When he stood, he was surprised to find that he was much less weak than he had expected.

The strength of weakness! It seemed to him still a mysterious thing. He had fought his way through the world with all the advantage of Herculean strength and a determined will. Yet in the end it was his weakness that saved him from death.

Well, Julie had always been the gate through which he passed to the contemplation of marvels! And this was only the latest of her bits of wisdom.

When he was dressed he found that he could stand and

204

walk well enough. He was pinched a little toward the left side, to be sure. And his knees were by no means the mighty supports that they had been of yore. But he felt that a few short mushes down the trail would make him a man again.

He went outside, and there he saw, talking with Julie, a young fellow he would never have recognized, straight, high-headed, with shoulders proudly and strongly thrown back. His face was covered with the soft beard of a youth. But his eyes were bright, keen and clear.

He came instantly to the giant and took his hand.

"What it does for me to see you up, Ned!" he said. "It's the greatest sight in the world for me!"

"Yes, pretty great," said Julie. "Six feet and a half, or so, of greatness. They don't come much bigger than that."

"Why didn't the Chandalars come booming down our trail?" asked Windham.

"It stormed like the devil for a few days," said the girl, "and maybe our trail was pretty well lost."

"Little Knife could have found us," he persisted.

She nodded.

"Yes, I don't understand it," she admitted. I've dreamed of seeing him coming alone, as tall as the trees, with a half a dozen of his pet Chandalar devils behind him. But thus far he hasn't come. That's all I know!"

"He was hurt," said Windham, "but more in his pride than his body. Bert, have we enough chuck to keep us going for a while?"

"We're not going to have heavy sleds," said Bert Fernal. He added ruefully: "But Julie and I have tried to map out the course. She knows it pretty well. We ought to be able to make it to the last cache that you and she left before you struck across the tundra. From there on it would be easy to get in to the Fort."

He looked askance at the long legs of Windham. The latter, understanding, said: "Three short marches and then I'll be able to keep up, I think. We start now, Bert. Line out the dogs. How long have we been here, Julie?"

She looked at him steadily.

"Don't worry about that," she answered. "You can find that out later on."

He went to the sleds and examined the size of the foo
pack. Then he understood clearly enough.

"A long time," he said. "And all the while I've bee
wolfing it down. You and Bert are thin enough. Why di
you give me so much chuck, Julie?"

"To put back the blood you'd lost," said the girl
"That's the reason. And you'd lost plenty."

So they lined out the dogs, and Windham fell in be
hind. On this first day's march he would have to take th
easiest, the most advantageous position. But Julie had
better idea.

She harnessed Chinook and put his traces into the han
of his master.

The word to mush was given, the toboggans were bro
ken out, the team swayed ahead, straightened, and the
were away across the snows.

But behind the last toboggan went Chinook, gla
enough to be deprived of his leadership, for he went alon
with his head often turned, and his brilliant eyes softene
as he looked back to his master, who strode along leanin
back a little, wavering somewhat in his gait, draw
strongly forward by the might of the dog, and ever and
again a thrill of joy leaped through the heart of Chinook
for he heard his master laughing softly with happiness.

# CHAPTER FORTY-ONE

It was not three days before Windham could make a
good march. His muscles were merely softened by weakness. The pure air, the familiar exercise, and, above all,
the glorious tonic of happiness restored him rapidly. His
third march was nearly up to the limit of the strength of
Bert Fernal.

From that point on all three raced together.

As the sleds lightened still further, with Chinook in the lead and the dogs straining, Julie Fernal had to spend part of every day riding, but Bert himself proved a musher almost equal to the long-legged Windham. He had the perfect style, the deep wind of an Indian, and he seemed to love the work as though he had been born to it.

He told them, during their pause at the fourth or fifth camp on the way toward the line of caches, what he had endured from the Chandalars. He told it with a voice that trembled and threatened to break now and then, but he persisted to the end. It was very much the same tale which Dean Carey had related, except that Dean had been wrong in thinking that the white man had failed in his promise to return with Carey to the Fort.

"They'd simply turned me into a woman. I was no good. I guess that I was no better than a half-wit, when you came for me, Windham. There's a weak strain in me somewhere, and that's all!"

He looked desperately before him.

Windham, his big hand stroking the head of Chinook, which was on his knee, made answer out of the conviction of his heart.

"What happened, Bert, was that you lasted a little too long. They broke down Dean Carey. He told us about that. They made a woman out of him, and he's man enough as the whole arctic knows. But a white man is not a brute or a beast. He has nerves. And the same nerves that keep him going when an Indian is giving up are the nerves that make him buckle when pain rubs him the wrong way. Julie, here—she could stand anything. She's one in a million. But then, Julie's a devil, and doesn't go by the rules of ordinary people."

He smiled at Julie as he spoke, and Julie smiled back. The understanding between them had become so perfect that it took more than ordinary badinage to upset them.

Windham went on, feeling his way, knowing that he had found the truth for this fellow with the desperately shamed and hungry eyes:

"The very thing that made you buckle in the end, under the tortures, was the very thing that made you a hard fighting man before."

"I'll never be again!" said Bert with a shudder. "The next half-grown boy that looks me in the face—I'll take water from him."

Windham shook his head. "You'll be different, now. You've got the cold steel in you, and other men will be able to see it shine so far away they'll let you alone."

"Do you mean that, Ned?" he said. "You're not simply trying to buck me up?"

"I mean it!" said Windham.

That talk seemed a turning point to Bert Fernal. His pride returned. And now, as one perfectly harmonious unit, they rushed the dogs forward toward the goal of the first cache.

A week out they put themselves on short rations. Something might have happened to that cache, they decided, and it was best not to make it their only bet.

They were right in their fears. When the long mush brought them to the place, they found that the bundle had been cut out of the tree in which it had been lashed. Some of the provisions might have been stolen. Some were burned. Some were stamped into the snow and ruined. Vandals had gone that way before them.

The three stood about, unable to look at one another.

Then, without a word, they mushed on toward the cache.

They had little hope, however. If this cache had been deliberately ruined, then others along the trail had been spoiled, also. If others had been spoiled, they would never reach Fort Yukon.

They knew it, but each of the three locked jaws and headed steadily onward.

When they camped at the end of this march, Bert merely said: "Who could have done it?"

After a pause the girl remarked: "Murray followed down this trail."

Bert nodded and looked far away, as one conjuring up a picture and a duty one day to be performed.

For food they had dried fish, like the dogs. And only a morsel all around. The dogs themselves had lost their bellies. Their eyes were red, and their coats stared upward, their tails dragged down. They stumbled and coughed along the trail.

The next day when the march began, the swing dog, a big, fine Husky, was found dead in the snow.

He had worked faithfully on the outtrail and on the in. So he was left in his harness and some snow thrown over him, and water over this to freeze. That was his grave!

Then they slogged on. It was a hard pull, a bitter hard pull. Then they reached the next cache their grim expectations were realized, for this one also had been spoiled.

"Murray," said Bert Fernal.

He even laughed a little, in a way that made the flesh of the giant crawl.

All had been done here as at the first ruined cache, except that apparently little or nothing had been taken. Those who went this way traveled with such a superfluity of provisions that they did not need to increase the weight of the load. It was pure vandalism. It was worse. It was blackest murder for those who had laid up the provisions. It was the ultimate crime of the Alaskan trail code.

The three, knowing this, still could not speak. They looked grimly about, Julie walking in a small circle at the outside.

Then she said: "Bert, when did that snow fall?"

"About thirty hours ago."

"Wet and slushy, wasn't it?"

"Yeah. The kind that freezes—slicks out into ice in no time. Why?"

"Look at this?"

She dropped to her knees and blew upon the ground. A surface coating of snow dust puffed away, and the imprint of a mukluk was plainly defined.

"What of it?" asked Bert. "I suppose that it's one of the devils! But what good is that to us? They're in Fort Yukon by this time, I guess!"

"They're not," she answered. "This trail was made after the fall of that slushy snow. Then afterward the snow dust covered it. This trail was made something less than thirty hours ago. Bert, Ned, we're going to give the dogs every last scrap of food that we have. Let them rest

209

three hours. Then we'll start slogging. We can pull up ou
belts instead of eating. And I've an idea that we may b
able to catch the hounds who're marching ahead of u
Mind you, they know that we've had two empty-bellie
marches before ever we get up to them. They're feelin
safe; they may be traveling slowly! Shall we try?"

Should they try?

What else was there to do? It was only maddening th
they must wait the three whole hours before making the
start! But they knew that Julie was right. The spent dog
needed food and sleep. Then they would mush on agai
and pray for a killing at the end of the journey.

So the dogs were turned out, a fire built, the dog foo
cooked and distributed with painful care. Chinook, fo
instance, got not a mouthful. He was in far the best co
dition of them all, though he had always done twice a
much work as the others of the team. While the food wa
being distributed, he simply lay at the feet of his mast
and pretended that he had heard and seen nothing, th
no fragrance of fish had reached his nostrils.

So the three hours went by.

They walked to find two more dogs frozen in the snov
The lips of Fernal curled like an animal about to bite. Y
they delayed to give the poor Huskies honorable buria
which is all that one can do in the arctic, even for th
most tired companion on the frozen trails.

Then they went on with their shrunken team.

But with Chinook in the lead, and a few hearty word
to him, with Windham breaking trail mightily most of th
way, they fairly flew, hunting for life or death at the en
of that march. For starvation kills quickly in the arcti
The bitter cold eats up the strength even as heat does i
the tropics, and saps the vitality far more rapidly.

They ate their hopes of revenge that day and pushe
relentlessly forward. When they were a few miles fro
the cache they sent Bert ranging ahead. It was more tha
possible, if the time schedule of the girl were correct, tha
they might find the enemy still camped near the thir
cache; and it would be well to have an observer far ou
ahead, scouting.

210

So, running straight and true in spite of his fatigue, Bert, as the most light-limbed member of the party, scouted ahead.

They followed at a more moderate pace. Julie was at the limit of her iron strength. The dogs swayed and staggered in their harness. Even Windham felt the strain to the soles of his feet, for he had made trail almost all of that day.

Now, as they moiled and toiled by zigzags up the side of a slope, through the dun arctic twilight, they saw a form coming toward them, waving both hands.

"It's Bert," said the girl with a shout of joy. "He's found them. It's Bert, come to warn us that they's just ahead."

# CHAPTER FORTY-TWO

It was as she said. Bert came up, fairly trembling with fierce excitement. "I found 'em smashing the cache, feeding some of it to the dogs, ruining the rest."

"Who?" asked Julie.

"I don't know. There's a pair of 'em. Average-sized, I'd say. That's all that I can tell you. They have eight dogs that look like good ones. That's all I know. But I'm going to know more pretty soon!"

"How does that spot lie?" asked Windham. "I've forgotten the look of the place."

"Right over the hill there's a little circular hollow. A good many trees. Just the place for a camp. Ned, we're going over that ridge like a pair of bull moose. They're turned the dogs out—"

"The dogs will warn 'em in plenty of time," said Julie.

"I'll take Chinook and a few more of the best Huskies," said Windham. "They'll give the other dogs enough to think about when I send 'em in. And then—"

He added: "You stay back here."

"Stay here?" laughed Julie. "When there's a party like this? Stay back here when we have three guns?"

She laughed again in defiance.

Windham took her by the shoulder.

"If you don't give me your promise, I'll tie you on the sled!" he told her.

"Why, Ned?" she asked almost piteously. "We've gone through everything together. Let me be with you at the finish. Because this is the finish! If we win here, we're as good as at Fort Yukon. If we lose here, we die. Let's live or die together, the way old partners should! Can you say no to that?"

"I say no," said Windham. "You're back here, Julie. You're more use to us this way."

"Look!" said the girl. "There's the rifle and two revolvers. Why should one gun be wasted?"

"It won't be. Bert will take the rifle and I'll take the pair of Colts."

"But how am I more use trailing behind?"

"Because we'll know that our woman is watching us, and that'll multiply us. But if you go along, we'll be more bothered to protect you than to polish off that pair of murderers!"

Suddenly she nodded. "I understand," she said. "I'll walk to the rim of the hills and lie there to watch."

They took Chinook and three more of the most powerful Huskies. And the procession went carefully up the slope.

When they came to the ridge they dropped upon both hands and knees, and so each was able to obtain a safe look into the hollow.

A fire was blazing there before a shelter tent, and the two men were busy, feeding the fire and cooking.

At a little distance, in a hungry circle, the Huskies waited to be fed.

It was this intentness of theirs that allowed the stalking party to come so very close, beyond a doubt. For the two

nd their dogs were far down among the trees before one
of the enemy Huskies pointed its nose into the air and ut-
ered the long wolf cry of alarm.

All the rest instantly replied and started in a swarm in
he indicated direction. The two men by the fire, catching
up rifles which had been left carefully at hand, ran one to
he right and one to the left, to gain the cover of the trees.

"Take the left-hander!" shouted Windham to Bert.
"I'll take the one on the right."

And he opened fire with a revolver.

He got in two shots before the man was in cover. But
he was more than reasonably sure that he had missed
both.

Glancing over to the left, he saw Bert's mark fling arms
nto the air, stumble for one stride, and then fall on his
ace, sliding a little on the frozen surface from the forward impetus of the fall.

Then the dogs met. Windham was glad that he had not
risked any of the weaker members of his team when he
saw what happened. There was no need of them. Chinook, two leaps ahead of the rest, led a charge that split
he other dog team apart.

His great body looked the size of a bear as he bounded
here and there, slashing. His size, his terrible tooth-work,
old the tale in an instant. It seemed to the watchers as
hough Chinook himself had accomplished all the rout,
although the other three were cut and bleeding after the
battle. Then the opposing Huskies scattered, yelling like
mad, scampering for dear life.

Windham hastily whistled to Chinook and started
scouting through the trees to get at the second man.

He had not escaped over the hills, he was sure. Why
should he, in the first place? If he did, he had only the
white arctic to die by, instead of the swifter mercy of a
bullet through the head.

By his side walked Bert Fernal, eager-eyed, stealthy-
footed, pressing ahead, while Chinook scouted just before, with his mighty head low. A crimson head it was
now, stained with the blood of his enemy.

Suddenly a voice ahead of them yelled: "Windham!
Let me speak!"

213

It was the voice of the breed, Murray!

"Windham!" screamed Murray again. "Call off th
devil dog. Let me speak!"

"Damn him!" said Bert Fernal. "We want his blood!"

"Steady," said Windham. "We can hear him tall
There's no harm in that."

So he called in answer:

"Drop your rifle and come out from the trees straigl
toward the fire, with your hands over your head. Her
Chinook. Back here!"

Chinook reluctantly turned back. Almost immediate
afterward they saw the form of the half-breed issue fro
among the trees with his obedient hands above his hea
That head was down, and he stumbled like a weary or
beaten man as he walked. When he was close to the fi
he turned to face them.

Windham and Fernal were already close upon hin
with guns ready. But the sight of them was not what trou
bled Murray. It was the dog at which he looked, with h
eyes starting from his head with horror.

"Keep Chinook back," he said. "Windham, send Ch
nook back, will you? Go back, Chinook! Back! Back!"

But Chinook, dropping his head, began to stalk fo
ward for a kill. A hoarse scream rose from the lips of th
breed before Windham, with a single word, brought th
great dog to heel.

"I've always dreamed it from the first," said the bree
"I mean, even that first night of all in your cabin dow
there in California, Windham. Either I'd be the master o
that brute or else he'd have my throat ripped wide ope
one day. Today I felt that it was coming."

His head drooped as Windham came up to him.

"Cover him, Bert," he commanded. "I'll see what oth
weapon he has on him."

But there was only a small hunting knife; nothin
more. Then Windham stepped back. Over the hill, at th
same time, they could hear Julie calling to the dogs th
still remained with her, mushing them forward with th
lightened sleds.

"I'd like to know," said Windham, "what the devil ha

214

een in you, and why you've hated me so, Murray? What
ad I done to you?"

"Nothing," admitted Murray. "It was only because I
ad to have the dog first of all. Then, when you got on
my trail again, I thought that there was hypnotism, or
spirit work, or something like that behind it. You didn't
seem to me like just a plain, ordinary man from that time
onward. I don't know how else to explain it."

"And that fellow yonder? The dead one?"

"That's Gus Aintree. He's the one that hated you.
You'd slugged him once with a woman looking on."

Julie came quietly up. Murray looked steadily away
from her.

"If you and Aintree wanted to cut us off," said Windham, "why did you wait so long before you started from
the Chandalars? We made a long delay. You could have
been here a week ahead of us!"

"You think that we're fools, I suppose," replied Murray. "But we're not! We saw the bloodstains in your foot-
marks where you went off into the woods. We figured that
if you were that far gone we had plenty of time on our
hands."

"That was it, eh?"

"Yes, that was big part of it. Then, besides, there was
Little Knife."

He shook his head and shuddered.

"What about him?"

"When he came out from the woods his face was all
muffled up, and he was walking pretty slowly," went on
Murray. "He went into a tent and stayed there by himself
for days, with the Chandalars all camped around and
wondering what was coming next."

"Stayed there by himself?" said Windham, wondering.

"Yes. He had them pass in food to him once a day.
Some days he didn't eat at all. After a while he came out
and called all the Chandalars together. They came, and
they stood pretty still. They were scared to death. They
thought that he'd been in there communing with the
spirits, or some such rot.

"Well, he stood up there before them with his face all
muffled, looking pretty much like a ghost, and he made

215

them a speech and told them that there was a curse on th Three Hills and their gold, and that they were never t come back there again, any of them. He told them that h would show them the results of the curse. One result the could see now."

Murray paused, took a breath, and went on:

"All at once he jerked the fur from about his face, an we had our look at it. It was smashed in, sort of, as thoug a horse had stepped on it. And it had frozen and black ened, and—"

He stopped, with a look of horror in his eyes at th memory.

"He went back into the tent, leaving the Chandalar pretty well paralyzed, and a minute later we all heard th boom of a gun. Nobody needed to ask any questions. was pretty clear what he had done. The Chandalars jus waited long enough to bury him decently, and then the scooted for home.

"We headed back for Fort Yukon. We knew if w could get in with our outfit and three hundred pounds c dust we could get together another outfit and send out a expedition that would lift a million from the bank of th river and—"

He stopped and actually clapped his hand over hi mouth, like a child that has spoken too much.

And much he already had said!

# CHAPTER FORTY-THREE

The situation was completely altered. Before them la caches, untouched beyond doubt, which they had estab lished on the way out. With them now was a plentifu supply of provisions from the outfit of the dead man an of Murray.

216

They found, upon examination, that Murray had three hundred pounds of gold on his sleds. Three hundred pounds of gold meant nearly a hundred thousand dollars of solid cash! In how amazingly short a time had the two breeds ripped that gold from the earth! Perhaps, during the time the Chandalars were there, they had been bribed to assist the pair.

They held a consultation. Then Windham delivered his judgment upon Murray.

"Murray, you've played the dog ever since I first met you. Leaving everything else out of the tale, you broke into two caches on the trail. You weren't dying of starvation. You were simply trying to secure the death of our party. Now, you know what comes to you for that?"

Murray nodded sullenly.

"What do you expect?" asked Windham.

"To be robbed, cleaned out of my dust," growled Murray.

"Robbed?" said Windham. "Who discovered that ground? Who led the way to it? You were the robber, Murray, in the first place!"

"The law'll see to that," said Murray, snarling and gaining courage with the distantly implied assurance that his life was to be spared.

"If we were like most of the old-timers up here," said Windham, "we wouldn't talk, Murray. We'd simply bash in your head and leave you in the snow."

Murray made no comment.

"Instead of that," said Windham, "we're going to give you one dog and one sled. You can put plenty of provisions on it. You—"

"One dog," howled Murray.

"Yes," said Windham. "That'll see you through. Better men than you have plugged along without any dog at all, and you know it. Besides, if you follow down the line of caches you'll find that one of them is left intact for you. Moreover, you can keep all your gold dust. We won't touch it."

Murray offered no thanks.

"Another thing," went on Windham. "When you come

217

in, you don't stop at Fort Yukon. I know your game. You'd spread the word of the gold strike, and we want that under cover for a time. If you get to Fort Yukon, you'll find the complete yarn about your breaking into the caches there ahead of you, and enough evidence to hang you by your scrawny neck. Do you understand? Go on!"

Still Murray was silent, his slant eyes filled with rage of insatiable malice. Windham left the rascal and began to arrange the packs.

For the dogs which they had lost they had ample recompense from the remainder of the team of Murray and Aintree. They made their pack on three toboggans, the best of the entire lot. They picked up the rifles which Aintree had dropped and the one which Murray had thrown away when he ran out from among the trees.

Then they gave the signal to the weary team, and with Chinook staunchly in the lead, they mushed on; not far, however. Five miles was their march, simply to put distance between themselves and the possible malice of the breed. Then they camped.

It was a joyous camp! Of all that Windham ever had sat in, there never had been one like this. They had food for their starved dogs. They had food for themselves; fat food, which fills the belly and lines the ribs at the same time—not the dry and almost useless slabs of lean old caribou meat which so many Indians often have on their sleds.

They had all the wood they wanted for fires, they had plenty of good axes for felling timber, they had strong hands to wield the axes.

Above all, they had one another, welded into the mighty friendship which only the long white trail can engender. Sometimes mad hatreds are bred on those trails, speechless contempts and disgust. But love and friendship as deep are born along them, also.

Ahead of them lay sure triumph. Nothing could stop them on their way to Fort Yukon. They could equip an outfit and one of them then could lead the trek back to the Three Hills. They could skim the cream before busy rumor located the diggings and the rush began. That cream would be enough to make all three of them independently wealthy for life.

The splendid acres of Wind Valley came up again before the eyes of Windham. But he shook his head at the vision. Wind Valley was not enough. Somewhere else along the range where the foothills break up from the plain; somewhere else, where acres were cheap and fertile he would begin again. Not with one valley this time, but with a half dozen. On every spreading bottom land his plows would turn the black, rich surface of the soil. His barns and shacks would rise. His farmers and cowpunchers would gather at long tables. His swarming cattle would grow fat along the blossoming hillsides.

As he made these plans one night, he was stretched at ease where the fire bathed him with light and its heat soaked through his body and bones, entering like wine through the old hurt in his side.

Then a shadow came over his mind. He listened for a moment to the murmurings of the brother and sister. Turning his head, he looked at them and saw that they were sitting hand in hand, like children, musing at the fire with smiles of content.

That shadow upon the heart of Windham grew larger. His comfort was forgotten, and all of his future grew dim. He sat up.

"Julie," said he, "do you—"

"Yes?" said Julie.

She was up in an instant, with that Indianlike quickness of movement which he so often had admired.

"Wait a minute," said Windham. "I'll come to you. I didn't mean to call you, but—"

He was rising awkwardly, but she was already beside him and had dropped to her knees. The firelight was at her back; only the glow of it was on her cheeks.

"Julie," he said, "it's no go to dodge it. You'll laugh, most likely, in my face. I won't mind. I've used some pretty strong words about you. You know the worst one of all. Well, the time has come when even that word won't stop me. Whatever your blood is, Julie, I want you. I love

219

you till I ache for you. Julie, I'm asking you if you wil
marry me. Don't say it fast. Wait a little. Think it over
I'm no bright fellow. I've got no graces. There's not much
to say for me. I'm no hero, either, as you pretty darn well
know. Only, I love you clear to the bone. Now tell me."

What he had dreaded happened. She laughed in his
face!

In a moment, however, when the first shock passed, he
realized that this was not the sharply ringing laughter
which he had heard rippling from her throat so many
times before. Instead, it was a soft, low-pitched, musical
flow. The sound enveloped and caressed him.

"Why should I take time to think, Ned?" she asked him
finally. "Haven't I known from the first minute what I'd
think about you in the end? Haven't you been able to
guess, you great dull-wit? *Hai!* What could a half-breed
ask better than a great warrior like Ned Windham?"

She leaned a little closer to him.

"And what more could even a white girl ask, without a
drop of Indian blood in her, without a trace of anything
but white; a girl, say, like Julie Fernal?"

"Julie!" he cried in bewilderment.

"Why, Ned," she answered him, "a thousand people
could have told you, if you'd only happened to ask the
right ones. Do you think that Bert, yonder, looks like a
half-breed, also?"

He glanced across at Bert. The young man was laughing cheerfully at them, and the luster of his skin was like
the whitest ivory.

"Julie," said Windham, "I've been blind. I'd like to get
on my knees to you—"

"You'd still be taller than I," said Julie, "and—"

A bulky body pushed between them. The strong
shoulder of Chinook knocked the girl away, but she
reeled lightly to her feet and laughed again. Chinook sat
down before his master and snarled savagely at her.

"Julie," said Windham, "I know how it is. If the
strength of weakness made Chinook love me, wasn't it the

220

ame thing that made you begin to like me? Wasn't it my very dumbness and blundering, Julie?"

"Hush!" said Julie. "How is a wife to speak of her usband?"

# "THE KING OF THE WESTERN NOVELS"
## IS
# MAX BRAND

# THE BEST OF THE BESTSELLERS
# FROM WARNER BOOKS!

**THE KINGDOM** by Ronald Joseph     **(81-467, $2.50)**
The saga of a passionate and powerful family who carves out of the wilderness the largest cattle ranch in the world. Filled with both adventure and romance, hard-bitten empire building and tender moments of intimate love, **The Kingdom** is a book for all readers.

**THE GREEK TYCOON** by Eileen Lottman     **(82-712, $2.25)**
The story of a romance that fascinated the world—between the mightiest magnate on earth and the woman he loved . . . the woman who would become the widow of the President of the United States.

**FISHBAIT: MEMOIRS OF THE CONGRESSIONAL DOORKEEPER** by William "Fishbait" Miller     **(81-637, $2.50)**
Fishbait rattles every skeleton in Washington's closets. Non-stop stories, scandal, and gossip from Capitol Hill, with 32 pages of photographs.

**THE WINTER HEART** by Frances Casey Kerns     **(81-431, $2.50)**
Like "The Thorn Birds," THE WINTER HEART is centered upon a forbidden love. It is the saga of two Colorado families—of the men who must answer the conflicting claims of ambition and love and of the women who must show them the way.

---

 A Warner Communications Company

- - - - - - - - - - - - - - - - - - - - - - -

Please send me the books I have checked.

Enclose check or money order only, no cash please. Plus 50¢ per copy to cover postage and handling. N.Y. State residents add applicable sales tax.

Please allow 2 weeks for delivery.

WARNER BOOKS
P.O. Box 690
New York, N.Y. 10019

Name ..................................................................................................

Address ..............................................................................................

City .............................................. State ......................... Zip ..............

_____ Please send me your free mail order catalog